Black Indian – Red Heart (White Justice)

Black Indian – Red Heart (White Justice)

A novel by:

Frederick H Savage

Oak Tree Press Hanford, CA

Oak Tree Press
Publishers Since 1998

Black Indian, Red Heart (White Justice) Copyright 2015, by FREDERICK SAVAGE. All rights reserved. Printed in the United States of America. No part of this book may be used or reproduced in any manner whatsoever without written permission except in the case of brief quotations used in critical articles and reviews.

For information, address Oak Tree Press, 240 N. 12th Avenue, Suite 109 #120, Hanford, CA 93230.

Oak Tree Press books may be purchased for educational, business, or sales promotional purposes. Contact Publisher for quantity discounts.

First Edition, October 2015

ISBN 978-1-61009-186-2
LCCN 2015939737

Although actual historic events are chronicled within, this book is a work of fiction. All characters, names, places and incidents are the products of the Author's imagination, or are used fictitiously. Any resemblance to actual events or locales or to any persons, living or dead is entirely coincidental. It is only a story and not intended to be slanderous to those on either side of the conflicts described.

All rights reserved. No part of this book may be reproduced or transmitted in any form or by any means, electronic, magnetic, mechanical, or photographic including photo copying, recording or by any information storage and retrieval system, without prior written permission of the author.

No patent liability is assumed with respect to the use of the information contained herein. Although every precaution has been taken in the preparation of this book, the publisher and author assume no responsibility for errors or omissions. No liability is assumed for damages resulting from the use of the information contained herein.

To my best friend, Marie

And...

A special thank you to my daughter, Sharon.
Your input and encouragement is greatly appreciated.

Sometimes fair or unfair is simply a point of view.

Table of Contents

Prologue
Part One: Indian Territory

Chapter	Page
1. A Property Issue	8
2. The Slavers	18
3. The Winds of Change	25
4. Wars and Rumors of War	40
5. Ass Deep	57
6. The Fever	66
7. The Three R's	73

Part Two: This Troubled Land

8. Red Calf the Hunted	79
9. Kegs of Powder	87
10. The Little Colored Boy	98
11. The Beginning of the End	106
12. Training Camp	110
13. White Man's Way	121
14. White Man's Law	130

Part Three: Black Bat from Hell

15. The Red Man's War	150
16. No More Chances	156
17. The Dare	170
18. Stirring the Hornet's Nest	182
19. Merciful Heavens	201
20. A Simple Minded Negro	218
21. Black Indian, Red Heart (White Justice)	229

Epilogue   247

Prologue

Minnesota Territory June 1836

The setting sun was directly in their faces as the soldiers topped the rise and reined their horses to a stop. Through squinted eyes they took in the macabre scene as they realized they had found the two wagons and the settlers that had been reported missing. Their Indian scout, a half breed who went by the name Sawyer, sat silently a few yards in the lead, his eyes taking in all that lay before them in the large clearing. The wheel ruts that served as a road disappeared about three hundred yards further on as they made their way into a maze of trees.

Midway across the clearing on a downhill slope, a wagon was turned over on its side. The carcass of a single horse was lying dead in its traces. Farther on, another wagon sat unscathed as if waiting for a team to be hitched to it. On the ground, much closer and in plain view, a woman's body and that of a young boy lay face down. Their hands were outstretched and nearly touching as if their last act had been that of reaching for each other. Slightly ahead on the road, another body, a white man, lay twisted grotesquely with several protruding arrows that appeared to have been shot into his body from different angles. Even from a distance of still fifty or sixty yards, they could see the swarm of flies buzzing angrily around the corpses.

The soldiers were well trained and believed they were ready for anything. What lay ahead had them all the highest level of alert; hearts beating fast, anticipation in every face, nerves on edge. The command to form a skirmish line, uttered by the commanding officer was instantly obeyed. They fanned out and moved slowly though the clearing in a wide single row. The soldier who had been last in line and holding the lead rope to their pack mule quickly tied the rope to his saddle's pommel and dropped back from the line just slightly, his rifle at the ready. In the lead, the Indian scout and a private approached the first wagon about twenty or thirty yards ahead of the rest. The commands from the patrol's leader, a lieutenant, now offered in a low and serious tone could be heard and understood by the twelve remaining. "Rifles at the ready," he said, "standard approach." Their eyes scanned the area ahead and despite still being nearly blinded by the setting sun, they urged their horses onward.

One soldier, a sergeant, muttered in a skeptical tone, "Hell, all them damn cowardly Indians are gone, Sir. These here dead people can't hurt anyone."

The lieutenant, a young officer new to the territory, ignored these remarks with an indifferent manner.

As the soldiers went over the rise started down the incline on the other side towards wagons, they were unaware of the events happening behind and around them.

A group of five hostile Indians silently made their way down onto the same wheel rutted road from the tree covered high ground on the north side. They had been well concealed and like ghosts, now silently followed the soldiers. At the urging of their leader, they had practiced this very ambush several times earlier in the day. They were crouched, keeping low, knowing that their success depended on surprise. Even the time of day was seen as a good sign to them. Blinded by the sun, the soldiers were surely at a disadvantage from what lay ahead.

As the soldiers neared the first wagon, from a brushy area further on and a little to the left of the road, there was a flurry of motion. Looks of surprise crossed the faces of several soldiers. It was a woman in a calico dress, bright blue in color and wearing a white bonnet. She sprang up and ran unsteadily away from them. She was only visible through the trees for a few seconds.

"Quick! Go get her!" the Lieutenant exclaimed as he instinctively urged his horse to a faster pace. The scout, the private and one other soldier urged their horses to a canter and disappeared from sight though a grove of scrub pine. The soldier who was third in line slowed as he came upon the dead settlers. He was nearly sickened as he guided his horse around the mutilated remains of the white man riddled with arrows. He was lagging behind the scout and the other soldier by about twenty yards as he tried to regain his composure and shake off the grip of ice cold fear that clouded his mind.

The remaining soldiers continued their approach, now in a ragged line as they urged their horses a little faster. Their attention was focused on the macabre scene. Moments later several shots were fired ahead followed by loud Indian war whoops. The soldiers pursuing the woman had burst into a small clearing and started to rein in their horses when the trap was sprung. The woman, lying face down by a large rock turned out to be an Indian warrior in disguise. He rose up with lightning speed and killed the Indian scout with a blast to the face from a double barrel shotgun. Enraged Indians appeared as if out of nowhere and the others were torn from their mounts and fiercely set upon.

The other soldiers too, were taken completely by surprise and at close quarters by a horde of angry and vicious savages who had silently maneuvered on foot into attack range from behind and from the high ground on the north side. Now a group of a dozen mounted warriors appeared thundering towards them from around the bend in the road ahead like a force released from Hell. The fighting was fierce and brief. Although many shots were fired, within minutes it was over. All save two soldiers were dead or dying. One of the surviving soldiers was a one eyed man, a private with a black eye patch, who appeared to be in his mid-thirties. The other was a younger man, also a private. Both terrified survivors were herded to the undisturbed wagon and made to sit on its seat, unbound and unharmed. Several of the severely wounded and dying soldiers were still being scalped and mutilated even as they screamed and begged for mercy.

The Indians were nearly beside themselves with excitement as they celebrated their victory. This raid was another of many made in retribution to similar acts of cruelty and savagery towards the Indian people by the white settlers and the soldiers. A short time before, in the dead of winter, the horse soldiers had wiped out nearly an entire village using cannon and all the military might at hand. They had claimed that several rogue Indians were being sheltered in the village. The denials from the Indians had fallen on deaf ears and the soldiers had opened up with the combined cannon fire of two gunnery units at the defenseless village. The slaughter was made even worse as the soldiers, alive with excitement, used their rifle stocks to crush the skulls of the younger and more defenseless women and children. They had spared no one.

Now this battle, short and decisive, was a true victory. No Indian had been seriously hurt in this skirmish. Eleven horse soldiers and a turncoat scout were dead or dying. Two soldiers had been captured alive and were essentially unharmed. The tally was fourteen mounts captured, a single pack mule and armament for fourteen warriors. It was indeed a great victory and to be remembered as one of the most carefully planned and successfully executed battles of the great Indian wars.

The Indian leader approached the two survivors. He was a young warrior chieftain, proud and ferocious. His war paint veiled a thin face and piercing eyes. He approached these white captives who were now surrounded by a bloodthirsty horde of savages who wanted even more blood. The chief's anger was apparent as he shouted down one of the more outspoken and angry braves who wanted to kill them both. None of the warriors wanted to challenge his authority and as a result, soon, all were silent. Over the sounds of still agonized moaning and the buzzing of flies around the corpses he spoke.

His English was nearly perfect as he addressed the soldiers, "The spirits have told me to spare you." He said in a commanding tone. They both showed expressions of amazement and then recognition as they realized who he was. The chief continued, "Tell the other white eyes that without peace this is the fate that waits for them." He slowly waved his hand in a sweeping motion taking in the ambush scene. "Tell your leader that you are my prisoners. With no jail to hold you, and no one to discuss terms of surrender, I am now setting you free." He pointed back down the trail. Darkness was fast descending. "Go." He said in a soft voice. "Go quickly."

Both men cautiously climbed down from the wagon and started walking, hoping that the Indian's word was good and that he had enough power over his warriors to actually keep them at bay. Their eyes took in the heinous sights of the fates of their fellow soldiers. The officer in charge was still alive. His breath was coming in short agonizing gasps as two Indians were carefully removing the flesh from the front of his skull. His eyes were deep blue and very much alive as his face was slowly cut out and peeled away all in one piece.

Even as several Indians feigned attacks as if they were walking a gauntlet, the two soldiers hurriedly made their way towards safety. They had gone about a mile and darkness had overtaken them when the soldier with the eye patch said, "Is that Indian who I think he is?"

The younger soldier replied in a whisper, "Yes. That was Tall Cloud himself."

"Why do you suppose he spared us?" When there was no response he added, "You don't suppose he could know that our troop was part of the attack on the village where all those women and children were killed?" He paused, then, his voice nervous, asked, "Do you?"

"Can't say," was the whispered reply.

They walked all through the night, each man busy with thoughts of his own. Just before dawn and nearing the point of exhaustion, they came onto a campfire and the safety of another army patrol.

Fort Snelling

From a vantage point high on a bluff overlooking the joining of the Minnesota and the Mississippi rivers it was easy to watch the wagons and commerce on the trails and roads below. This army outpost, a beacon of hope and safety in this nearly uncivilized land, was now host to a very serious meeting.

From his commanding position at the head of the long and narrow table, the General seemed uncomfortable. It was obvious that the topic and the agreement reached were not of his choosing. It was with great reluctance and a forced patience that he gave the order.

"I want you to find this Indian chief." his command was directed to a young Captain, new to the territory. "Find this Tall Cloud and tell him we are ready to sign a new treaty. Give him assurances of parley. He and his kind will not be harmed or interfered with in any way as long as he is serious about talking peace."

"That son of a bitch!" a Colonel seated at the table muttered bitterly. "I still say you should keep up the pressure and kill that bastard."

"These are the orders, Colonel," the General said, his voice stern, "Straight from Washington. You are to accompany me back there for reassignment."

The colonel didn't seem surprised at this news. He had requested a transfer back east several times in the past and was hoping for a Washington DC transfer.

Another soldier, a major, interjected softly, "The Indian Affairs department can only cover up so much of what has happened here. We can't let the newspapers back East get wind of any more of this. It is time for it to stop."

"Easy for you to say," Was the colonel's bitter reply, "it wasn't your son who had his face scalped off by that rotten heathen."

The General, who had obviously heard all he wanted to hear on the subject, declared in a loud tone of voice, "That's enough, gentlemen. Meeting adjourned."

Part One

Indian Territory

Chapter One

A Property Issue

Colton, Minnesota, Late August 1844

It was late afternoon when the two small and nearly empty wagons approached the center of the isolated and practically deserted community known as Colton. This dying settlement was located near the edge of the bleak Indian reservation nearly thirty miles from the Minnesota River.

Tethered like animals to the back of the lead wagon, a Negro man and a pregnant Indian woman staggered along on unsteady legs. They were secured to the wagon by ropes that had been tied around their necks. Both had their hands tied together, in front, allowing only enough freedom to cling desperately to the ropes in an effort to avoid being dragged. The man's face was awash with sweat as he tried, to no avail, to offer assistance to the woman. An expression of dismay was etched into his dark features. They were nearing the point of exhaustion. Strained almost beyond human limits, both seemed unaware of their surroundings as they followed blindly behind the wagon and the cruel slave hunter who sat comfortable and uncaring on the seat.

The Colton area had a shady reputation as being a safe haven for runaway slaves and those who would offer them comfort and shelter. Angry bounty hunters had burned nearly the entire town to the ground only last spring. Now, all that remained of a once thriving town were a dozen or so weathered buildings, a trading post and the oldest building, the mission.

The government was in the process of changing the reservation boundaries. A new road had been built twenty miles to the south. It was only a matter of time until this trading post, and the mission, would be forced to move to the lower reservation, near the town of New Ulm, if they wanted to remain within its new borders.

The lead wagon, pulled by a fine team of horses, was the first to stop. The driver, a lean man with bushy whiskers, reined the horses to a halt in front of the trading post. The corners of his mouth were stained brown from a constant drool of chewing tobacco. He wore what had once been a wide-brimmed felt hat that now sagged equally around his unkempt features. His shirt and heavy canvas pants were filthy and stained from countless days and nights on the trail.

Several faces were pressed to the glass windows that lined the town's remaining boardwalk as the people within peered out, curious to see who it was. A number of Indians, who appeared to be passive and uninterested, sat watching silently. It was obvious that they had nothing else to do and no place to go as they waited expectantly to see what was going to happen. Although it wasn't all that uncommon, seeing an Indian woman in captivity was still a bit unusual. They stayed in the shade cast from a clump of tall maple trees that bordered the town's only livery stable.

The August heat and humidity was stifling. Ominous storm clouds appeared overhead as if threatening, almost mockingly, to end the solace of this idle afternoon. An extremely overweight white man was sitting lazily on the top step of the building with a faded sign that read 'Barber Shop.' He watched the procession with a look of idle curiosity. It seemed to require all of his energy as he slowly wiped the sweat from his forehead with a rag.

A thin, middle-aged woman wearing a black dress was watching from the open doorway of the mission house that was located across this main street from the trading post. She wore her dark brown hair in a bun, fashionable and practical. Her expression showed amazement at the sight of the Indian woman, obviously heavy with child, and the Negro man tethered like stock animals to the back of the first wagon. She remained still as her fierce blue eyes, set narrowly in a thin and once pretty face, took in the scene. She gasped in astonishment as the wagon stopped and the Indian woman dropped to both knees. The Negro man had been staggering along trying to assist her as he struggled to maintain his balance. It had been all they could do to keep from being dragged behind the wagon. He also fell to his knees, his chin resting wearily on his chest, as the wagon stopped.

The second wagon came to a halt. The lead horses were only a few yards from the rear of the first. The gentle 'whoa' coming from the driver belied a hardened face and nasty manner. He cursed softly as his team pranced in place as they tried not to trample the Negro who was now collapsed face down on the ground. His temper was apparent as he quickly climbed down from the wagon. He was cursing profusely as he approached his exhausted prisoners.

The Indian woman, who was still on her knees, had leaned over the Negro. The angry white man pulled her back by the hair of her head and struck her several times with a riding quirt. She made no sound and only a weak attempt to protect herself from the cruel blows. Her face was bleeding from the stings as she silently drew back from her failed efforts to provide help to the fallen man.

The white man's angry words, "Leave that worthless darkie lie right there," could be heard plainly. The sound of his hand slapping the woman's face was exceptionally clear as he added, his voice vile, "Do you hear me? Whore?"

From within the trading post, a tall, lean white man walked slowly onto the porch and took a station on the top step. He stood calmly with one hand on the railing almost as if he were posing for a picture. He was a stereotypical southern gentleman dressed in a white suit. Due to the stifling heat, he was holding his hat in his hand and fanning his face with the wide brim. He ran his hand slowly across his large white mustache as if to smooth it and stroked his neatly trimmed goatee. It was he who spoke first. He addressed the man still sitting in the seat of the lead wagon.

"Which of you is Riley?"

The man jerked his thumb over his shoulder indicating the man from the second wagon. He wiped the drool from the side of his mouth with the back of his hand and said, "The tall, skinny fella back there be Riley." He grinned, showing upper and lower front rows of stained and rotting teeth. "Just give him a minute. He be a little upset with the whore right now." He leaned over the side and spat.

"I got word you were coming," the southern gentleman said. He craned his neck to look towards the back end of the wagon. He directed his next question to Riley, "Is that the run-away son-of-a-bitch we been hearing about?"

"Yes indeed, Colonel." Riley answered. "We just need to get this here paper signed by a government official such as you and we'll be on our way."

The colonel said in a matter of fact tone, "This darkie makes what? Six of 'em - this trip? I guess it isn't as easy as it used to be for them to hide amongst the heathens. Come on in with your paper and I'll sign it. The fee is the same as it has always been."

As the bounty hunters were joining him, the woman who had been standing in the open doorway of the mission building took a few steps towards the center of the street. She placed her hand across her forehead to shade her eyes from the sun with her palm. With her other hand she clutched the large silver cross that hung from a silver plated chain around her neck. Her voice was surprisingly clear and calm as she spoke loud enough to be heard,

"Colonel Farley. Colonel. It won't hurt anything to give these poor souls a drink of water." When there was no immediate response she raised her voice another level and added, "Will it?"

"Suit yourself, Lillie," the colonel answered.

"She's a Santee, Colonel!" Lillie exclaimed, pointing to the woman. "Lakota Sioux. These bounty hunters have no right to her. Not as long as she is on the reservation."

"I'm dealing with it, Lillie," the colonel said in a sarcastic tone.

"Go ahead and get them some water. Pray over 'em if you like." He met her look with one of authority as he added, "I'll decide who is a Santee Indian and who is not. This here is a property issue and I'll thank you to keep your opinions to yourself."

Riley joined the colonel on the porch and shook his hand. "Good to see you, Colonel." He was obviously still angry as he muttered something about not wanting to be cheated out of what rightfully was his.

"Don't worry about it, Mr. Riley," the colonel said. He glanced at the pregnant woman and added, "It don't look like she'll be keeping us guessing for long."

Lillie hurried to the mission building and returned to the street moments later carrying a wooden bucket full of water and a tin cup. She knelt down and offered the woman a drink. To her surprise, the woman took the cup from her and gave it to the fallen man. He was gasping and nearly chocking as he drank holding the cup unsteadily in both hands. He gulped the water and slumped back to a prone position on the ground. He was barely conscious as he lay on his side with his head rested on his outstretched arm.

The small group of Indians still sitting in the shade next to the stable looked on. One young boy in particular was watching with an unmistakable look of hatred. He was barely ten years old and already sick to death of how life on the reservation had deteriorated over these last few years.

It was only a few minutes later when the bushy faced man came back outside. Without a word, he walked to the rear of his wagon. He grabbed onto the rope that still held the Indian woman tethered to the back. It was tied tightly around her neck. He yanked on it, dragging her from her kneeling position by the Negro and causing her to fall prone on the ground. Lillie had been administering a drink of water to the man and wiping his face with a wet cloth. She looked up, startled at this interruption.

"Stop that!" she exclaimed. "This woman is protected by the tribal agreement."

The man muttered, "Shut the hell up, preacher woman." He fumbled for his knife and prepared to cut the rope up close to the woman's neck. At the same time, Lillie got between them. For a moment, it appeared as if he was going to strike her as she gently removed the rope from around the woman's neck. Expecting no answer, she asked, "See? Wasn't that better than trying to cut it?"

She was aware that these men were slave hunters. They were heartless men who hunted runaway Negroes for the bounty money. She knew that there were others, just like these two, waiting for these men to return to their camp.

Lillie helped the pregnant woman to her feet and then to back up a few steps.

The man, determined to get his point across, lunged close and with his face only inches from hers, he snarled, "You're lucky I don't cut her damn throat!"

Lillie remained silent. She suppressed an involuntary shudder as her gaze fixed on the madness in his eyes.

With unabated anger he added, "I still think that damned unborn whelp is a darkie, and if so, it belongs to us." He slapped the woman's protruding stomach with a heavy backhand, "You're lucky I don't cut the damned thing out of her right now just to see." He grinned at the look of horror on Lillie's face. Through tobacco stained teeth he added, "Maybe I will after all." Without warning, he struck the pregnant woman a violent blow to her midsection with his clenched fist. She fell gasping and retching to her knees feeling as if her insides had caught on fire. Lillie's heart was racing with fear and excitement as she crouched and twisted around to place herself between the helpless young woman and the cowardly attacker.

The black man made a futile attempt to thwart the assault as he lunged at the man. With his hands bound and the rope around his neck, he need not have bothered. It cost him a hard kick to his ribs. He gasped in pain and lay curled up on his side catching every breath. He hatefully watched the white man as if trying to anticipate his next move.

"That's enough of that shit, Earl," Riley said, his voice surprisingly calm, "We don't want to damage the goods too much." He was already standing with one foot positioned on the front wheel of his wagon to climb up onto the seat. His tone of voice was commanding as he added, "Make the darkie stand up. We've got to get a move on if we're to join with the rest of the boys before dark. We'll throw him on the back of the wagon in a while."

Riley climbed onto his wagon seat and looked for a moment at the young Indian boy who was now standing silently only a few feet away. He met the boy's harsh stare with one of his own and without a word picked up the reins.

An old man placed his hand on the Indian boy's shoulder. Only the boy could hear the words as the old man said, "Come, Red Calf. This is none of our affair." The boy silently turned and rejoined the others sitting in the shade.

Once again, the sounds of the creaking wagons and plodding hooves filled the still, humid, air as the teams were reined and made to move out.

The Negro, refreshed a little from a few moments of kindness and with renewed energy, silently followed along. It was that brief moment of eye contact between him and the pregnant woman that caught the mission lady's attention. Lillie felt a wave of faintness overcome her as she realized that the man and woman had just said their final goodbyes in a glance that lasted only for a moment.

Colonel Farley stood silently watching as the wagons slowly rounded a bend in the road. He turned and focused his attention on the Indian woman and her benefactor.

"Lillian Taylor, I swear. These damned redskins will be the death of you yet if you don't learn to mind your own business." He smiled mockingly at her bitter expression. "Aw, come on now, Lillie!" he exclaimed. "Where's all that love of Jesus? Eh?"

Lillie offered no reply as she poured more water onto a small hand towel and continued to wipe blood away from the young woman's face.

The Colonel raised his voice. He was nearly shouting as if for everyone in town to hear,

"I told them two bounty hunters that if the squaw's whelp is a Negro, they could stop in and buy it back come spring."

Lillie glanced back over her shoulder with another look of contempt. There was no ignoring him as he added, almost defensively, "It's the right thing to do, Lillie. Might even be a couple dollars in it for you, if it's a boy."

The colonel turned and went inside to the relative cool of the store. This left the two women alone in the hot sun. The Indian woman was prone on the ground at the side of the street. The preacher lady continued tending to her, wiping her face gently with the wet cloth and assuring her soothingly that she was now among friends.

Lillie looked up in surprise as a young Indian boy came over and motioned that he wanted to help. She recognized him as the younger brother of a tribal leader, Tall Cloud. "It's good to see you, Red Calf," she murmured. "Thank you." As he got on one side of the woman to help her across the street, she added, "God will surely bless you." His return smile, set in a ten year old face of stone with hollow eyes, was such that she had nothing more to say.

That same evening, the young woman, whose name was Sage, went into a premature labor. Knowing that this was her first child and sensing that the time was too soon, Lillie sent for a reservation doctor.

It was doubtful that Sage ever fully regained her senses. She was burning with fever and kept asking, in her native tongue, where she was. Even though Lillie told her, 'Colton,' over and over again, she never did seem to understand. It was late in the afternoon the next day when Sage gave birth to a son. Ominous clouds had gathered and the baby was born during a fierce thunder and lightning storm. Sage asked Lillie, this time in broken English, that her son be baptized. Lillie assured her that it would be so. When Lillie asked what his name was to be, the new mother spoke one word in a questioning tone, "Colton?"

Lillie exchanged concerned looks with the doctor and took the baby from the room to clean him up. She wrapped him in a soft blanket and brought him back to his mother. Sage smiled softly. She died minutes later with a faint smile on her face. It was determined by the doctor and the missionary lady that the baby was Indian and not Negro. Dr. Morrison was new to the area but had caught on quickly in the ways and realities of everyday reservation life. On the official reservation records, they recorded the boy's Christian name as Colton Sage.

Several Indians who were present when he was born affectionately referred to the baby as a little black bat. It was a nick name that would catch up to young Colton in the future.

The news that the 'squaw's whelp' was an Indian upset the Colonel for a short time. It really made little difference; just another reason to refer to the dead woman as another Indian whore.

The following spring, the entire town of Colton was abandoned and everyone moved closer to the township, called New Ulm, which was still within the reservation's new boundaries. The Colonel got completely out of the business of selling to the Indians. He sold his inventory and transferred his government sales lease to another white man. Word was that he took his money and moved somewhere back East.

The surrounding area was growing rapidly. Settlers arrived in droves with visions of cheap land and a better life. Rumor had it that the railroad would soon be heading towards nearby Mankato from St. Paul and word was that the Minnesota lands were soon to be organized into a territory with its own territorial governor.

Miss Lillie was unwavering in her desire to start another mission. Her fierce determination finally paid off when the reservation officials agreed to fund a new school. This one was to be located in the heart of the newly created lower agency and a short distance northwest of New Ulm, which was about twenty miles from Mankato. It wasn't long before routines settled in as before and life went on.

The young Indian boy, Red Calf, had also been taken in as an infant. During the infamous Indian wars, now only memories, his life had been spared by an act of kindness on behalf of a tribal leader,

Tall Cloud. It was Tall Cloud who had adopted him as his brother. For this reason, he was pleased to learn that Miss Lillie was going to keep the orphaned boy and raise him as her own. He had decided that day on the street, even before the boy was born, that little Colton was family.

Chapter Two

The Slavers

The slavery issue was one that ran hot in nearly every western region. The vast Minnesota Territory was no exception. As civilization spread steadily west, so did the opportunity for more Underground Railroad activity. The Colton area, not far from New Ulm, was such a place. Not far from a trade route that led straight to St. Paul and northern freedom, it was a goal, a little known destination for many Negro men, women and children. Another plus, was that it was in the heart of the Sioux Indian reservation and thus considered much safer than most areas.

The spring of 1844 was a time of darkness for the region. Several roving groups of slave hunters banded together and raised all kinds of mischief in the area. They burned nearly the entire town to the ground, in a single day and night of rampage. With no law around to stop them, they operated with complete immunity. Only the threat of justice metered out from the soldiers assigned to the reservation kept them from committing even more heinous acts.

The government officials decided on a new treaty with the Indians that changed the reservation borders. This assured that Colton would soon be a forgotten town, a mere memory of those who had been there with not even a mention on any map. The next spring, hateful whites, suspected to be bounty hunters, torched the abandoned mission, the vacant trading post and the remaining buildings. Some say they did it just for spite. With the roads abandoned this once hub to freedom would soon be simply another part of the forest. Within a few years, the remnants of stone foundations and streets that once showed signs of commerce would be overgrown with trees and saplings as nature took her course.

September, 1844

The slavers' camp was actually an old French settlement that had been abandoned many years before. Originally serving as a place of refuge for French trappers, these dilapidated shacks were home these past two seasons to a cruel and violent bunch. The forest had nearly taken over most of the buildings; trees and saplings were growing in and out of most of what remained. Only two or three of the remaining structures were still sturdy enough to offer shelter.

With autumn fast approaching, the slave trader named Riley was anxious to get his covey of captured run-away slaves to the railhead and then back to Atlanta where his bounty money could be collected. He was looking forward to another long and boisterous winter chasing after saloon whores, cards and whiskey.

It was early morning, only a few days after they got word that the 'squaws whelp' had indeed been an Indian that they started on their journey. The overcast sky gave warnings of afternoon thunderstorms. Riley gazed skyward and then at his right hand man, also his half-brother, Earl, and said,

"Let's get them niggers that we have to load, loaded on the wagons. Those who can walk, tie to the back the same as usual."

In addition to Riley and Earl, there were two others who made up the crew. One was a scrawny young man called Clark that they had picked up late that spring along the way. The other, a heartless man named Bentsen, had been with them for nearly a month longer than Clark. This was also Bentsen's first trip with them on the slave route.

"Let's get a move on!" Riley growled.

In a very short time, Bentsen and Clark had the teams hitched to the two wagons and were ready to go. Then, they made two of the captured slaves help load their supplies. They double checked the area to be sure that they had not forgotten or overlooked anything. Now they were ready to pull out.

Three Negros were loaded onto the back of the wagons. The one with a broken leg and arm was roughly tossed, screaming in pain, over the side and into the bed of the first wagon by Clark and Bentsen. This one seemed to have internal injuries and wasn't expected to live so they saw no need to be gentle. Two others were allowed to sit in the second wagon among the supplies and equipment. Their injuries were such that there was no way they could be expected to keep up with the wagons on foot. Their hands were securely bound in the front to deny them any chance of attacking their captors. The remaining three, all able to walk, were tied to the back of the first wagon. They were held by ropes that were first tied around their necks, then to the wagon. Their hands were bound together in front so they could clutch the ropes that tethered them like stock animals.

Riley's voice was vile as he addressed the slave tied in the middle. "That squaw's whelp wasn't even yours. I'll bet you wish now that you hadn't made such a fuss over that whore."

Earl cut in, "Hell, Riley, I can't say as I blame this fool. She was a good looking squaw after all," he paused to spit before adding, "I tried that whore out a couple times myself. Not that bad, not bad at all."

The Negro man had no reaction to their comments.

Riley turned his attention to the remaining two captives who were also tied to the back of the wagon, "Each of you turn around and hold hard onto the horses less they get spooked and tread all over your worthless black asses."

They did as instructed, standing silently, holding the halters of the team that was hitched to the second wagon. Then Riley took a position on the right side of the first wagon, holding the reins firmly as Clark was climbing onto the seat.

"We're about ready to move out," Clark said. His voice sounded almost gleeful as he added, "We got us some reward money to collect!"

Clark never saw or suspected a thing as Riley pulled his cap and ball revolver and cocked it. He died instantly from a bullet in the side of his head as the force of the shot knocked him off the wagon. His body trembled and twitched briefly on the ground. Riley maintained a firm grip on the reins, calming the horses. The team hooked to the second wagon, stomped and snorted fiercely. The two slaves continued to hold a tight and now desperate grip on their halters.

The one called Bentsen had just coiled up a long rope and placed it on the back of the first wagon on the side opposite and out of sight of Riley. Earl was standing only a few feet away, near the second wagon. Bentsen shouted in amazement, "What the hell just happened, boss?" He had turned and now stood only a few feet from the dead man. His eyes were fixated on Clark as he started to say, "Did he..."

"Just making it easier to divide the reward money," Riley answered, interrupting Clark's train of thought. His words were followed closely by a shotgun blast fired by Earl from only ten feet away. The blast killed Bentsen dead in his tracks as his body was slammed instantly to the ground. The loud report of the shotgun fired within a few feet of the horses caused them to rear on their hind legs despite the grip the slaves had on their halters. "Whoa, damn it," Earl exclaimed as he reached for and grabbed onto one side of the halter of one of the horses. With the horses calmed down a bit, Earl said, talking to the two dead men, "Don't you boys know that equal share doesn't include you?" His nearly toothless smile was matched by Riley as he tied his saddle horse securely to the back of the second wagon.

As Earl snapped the reigns to move out the first wagon, he spit over the side hitting Clark in the forehead with the nasty gob of tobacco juice. "Hell," he said loudly over his shoulder to Riley, "this time was even easier than last year."

Riley grinned and snapped the reigns urging the team to follow the first wagon.

The three slaves tethered to the back shuddered as they took in the sight of Clark's body, and Bentsen's, as they walked silently past. Bentsen's body was by far the worse; the shotgun blast had hit him squarely in the throat, nearly severing his head from his body. They had no doubt these slavers were mad men and could only hope that they would be spared a similar fate.

The slave tethered in the middle plodded on surrounded by the others. A feeling of hope was welling up deep inside him. He was hopeful for the fate of his son. He believed that the Indian officials and the white lady, of whom he had heard, would never offer up a newborn to slavers like these. For this reason, his belief was that the child had been a boy, it was his son, and he had been born free. Knowing this caused him to find inner strength as the journey dragged on.

A severe thunder and lightning storm overtook them just before dark that first day on the trail. The horses were terrified and even though they were hobbled and tied securely to a rope line, it seemed a miracle that none of them were hurt as they bucked and strained to be free. The storm blew over and a calm settled in just as darkness fell.

Earl and Riley were both upset over the effects of the storm and extremely busy keeping up with all that was happening. The Negros considered being flight risks had been made to lie beneath the wagons where they could be seen and easily guarded. Fear and feelings of sheer terror knowing what their captors were capable of kept them from trying anything that could even be considered out of the ordinary.

The one named Arthur was made to cook and do the miscellaneous camp chores. He was one who was allowed to ride in the wagon due to his injured ankle. They thought him to be a very low flight risk.

"What the hell were you thinking, Riley," Earl asked, "We could have waited a day or so before disposing of them two partners of ours."

It was after dark, the camp was quiet. They were sitting near their campfire on wooden boxes sipping coffee laced with whiskey.

"I'm regretting it already," Riley snarled, "I'll be damned if I ain't."

"At least we got these black bastards to help out with the chores," Earl stated. "Just don't take your eyes off them."

"Everything will be fine come morning," Riley said, his voice hopeful. "This damn storm is something we just could never know about ahead of time."

"I recon you are right about that," Earl said. "Still, I'm a wishing we had them two fools here to divide up the night watch like before. Last year, when we thinned them out, we only had three captured slaves to worry about, now we got six."

"God-damned if you ain't right, Earl," Riley said grudgingly, "I guess I figured killing them now, this far out, and we don't have to worry about burying the bodies."

"Hell," Earl said, his voice insistent, "we've got us a whole passel of niggers right here to handle that."

"Damned if you ain't right," Riley allowed. "Next year you be sure to remind me and we will wait till we are only a day out from the railhead before we get rid of whoever it is we hire for the season. Is that all right with you?"

"Couldn't have put it better myself."

The next morning they got off to an early start. The slave named Arthur warmed up leftover beans and molasses and served it up hot first to the white men, then to the slaves.

Earl was still missing Bentley and Clark as he was the one who had to work with the captives to hitch up both teams. Riley was in a bad mood again and Earl felt it best not to bother him.

Riley and Earl got to the railhead with five captured slaves three days later. The more severely injured slave, whose name according to the reward papers was Ramses, had died on the trail. His condition had worsened to the point that Riley felt obliged to 'put the nigger down,' and had done so with a single shot from his revolver. As he was holstering his revolver, he said loudly, to no one in particular but for all to hear, "What I just done was a true act of mercy."

The next morning they continued on, leaving the body where it was the same as they had done for Bentsen and young Clark.

The fee to transport the slaves was the same as for the horses or any stock animal. They rode in the same box car with their captives. Riley, sitting on a bale of hay was smiling as he went over the papers with his brother, Earl.

"That first one we caught, the one named Arthur, is in pretty good shape and worth three hundred dollars, gold, to us." He smiled and clinked his whiskey bottle with Earl's and drank a toast. "The next two," he hesitated, "no, the next three, are all worth a hundred dollars each and the big buck, the one named Grant Washington on the reward paper, well, that buck is worth five hundred dollars."

"Damn, that's a lot of money for one nigger." Earl said.

"Look at him," Riley replied, "I don't see nothing special. I think his reward is higher due to his being educated."

"Educated?" Earl said uncertainly.

"Yeah," Riley said, "The reward paper here says he can read and write. Maybe that why they gave him such a fancy name."

"Grant Washington," Earl snickered, "I'll bet that if that whore's whelp had been his, they would have named it after him." He took another pull from his whiskey bottle as he added, "Ain't that just one a hell of a name for a low-down darkie?"

"Go figure," Riley said.

"What's that all total, Riley," Earl asked.

"Well, if they all pay up as advertised, one thousand and one hundred dollars."

"That's a lot of money," Earl murmured. "Can you really count that high?"

The rest of the trip was uneventful. They met up with the proper authorities in Atlanta and had no trouble collecting the reward money. Over the course of the next ten years, each spring they were destined to make the same trip after runaway slaves using the same tactics and in basically the same territories.

Chapter Three

The Winds of Change

Nine years later

The spring of 1853 was an uncommonly wet and miserable one. It followed what had been an unusually harsh winter. Rumor had it that hundreds of Indians living on the upper reservation in the area closest to the river had starved to death. Those responsible for delivering the supplies that were due these people from the white man's government claimed that the deep snow had prevented them from getting through.

The previous summer's crop had been very poor. The corncribs, root cellars and storage bins had been empty for a long time. There was also a lack of wild game for the men to hunt. This was due in part to the hunting pressures brought on by the steady onslaught of white settlers. It was a volatile situation that only added to the downward spiraling plight of the local Indian men who were accustomed to being hunters.

The government had broken yet another treaty and had made the boundaries of their world even smaller. They had assured the Indians that this change was good. They said that with less ground to cover, the distribution of food would be much easier and more reliable during the winter months. The treaty of 1851 still caused much unrest even with the most agreeable members of the Indian council. Too much land and control had been given to the white man. The continuing intrusion by the white settlers was causing all kinds of problems and unrest. Something needed to be done to resolve these issues, and soon, or there was sure to be more trouble. The area was viewed by many as a virtual powder keg that could explode at any time.

The new Indian agents, who were now being appointed by the acting Governor, had decreed that only those Indians designated as hunters would be allowed to possess guns. When these same officials were asked by the council to provide a list of those who were eligible, the answer was always the same. "We are working on it." For those who did have guns, getting ammunition was next to impossible. Many of the young Indian men were ready to fight back. Talk of another war with the white man became common around campfires and in the many meeting places throughout the upper and lower reservations. There was no doubt that trouble was brewing.

Red Calf had taken it upon himself to help raise the young black Indian, Colton. He practically lived at the mission school. He turned out to be one of her best students as Miss Lillie taught him to read and write. She convinced him early on of how important it was to adapt. He became determined to learn the ways of the white man. He was now nineteen years old. His reputation for being a wise young man grew and the tribal elders listened to his words. He urged education and change for his people. His skills in the white man's language, both spoken and written, were much better than that of his older brother, Chief Tall Cloud. He often served as a spokesman for his brother at many of the tribal council meetings.

"Let us learn the ways of the white man," he said each time he addressed the tribal council. "It is the only way for our people to live in peace."

Many Indians had already resigned themselves to learning the white man's trades and skills. There were many who decided to be carpenters, merchants and farmers. It was with the realization that old ways needed to give way to new ideas that many young men decided to heed Red Calf's advice. A lot of these lifestyle changes were for the best. Those who adapted to a life of farming and putting up winter stores soon realized that this made the difference between life and death during the long and lean winter months. Many now lived in sturdy farm dwellings with barns and stock houses. For the most part, they raised pigs, cattle and chickens.

Still, the Sioux were a people born to be free and not meant to live under the control of anyone. As the white man's grip on their everyday lives tightened, more and more young Indian men longed for a return of the days when they had roamed the land as they wished.

Miss Lillie knew that the Indians who lived in this area, near the central agency, were the least affected by the government's callous attitude and broken promises. The main agency store and trading post was about twenty miles away. A white trader named Myrick operated it and several other smaller stores. This included Carlton's store which was about nine miles away in the opposite direction. Being this close to it had insured that their supplies and rations had always been available.

These past nine years had passed quickly for Miss Lillie and her little man. Although his given name was Colton, she and everyone else called him Colt. He had been a very easy baby to bring up. He seldom fussed and seemed to be resistant to every form of sickness or ailment that came around. She had never seen such a happy baby. Those in her circle of friends, both white, colored and Indian, were amazed at how quickly he had learned to talk and take care of himself. Colt was reading from the grade seven primers by the time he was eight years old. There was no question that he was a very smart boy.

One of the white settler's wives, while passing through, had made the mistake of asking, "What on earth inspired a white Christian woman like you to take in such an ugly little Negro whelp? Don't you think he would be better off with his own kind?"

Lillie's anger had surfaced instantly. The woman was put in her place as Miss Lillie displayed one of her rare temper fits. She was determined to raise young Colt in the same fashion she would have had he been her natural child. Since the death of her husband, the first year they had been in the territory, she had been a loner. Her reputation for being fair and unafraid had earned her respect and numerous friends on both sides of the Indian issues.

The Reverend Jim Hastings and his wife, Amanda, ran an Indian school in the upper reservation. Several times a year, usually the first week in October and again the first week of June, Lillie's school and theirs got together to hold spelling and math competitions for their students.

The students were either pure Indian or a mix of white, and sometimes colored and Indian. Starting with the second year, Red Calf won the competitions every time. This had continued until he was fifteen years old and declared to be too old to participate.

The student from Reverend Hastings' school who won the most times and gave Red Calf a real challenge, was a young Indian girl whose Christian name was Marion. Like Colton, she was an orphan. The Hastings had taken a personal interest in her. They swelled with pride whenever they talked about her.

As the years went by, it became obvious that Red Calf and Marion were meant for each other. It was with great pride that Reverend Hastings joined them in marriage on Marion's sixteenth birthday in March of 1854.

June 1854

Typical of most rural schools, Miss Lillie's was one that was open all year around. Even as it was being built, she had insisted that a sign be erected in the center of the circular drive that read, "Sage Elementary School,' named in honor of Colton's natural mother.

There were no school semesters and no breaks other than harvest time. There were no grading standards. When a student was able to pass the current level testing they moved up a grade. Along with Bible study, Reading, writing, ('Riting') and arithmetic, ('Rithmetic'), the three R's, were the major areas of study.

Young Colton, at ten years old, was by far one of the brightest students she had ever had. Although she freely admitted that her opinion was prejudiced in Colton's favor, his test scores led her to believe that he was indeed, a gifted young man. His primary tutor and mentor, Red Calf, bragged on him all the time. Over the years, he had encouraged Colton to study hard and championed him in all ways. Like Colton's foster mother, Miss Lillie, he was determined that this orphaned Negro half-breed would get the best of what limited resources were available. He often said the Colton, though half Negro, had a heart as red as any Indian.

The hardships and realities of reservation life and open prejudices displayed towards them were overwhelming at times. The outright cruelties and injustices imposed on the Indian people were often greatly enhanced towards Colton, due to his being of mixed race. On several occasions, he had asked his foster mother questions about his natural mother and father. These were questions for which she had few answers.

It was the first week in June. Red Calf had taken a job as a carpenter building a house a few miles from the nearby town of Mankato. Miss Lillie agreed, halfheartedly, that Colton could spend a few weeks with Red Calf and Marion and perhaps help out on the construction job. Colt viewed them as family. He was excited when his mother gave permission for him to spend a few weeks away from home.

Red Calf and Marion also had another child who lived with them, an eleven year old Indian girl whose Christian name was Ruth. She was a very bright child and had beaten Colton in the schools' spelling competition just last spring.

Red Calf had been provided a small house, barely more than a shack, to live in while he worked on the construction of a farmhouse for a family who had recently moved to the area. The farm was located about a quarter mile from a fork in the main road that led south out of Mankato. The farmer was a smooth shaven white man named Tanner. He was known to be harsh at times and was in need of a competent worker and other helpers who would work for a lower wage than the whites demanded. He treated them decent enough, but Red Calf, being wise in the ways of the times, was always on alert.

Colton and Ruth got along well together. They played together as any children would. They enjoyed helping out as the new house was framed and built. They were enthusiastic and proud to help in any way they could.

It was mid-morning on the fourth day when a wagon and two riders came into view following the wheel ruts of the road that passed by the front of the house. Red Calf was working with several others on the second floor. He had just installed a window, and was raising it up and down to insure that it was working properly. He paused for a moment, almost in amazement, as he noticed that a Negro man was tethered to the back of the wagon by a short length of rope that had been placed around his neck. His hands had been tied in front and he was struggling to hold onto the rope and keep up alongside a horse that had also been tethered to the back of the wagon. On the wagon's seat, two white men were riding in apparent comfort. The wagon's bed was nearly full with supplies and miscellaneous items. On either side, in the front part of the wagon's bed, two Negro men were seated. If not for their many bruises they would have been riding almost at the same level of comfort as those on the front seat. Two other riders followed a short distance behind.

As the wagon neared, Red Calf stopped what he was doing to watch. He was vaguely remembering another scene, from a long time ago, as the wagon came to a stop in front of the house.

Tanner walked the few yards to the road and greeted the men.

"Good morning," he said. "Need a little water?"

"No, but we'd sure be obliged for some directions," the man nearest said. "I think we took a wrong turn. Will this road take us to Mankato?"

"Sure enough," Tanner replied. "You men must be bounty hunters." He looked the Negroes up and down for a moment and added, "Them niggers look a bit worn."

"Hell," the man answered, "It's a living."

"You're welcome to rest for a bit," Tanner said. He introduced himself, "My name's Tanner."

The men on the wagon's seat got down. The two riders also dismounted and came closer.

"I'm Riley," the first man said, "This here is my partner, Earl. The boys," he said as he thumbed over his shoulder, "are John and Michael."

"Rest awhile," Tanner said.

Red Calf was wishing that he could hear what was being said as the men below talked among themselves. A feeling that something was dreadfully wrong swept over him as he tried to remember.

Tanner smiled smugly as the wagon and two riders disappeared from view around a bend in the road. One of the first things they had wanted to know was where to find a good whorehouse once they got to Mankato. In his conversation with the bounty hunters he had been very descriptive about Marion and the cute little Indian girl. For a small fee he would tell them where they could stop and take their pleasure. As the wagon drove out of sight he patted his shirt pocket as if to be sure that the four silver dollars were still there.

Colt and Ruth were helping Marion with a few chores. She had just finished hanging a new curtain in the single window that faced the road. "When we are done, you and Colt can go fishing again," she said. "Red Calf will be so pleased to come home and have fresh fish for dinner."

Colt was excited; he loved whiling away time on the banks of the small river about a quarter mile from the back of the house. He and Ruth had caught 'dinner' there only two days before and he was anxious to try it again. For some reason, Ruth didn't want to go.

"Let Colt catch those slimy fish," she said. "I want to stay here with you." Marion was standing with her back to Ruth when she stuck her tongue out at Colt.

"That's fine with me," Marion said with a smile. "You can help me finish getting Red Calf's lunch ready. Do you want to walk with me and take it to him or are you just going to stay here and be lazy?"

"If it's okay with you, I'll just stay here." Ruth replied.

Colt was only a little dejected, "I always said you were a sissy girl," he said teasingly to Ruth. "You'll be so sorry when you see the gigantic fish I'm going to bring home."

This time Marion laughed as Ruth once again stuck her tongue out at Colt and retorted, "Girls are smarter than boys, you just go and get bug-bit all by yourself."

Colton got the fishing line and several spare hooks from the shelf and asked, "Can I borrow a sharp knife to cut the fishing pole?"

Marion gave him a sheathed knife and said, "Be careful with this, it is Red Calf's favorite."

Marion went out the door with a small basket and crossed the road to a trail that was a shortcut through the forest to the farmhouse. She was smiling, amused at how Colt and Ruth had exchanged words. As she distanced herself from cabin, she thought she could hear a wagon on the road.

As Colton was leaving on his quest, he saw a wagon in the distance. He noticed that there was a man walking behind and two riders following. He considered waiting for a few minutes to see who it was, but decided that he had rather get to the river and start fishing. For some reason, he was wishing that Ruth hadn't turned sissy and had come along with him. After all, she was his best friend.

The wagon was nearly even with the house when the driver, a scruffy man with bushy whiskers, noticed the very attractive young Indian girl standing in the open doorway.

"Riley," he murmured, "will you look at that."

"Hell, Earl that is nice. An early bloomer, just like Tanner said." Riley answered. "I sure as hell intend to get my dollars' worth."

Earl looked over his shoulder at the two riders who were now reined up alongside the wagon. "What do you think, boys? Was that farmer right?"

"What the hell, Earl," Riley said, "I don't see that grownup squaw he talked about."

Ruth was nervous as the wagon came to a stop in front of the house. She quickly closed the door and moved to look out the window. The two men dismounted and started walking towards the house. Earl approached and knocked on the door.

"Hello, inside. We're a little lost and are in need of some directions."

From within, Ruth replied, "Just stay on the road and it will take you to Mankato."

"What we're looking for is right here," Earl said. His voice elevated, "Open the goddamn door."

Ruth, her young voice filled with apprehension answered, "My uncle and his brother are in the back, talk to them if you need something."

She heard the man laugh and then gasped, as the door was kicked open. She cried out in terror as two men quickly entered. There was a short time of deafening silence as the men stood there, eyeing her up and down.

"We heard there was another squaw here as well," Earl said.

"Where is she?"

Ruth was nearly chocking with fear as she answered. Her voice was barely audible as she hoped they would believe her story, "She's in the back, too."

Riley crossed the small room and grabbed Ruth by the hair. "I know you're lying, you little whore," he growled. "Where's the other goddamn squaw."

"She left," Ruth said as she broke down in tears.

"Damn, Earl." Riley said. "That hayseed was right. "Ain't' this just the cutest little whore you ever seen?"

"Yeah," the man called Michael murmured. He was standing watching with his shoulder leaned against the open doorway, "Cute little tits and all."

"Let's do this like gentlemen," Riley said with a smirk. "You all wait outside and choose who is next."

Ruth was trembling in fear as the others went outside. She had heard rumors of these kinds of things happening and was terrified. The man called Riley kept his grip on her hair and holding her at arm's length peeled the calico dress up over her head. Her mind went blank.

The man named John was the last to have a turn. He was upset at his order of the draw due to someone having to keep a close watch on the three runaway slaves in the wagon. When he was finished taking his pleasure, he called out in a jovial tone, "Next."

Riley came back inside. The girl was beyond feeling as she remained in place; face down on the tabletop, her eyes glazed over. John left the room, smiling broadly. He watched over his shoulder, more curious than anything, as Riley went over to the girl. He took a firm grip on her head with both hands and broke her neck with one violent motion.

"Ain't any witnesses now," he said to the others.

Riley joined Earl on the wagon's seat and braced as Earl snapped the reins. John and Michael were already mounted. As before, they followed closely behind the Negro tethered to the back of the wagon.

Marion had decided to stay and help Red Calf finish out the day. It was late afternoon when they started walking home following the road. They were almost within sight of the house when a wagon came thundering up to them and stopped. They recognized the driver, a white settler named Gus. He was a friend and a neighbor. He shouted, "Red Calf! Thank God I've found you. You had better get home quick! I'll turn around and you climb on board."

A mutual feeling of dread swept over them as Gus reined the team around. They quickly climbed onto the seat. "What is wrong?" Marion asked.

Gus made no reply as he reined the horses to a dead run. A few minutes later he brought them to a fast stop in front of the cabin. His wife, Clara, came to the door. She had tears streaming down both cheeks.

"You had better get inside," she said as she wiped her face with her apron. Then, she chokingly added, "Colton got back from fishing at the same time we were stopping to say hello. He was the first one to go inside the house."

"Oh, my God," Marion murmured. "Ruth?"

Clara tearfully nodded her head.

Red Calf and Marion crowded past her. Colton was kneeling beside the bed holding Ruth's hand. He twisted around to make eye contact with Red Calf. His voice was surprisingly calm and clear as he said, "I saw a wagon followed by a man walking and two riders as I left to go fishing."

Red Calf's face was ashen as he took in the scene. Clara had placed Ruth on the bed. Her eyes were wide open. A grotesque expression was frozen on her dead face.

Marion had been silently watching. She fell to her knees as if she had been struck; a look of horror was frozen on her face as she took in the scene.

"I know who they are," Red Calf murmured. "They stopped

at the new farmhouse." His body stiffened as if he had been shocked as he instantly remembered back to that time ten years before when he had been a young boy. He felt nauseous. In his mind he could see the man called Riley and his partner, Earl, beating and terrorizing Colton's mother, causing her death, all those years ago. He shuddered as he came back to reality with a start. Anger started boiling within as he added, "Those animals must be stopped. I need to go after them, they can't have gone far."

"Clara will stay here with Marion and Colt," Gus said softly. "Come with me if you wish. I'm going for the law."

Gus and Red Calf hurried to the wagon. Darkness was descending. As Gus reined the team hard, Colton scrambled to climb on the back. He had Red Calf's 'favorite' knife in his hand. As Red Calf glanced back over his shoulder, he noticed for the first time, the catch Colton had brought back from the river, laying on the ground beside the door.

The sheriff in Mankato listened closely, first to Gus, then to Red Calf. He offered his condolences and said he would send a deputy back to the scene with Gus. He stated that there really wasn't much he could do other than keep an eye out for those described by Red Calf. Sensing trouble, he immediately sent a rider to the new army outpost, Fort Ridgley.

"Me and Clara will stay the night with Marion," Gus said to Red Calf. "I can see from the look on your face that you ain't coming back for a while."

"Thank you, my friend." Red Calf said. Then, he added, "Colt must go with you."

Colton had backed up a few steps and waited silently. He shook his head 'no.' His expression, set in a ten year old face of stone with hollow eyes, was such that Red Calf had nothing else to say. He motioned for Gus to get going.

For the next several hours they combed every livery stable in town with no success. They reasoned that the man called Riley and his friends had continued on their journey. Darkness was descending as a small group of Indians, several riding in a small buckboard and others on foot, caught up to them and silently shadowed their every move. They were aware of what had happened and hoped to be with Red Calf should he catch those responsible.

Colton was nowhere to be seen when Red Calf went into a small store on the edge of town to ask if anyone knew of the people they were after. Another young Indian, named Wild Fisher, had accompanied him and waited patiently on the boardwalk. When he walked back outside, he was surprised to find Colton standing calmly in front by the hitching post. He was holding the reins of two horses. The glow of a setting sun was gone and it was now dark. In the dim light cast from several boardwalk lanterns, he was surprised to see that Colton was smiling.

"Two drunken white men at that saloon," Colton said, nodding his head over his shoulder, "paid me a dollar to take these horses to the livery stable." He grinned at Red Calf's astonished look and added, "They think I'm a good little nigger."

Red Calf exchanged concerned looks with Wild Fisher. They both knew that the penalty for stealing a horse was death. A fleeting smile crossed his face as Wild Fisher shrugged his shoulders. They had no doubt that those they were after had left town. Since it was dark and there appeared to be no witnesses, they got astride the horses. Colton rode double behind Red Calf and Wild Fisher rode the second horse. Soon they were thundering down the road out of town. The buckboard with several Indians was close behind and those who were on foot followed doggedly as fast as they could.

They caught up with slave traders, Riley, Earl, John and Michael an hour before sunrise about five miles outside the reservation border. They were camped near a slow moving stream a short distance off the new road to St. Paul. There were now nearly a dozen braves accompanying Red Calf. The Indians approached the camp silently, like shadow warriors. In the darkness of a pre-dawn sky, the slavers were able to put up only a token fight. Soon they found themselves bound and helpless. As the sun rose in the new morning sky, they began to experience a very long day of true frontier justice.

Miss Lillie got the news early the next morning after Ruth had been killed. Word of the incident was spreading like wildfire throughout the reservation. An older Indian man named Dove of Day hitched up the buckboard and drove her in a hurry to be with Marion.

An Indian deputy marshal from the Redwood agency was there to greet them. He had been dispatched to the scene by the officials in a veiled attempt to show that the Indians did have authority in these matters. Although his show of support was appreciated, it came as no surprise to Miss Lillie, or anyone present, when he solemnly told them that he had no real authority to help. Those in charge would never allow anyone in the agency police unit to pursue white men.

The funeral services were held at Miss Lillie's mission the third day after Ruth's death. Indians had come for miles around. The Reverend Hastings came down from the upper reservation to conduct the service.

Red Calf and Colton showed up at the mission just as the services were about to start. Both were wearing freshly laundered clothes with their hair combed neatly. Marion and Lillie were worried about Red Calf and Colton. They hadn't been seen or heard from since they left the sheriff's office the day of the tragedy. They were both surprised when Red Calf came into the mission and took a seat beside Marion. Miss Lillie's face lit up with delight and relief when Colt squeezed into the bench seat between her and the person seated alongside. She smiled seeing that he was already cleaned up for church services. An eerie feeling came over her when he tensed up as she gave him a hug.

For the next few days, the reservation was abuzz with rumors and stories about four white men who had been found dead just outside the reservation borders and mutilated beyond recognition. Apparently, theirs had been a slow death. Rumor had it that a group of Indians had happened on them and exacted their revenge. These rumored accounts said they had been asked many questions.

It is said that a single silver dollar was found clenched in a death grip in the right hand of each man. The runaway slaves were never seen or heard from again.

The farmer, Tanner, immediately ceased all work on his new farmhouse and moved for a time into the town of Mankato. Little did he know that the only reason he was still breathing air was due to the fact that an incident within the reservation borders would have resulted in more grief and problems for the local Indians. Those in the know had near unlimited patience. Time was on their side. Justice and revenge would eventually be metered out.

For a short time, the horse soldiers were everywhere, making their presence known to all. During this time, food was plentiful and supplies were delivered on time.

Chapter Four

Wars and Rumors of War

May 1855

    Another harsh winter, one that they had thought would never end, had come and gone. The spring rains had brought with them the hopes and promises of better times. Hope was something that was in short supply throughout the upper and lower reservations. The past few seasons had seen more and more grief for the Sioux as the white man continued to box them in. Another army post had recently been established much closer than Ft. Snelling. Fort Ridgley was laid out in a manner similar to a regular town or settlement with no surrounding walls. It now housed a full garrison of government troops, always on the ready.

    More delayed payments of government annuities and more broken promises had created a division within the tribal council members. Even the most basic meetings often ended with angry shouting and hard feelings. Conflicts between the white settlers and Indians were becoming an everyday occurrence. Any grievances were almost always decided in favor of the settlers who continued to come in droves. The summer months came and went. July and August were two of the driest months on record. Hopes of having a good harvest of the corn and potato crops faded as the drought wore on.

The white settlers and the army soldiers seemed to share an open contempt for the young Indian, Red Calf, and his wife, Marion. There was no denying that there were those who resented the fact that they were both better educated than most whites. These were the same people who were determined to keep the Indians, educated or not, in what they deemed to be their proper places. To these people, good intentions made no difference. In nearly all things, the Indians were 'damned if they did' and 'damned if they didn't' in their eyes. With no way to win, and no hope in sight, it was no wonder that many Indians refused to give an inch in adapting to the so-called civilized ways of the whites.

There were many settlers in the area that would forever hold a grudge against Miss Lillie. They thought her to be untrue to her race as she kept turning out one educated Indian after the other. She was talked about unfavorably in the gossip circles of the white women in town. They spoke of a great mistake on her part due to how she had taken in the orphaned colored boy. About the only Indian trait that showed in him was his straight black hair that was always neatly trimmed.

There were those busybodies that said that if not for that boy, Miss Lillie could have found herself another husband. After all, she was viewed as an attractive woman. Those who talked this way were the same women who snubbed her and her foster son openly whenever they came to town. She tried to ignore them, knowing that they were a bunch of small-minded people. Her hope was that they were not the majority. Still, she resented being slighted during the religious events participated in by the churches in town and those spread out over the reservation lands. She believed that there was no need for that kind of behavior in God's house. After all, everyone was welcome at her mission. This same bunch also showed a high degree of bitterness towards the Reverend Hastings and several other area missionaries. They believed that they had no business mixing the races and uniting what they referred to as 'two heathens' in holy matrimony.

The gossip community was a-buzz with scandalous stories every time a missionary Reverend or Miss Lillie announced a Christian marriage between anyone not of the white race. It was understood that the churches in town were reserved for whites only. Occasionally, there were those who would allow their colored servants to sit in the back pews. This was rare. The coloreds were expected to attend their own church.

Colton was one of those types who always seemed to be happy and upbeat. It was his nature to smile a lot. His was a somewhat sheltered existence, far away from the realities of the outside world. This was in part because his foster mother did all she could to protect him, especially after the heinous incident that had resulted in the death of his friend, Ruth, the year before. She did her best to keep him away from situations that could conceivable get ugly. This included never allowing him to be alone around the adults or white children from town. As a result, he was her constant shadow. Most of their time was divided between running the school and conducting the religious services. As protected as he was, young Colton was quick to catch on.

Since Ruth's death, Colton had experienced many incidents of which his foster mother would never know. This included the time he was set upon and severely beaten by three white boys. It happened while Miss Lillie was away for a few days serving as a midwife delivering a baby in a nearby settlement. Colton felt embarrassed over the incident and was determined that she never find out about it. He had managed to get away from his tormentors. Although they chased after him, it was his speed and agility that saved the day. Almost no one could keep up with him in a foot race.

The white boys had come upon him at the shore of the small lake near the school. It was just before dark and he was setting several fishing lines for the night. He had baited the large hooks with pieces of rancid salt pork. It was his plan to check the lines several times during the course of the night and if lucky, he would have a catfish or two for tomorrow's meals.

He soon discovered that he wasn't the only one fishing. He felt embarrassed that he had been so focused on what he was doing that he had no idea that the three boys were near until one of them called out to him in a loud rude voice.

"Hey, Nigger, what do you think you're doing?" the boy speaking was probably twelve or thirteen years old. He carried a long fishing pole that he had cut earlier.

Colton's surprised look was comical to the boys. They laughed as he replied, his voice shaking, "I'm setting a couple lines to catch some fish." Although he had no idea of their names, he recognized them from having seen them in town and on occasion, riding in a wagon past the school. They had never been rude or disrespectful before, but then, he had always been with his foster mother.

"Not here and not today you don't," the oldest boy said with authority, "we've got rules and we don't let no niggers' fish in our lake. You had better be moving on."

"I've got as much right to be here as you," Colton said defiantly. "You don't own the lake." He was afraid as he eyed his antagonists. The oldest boy was nearly a grown man, and had an obvious mean streak. The two lackeys were also around twelve or thirteen but were average size. One, wearing a pair of red suspenders, tossed down his fishing pole and said, "Maybe we should teach this mouthy little nigger some respect for white folks."

The fight was on as the big kid attempted to grab Colton. He may as well have tried to catch the wind. Even though Colton had his back to the water, he ducked and dodged out of reach before the big kid could lay a hand on him. It was the other two who got a hold of him as he tripped over one of their fishing poles. He was thrown to the ground and all three boys started pummeling him with punches and kicks to his midsection. One of the boys hit him hard alongside of the head with a fist sized rock. Through waves of pain and dizziness he writhed and wriggled loose and sprinted a few feet away. After that, the white boys had no chance of beating him anymore. Colton ran like the wind to high ground and stood bent forward with his hands on his knees, gasping for air, reeling in pain. His nose was bleeding and he had several bruises on his face. The boys followed still wanting to beat him some more. Then it became as a game to Colton. He realized fear was his true enemy. He got a tight grip on his emotions and waited calmly as they neared. As they got close, thinking they had him, he would sprint away at such a speed that they couldn't hope to catch up. After getting away the first time, he started laughing and taunting them.

"What's the matter?" he said. "Can't you three cowards catch this one little nigger?"

They screamed at him in rage as he led them farther from the lake towards a wooded area. "Come on, fat boy, catch me." He taunted, "I guess cowards are slow; slow and stupid." When they finally realized that they would never catch him, they gave up and started walking angrily back to where they had left their fishing poles. They cursed him over their shoulders and tried to hit him with thrown rocks as he shouted from high ground, "Is that all you've got, cowards? Hey you, sissy boy, did your mommy dress you in those red suspenders?"

The boys had left their wagon, hours before, a short distance away and very close to the lake. Colton spotted it from the high ground as the boys were retrieving their fishing poles to save the hooks and lines. Apparently they hadn't caught anything. He came up with an instant plan of revenge. Smiling with delight, he silently raced around the high ground out of sight from the boys and quickly approached the wagon. He took hold of the reins and urged the horses to walk backwards just a little. When the wagon was positioned just right with the rear wheels just over the downhill slope of the embankment he hurriedly pulled the connecting pin. His smile was ear to ear as the wagon coasted and rolled the last fifty or sixty feet down a very steep and rocky embankment and went crashing into the water at the lakes edge.

"Let's see how the cowards get it back," he said softly to himself as he hurried out of sight. He watched from a place of concealment, silently in the near darkness, as the boys returned to discover that the wagon had come unhitched and had rolled into the lake. To make things worse, the pin was missing and they had no way to get the horses close enough to the wagon to pull it out. They left in a hurry; riding the team bare back and hoping their parents wouldn't be too hard on them over losing the wagon.

Colton smiled as he limped on his way home. Today had been an important learning experience, one to remember. Yes, they had beaten him and he was the only one suffering in pain and discomfort, but still he felt elated at how he had outmaneuvered three white boys and shamed them in a most humiliating way.

The next morning he awoke early, wincing from the pain of his many injuries. Then, remembering that he had left his fishing lines in the water and hadn't checked on them during the night, he rolled out of bed. Several Indian women had been staying at the mission while Miss Lillie was gone and were instantly concerned as they saw his face and the bruise where he had been struck with the rock. They fussed over him for a while. It was with great self-control that he nearly begged and then finally convinced them not to mention it to his mother when she returned. He bribed them with the promise of fresh catfish for breakfast. They smiled as he left to check his lines.

Colton walked quickly to the lake where he had left his fishing lines. His eyes constantly scanning the area, he was determined not to have anyone sneak up on him again. He topped the rise where he had a view of where the wagon had gone into the water. He smiled as he noticed that one of the boys who had beaten him was there with two adult white men. They were just hooking a pull line onto the wagon. He hurried to the lakeshore and checked his lines. He pulled in two very nice catfish and put them on a stringer. Next, he gathered his fishing line and hooks and started back towards the top of the rise. The white men had pulled the wagon out and were slowly driving it back to the road. They looked up and smiled and waved to the little colored boy standing there atop the rise, proudly holding two very nice fish for the world to see. The boy with them acted as if he didn't see anyone. Soon Colton was back at the mission and the two women were beaming when they saw the very nice fish.

Over the years, he learned the ropes from perhaps the most set upon people in the world, the reservation Sioux and his Indian brother, Red Calf. He instinctively understood the meaning of prejudice and injustice. He considered himself to be a Redman and got his most memorable lessons by merely observing the treatment of his Indian people. He believed that there was good in most people. The three boys who had assaulted him, he was sure, were products of their parents' prejudices. He tried to be in agreement with his foster mother in all things. Over time, the truths and harsh realities that he witnessed daily were the things that really molded him in his views. Living on the reservation and seeing the devastating impact and terrible results that lies and broken promises caused for his people, his beliefs were soon unshakable.

October

The fall foliage was in its full splendor of color. The early morning sun radiated off the many shades of red, yellow and green. The heavy morning frost was glistening and shining with a beauty of its own adding to the grandeur of a living forest. As the small buckboard made its way along the narrow road, Miss Lillie was nearly overwhelmed by the beauty of it all. She smiled each time her foster son would comment about something that was really obvious.

Colt was now eleven years old. He proudly guided the horse along the road, feeling much older than his years because he was allowed to drive. Since he had been old enough to talk, autumn had been his favorite season.

"Look at that one, Momma!" He exclaimed as they rounded a bend and was faced with an aspen grove that had turned brilliant yellow. "Isn't it beautiful?"

"It surely is," she answered softly, "I think God was really smiling when he painted those leaves. Do you think we should stop and collect a few?"

"Whoa, boy," Colt said gently as he pulled back on the reins. As soon as the wagon was stopped, he passed the reins to his mother. Next, it took all of his strength to set the handbrake as he stood upright and strained to pull the wooden lever into place.

"I'll be right back," he said as he jumped from the buckboard to the ground.

"Colt!" she said in a scolding tone, "how many times have I told you to climb down? You're sure to break a leg or something if you keep jumping like that."

His smile, as he picked off several brilliantly colored leaves and turned to face her, wiped away any chances for a serious scolding.

"These are just for you, Mother," he said, as he quickly approached another tree and picked several bright red leaves. "Don't you just love 'em?"

He climbed back onto the seat and gave his mother a quick hug. He placed the leaves into the sack that she was holding open.

"Thank you, young man." she said.

"You're welcome," he replied. "Can we put them up in the school room windows when we get back?"

"Sure, and maybe if Mr. Carlton has any of that new waxy paper, we can iron a couple together."

"Just like last year?" Colt exclaimed.

"Uh-huh. It will be fun and we can enjoy how pretty they are all winter long."

This idea sounded fine to Colt.

"Red Calf said you are right, Mother," Colt said breathlessly as he took the reins back from her. "I even asked him if he was sure."

"Red Calf?" she asked. "What about him?"

"He says that God painted them too."

"Red Calf is the second best student in the whole world," she said. "Do you know who the very, best is?"

Colt smiled and proudly said, "Me."

He gave the reins a sharp slap on the horse's back and got the buckboard moving. Soon, they came to Carlton's trading post. At first, they didn't notice that the area and the few scattered buildings were nearly deserted. As they reined to a stop, Lillie was caught up in an eerie feeling as it dawned on her that the usual groups of natives were nowhere to be seen. She wondered if the absence of people would have anything to do with the stories and rumors that were spreading. Even back in their small settlement she had heard rumors of serious trouble with another Indian tribe, somewhere out west in the Wyoming territories. She hoped that those in the trading post would have the real story.

Colt swelled with pride as he quickly tied the horse to a rail that projected into the street at an angle. He stood on his tiptoes and removed the bit from the horse's mouth. He smiled happily at his mother as he spoke soothingly to the horse.

"Old Winston is one lucky horse to have a good man like you taking care of him." Lillie said. They joined hands and went inside.

The proprietor, Mr. Carlton, greeted them warmly. He was a white man in his early fifties. He made no secret of the fact that he had wanted to court Miss Lillie for years.

"Howdy!" he boomed. "Miss Lillie, Colt, I haven't seen you two in a dog's age. How have you been?"

"Hello," Lillie replied. "It has been awhile." She offered her hand across the counter, "We've been doing just fine. How about yourself?"

"Lillian Taylor," Mr. Carlton said accusingly, "don't you think for a minute that you're going to get by this counter without giving me a hug."

Colt smiled gleefully at his mother's apparent self-consciousness as she leaned across the counter to accept an embrace from Mr. Carlton.

Another voice cut in, "Well hello there, strangers." It was one of Lillie's friends, Amanda, whose husband also ran an Indian school and a house of worship. Their small mission was located about the same distance from the trading post as Lillie's, only in another direction.

"Amanda. It's so good to see you," Lillie said. "How have you been? Where's Jim?"

They embraced, as Amanda replied, "He's around here somewhere." They immediately began to catch up on the latest news. A few minutes later, Jim joined them along with another woman and her husband.

"Jim," Amanda said, "be sure to treat Lillie's boy to a stick of sugar candy."

Jim shook hands with Lillie and answered, "Don't I always?" They shared a laugh as Jim reached across the counter and took a peppermint twist from the jar and passed it to Colton. "Just for you," he said.

"Colt," Lillie said, "What do you say?"

Colt bashfully took the candy and murmured, "Thank you, Reverend Hastings."

Jim smiled and said, "Think nothing of it, Colt."

"Hey," the other man said, "what about me?" He was an older man with flowing white hair and long sideburns. He stood smiling beside his wife. "Clara and I have an extra treat for Colt, too."

For the next few minutes, Colt enjoyed being the center of attention. The man reached inside his coat pocket and handed him another stick of peppermint. He leaned down and whispered, "Save this one for later."

Colt murmured, "Thanks, Mr. Bedew. I'll share it with a friend." Then, he winced as Mrs. Bedew leaned down and gave him a hug. "Thanks, Mrs. Bedew," he said.

It had been several weeks since any of them had been near the trading post. Miss Lillie, Mrs. Bedew and Amanda took this time to get caught up on local gossip and news.

Colt sat politely listening as the women talked about all kinds of things. Once the men joined them, it wasn't long until the subject of the recent massacre of the entire Brule Sioux Indian tribe came up.

"Is that why this area is so deserted?" Lillie asked. "Where is everyone?"

"They're afraid," Mrs. Hastings softly replied, "afraid to be near where the soldiers are usually seen."

Miss Lillie was incredulous as Mr. Carlton told his version of what had happened far away in the Wyoming territory. The Bedews and the Hastings already knew the story and listened somberly to its retelling. Lillie felt lightheaded as Mr. Carlton offered some advice.

"I'm serious, Lillie," he said, his voice stern. "They killed every damn one of them. The local Indians are already talking about revenge. You really need to think twice about wintering somewhere other than here in the heart of the reservation this year."

"Leave the school," she replied, "and the mission? We can't do that. It is home to us. We are safe there."

"I hope you're right," Mr. Hastings cut in. "Still, we've been advised to move into town for a while and that's just what we are going to do."

Mrs. Hastings met Lillie's questioning look and said, almost defensively, "We're going to move into New Ulm. It's not safe out here, Lillie, despite what you think."

"What about you?" Lillie asked Mr. Carlton, "Are you leaving as well?" She looked around the room and added, "I don't see you packing."

"I will be and soon. They've already cut off all of my supplies." Mr. Carlton said, "What you see right here is all that's left, when it's gone, there won't be any more, at least not at this post."

"Where are the people supposed to get goods this winter?" Lillie asked.

Mr. Carlton shook his head sadly and said, "The commander at Fort Ridgley is sending an entire troop of soldiers to winter it out right here." He scowled and thumbed in the direction of the rear of the store. "They're taking over. There's plenty of room back there and it'll put 'em closer to an insurrection should one happen here."

"My God," Lillie said softly.

Mr. Carlton glanced over Lillie's shoulder at Colton. "I'd consider moving very seriously, Lillie." he whispered. "If something happens, those soldiers won't think twice about bashing your boy's head in." He paused again at her startled look. He leaned to one side to spit into an old metal pail on the floor beside his counter. He continued in a whisper for only her to hear as he added, "It's a fact that most of 'em hate his kind."

Mr. Bedew said, his tone somewhat bewildered, "I never would have thought that it would come to this."

"Still, Lillie, I hope you know that I'm only trying to give some friendly advice," Mr. Carlton said in a matter-of-fact tone. "You and Colt, well, you both really mean the world to me. I'd be very upset if anything bad ever happened to either one of you."

A somber mood overcame them as the conversation stayed serious. The subject eventually switched to some of the recent stories that were spreading. There were far too many stories of cruelty towards the local Indians to ignore.

Mr. Carlton told them that he was afraid for his job. He thought for sure that those above him in the agency chain of command wanted him gone. He knew that this was because he actually tried to be fair to the Indians. "They'll probably have me out of here within a week," he added.

No one doubted that. They all knew that those who ran the business affairs of the agency were capable of just about anything. Mr. Carlton was one of the few agency people they knew who could be trusted.

"Most of 'em will use this Brule massacre story as an excuse to clamp down even more in these parts," Mr. Carlton stated somberly. "It's not too late, Lillie. I think you should go to New Ulm with the Hastings."

Colt stood silently beside his mother with his arm around her waist as he took in the conversations. Soon, it was early afternoon. Mr. Carlton and Mr. Bedew served up stewed chicken and potatoes for lunch. They enjoyed this time of togetherness. Soon after, the Bedews and the Hastings left the store to begin their journeys home. Mr. Carlton loaded several sacks of flour, oats and corn meal onto the back of the buckboard.

"We didn't ask for all that," Lillie said.

"I doubt if I will be seeing you folks for a long time," he replied. "Not a bad idea to stock up a little. Please consider my advice and winter it out in town."

"We'll think about it," Lillie answered softly. "Thank you for your concern."

Mr. Carlton bent down and whispered in Colt's ear, "Maybe stash some of these supplies away. Somewhere secret: somewhere safe.

It's a long time until spring."

Colt nodded his head and climbed into the wagon seat. Even though it seemed as if the tension in the air could have been cut with a knife, Lillie smiled and then, laughed out loud as Colt stood tall in the wagon and reined the horse around to begin the drive home.

"You've got quite a little man there," Mr. Carlton said as the wagon pulled away.

Lillie smiled softly and waved good-bye as she said, "Thank you. I know."

Mr. Carlton stood watching silently as the wagon disappeared from view around a bend in the road. He shook his head and murmured, "I hope you know what you are doing." He glanced up and down the deserted street and at the empty shacks that lined both sides. He went back inside and began packing his things.

They were no sooner around the corner that took them out of sight of the trading post when Colt twisted in his seat to gaze at his mother. Her face had taken on a serious look that he had never seen before,

"Mother," he said, "there's no need to worry. I know what Mr. Carlton meant."

"About what?" she replied.

"About my kind," he said.

He reined the horse to a stop and drew closer to her with an embrace of his free arm around her waist. "Mother," he said, "there's no need to worry. Red Calf already told me everything I need to know." His words, spoken as if he were years older, caused her to shiver as he added, "I know what I am, Mother. I also know what they are."

"They?" Lillie asked, her voice shaking.

"The white people," Colt said, "except for you and a few others."

"I sure wish it could be different," she said, her eyes tearing up.

"I know Mother," Colt said, "but don't worry. Like I said, Red Calf already taught me all I need to know."

She offered him a weak smile. "Let's talk about something else. Okay?"

"Sure, Mother." he twisted back to face the front and snapped the reins.

"We'll never get home if 'old Winston keeps standing here," Lillie said. Her voice rose and changed back to cheerful as she said. "Let him know who is boss and let's get going."

"Yes, Mother," he returned her smile and snapped the reins again.

A few minutes later, Colt exclaimed, "Mother! We forgot to ask Mr. Carlton if he had any of that waxy paper."

Lillie's laugh blended with his as she replied, "Oh yes, I did. See?" She opened a sack and took out several sheets. "In fact," she confessed, as she held them up for him to see. "He is the one that actually remembered."

"Thanks, Mother," Colton said. He urged the horse to a slightly faster pace. He knew that it would be dark in a couple hours and wanted to be home by then.

The stories of the Brule Indian massacre, somewhere out west, had spread fast. No one had ever heard of the Wyoming Territories before this horrible incident. For a while, no one talked about anything else. Talk of the massacre was on the lips of every young Indian who believed himself able to bear arms against the white man. Most agreed that they would rise up and fight if given a chance. The accounts of the massacre told them that everyone; all of the brothers and sisters of the Brule tribe had been slaughtered by horse soldiers. It was said that a cowardly horse soldier, a general, had led these heartless butchers.

The word was that it had all started over an argument with a few white settlers about a single lost cow. Someone said that the cow had been killed and eaten by Indians who were long since gone when the whites showed up. They blamed it on those Indians who were present and the trouble began. The cowardly horse soldiers had opened fire on the Indian encampment with a cannon; killing many men, women and children. A well-known Sioux chief was also killed in that first attack.

The Indians had been enraged and they had launched their own counterattack. A fierce battle between only a handful of warriors and the soldiers, thirty in number, ensued. It had been a running battle and one of which the Indians spoke proudly. This part of the story caused many young Indian men to swell with pride. Their brothers had stood up against the injustice of the white soldiers and they had won. Thirty white soldiers lay dead before that infamous day had ended. The elations of victory, however, were to be short lived.

It was revenge for this Indian triumph that had motivated the horse soldier general to butcher the remaining innocent and unarmed people of the Brule tribe. The horse soldiers had started the battle on an unsuspecting village by firing heavy artillery pieces into the defenseless teepees. They attacked without mercy and spared no one.

As the reality of the story and their lot in life was realized, many Sioux came to the realization that they could be next. Without guns to defend themselves, the whites could easily do the same to them. This was talked about in many meetings. It was with these stories in mind that they became more aware of the constant danger presented to them; each day, by the white man.

The winter months were a time of extreme vulnerability for the Indians. They had no choice but to rely on the white man for everything essential to survival. During the so called good winters when the snows weren't too bad, the reservation officials could keep most of the roads open most of the time. In those times of heavy snow and extreme cold, roads were closed and supplies could not be expected.

Many Indians still lived in teepees that could be moved each season as they wished. Still, many others, now the majority, lived in small houses hastily built by the reservation officials to house them. These structures were always of poor design and workmanship. Those lucky enough to have an iron wood burning stove were considered rich. Most buildings were to be heated by a fireplace on an end of the one room structure. The roofs nearly always leaked. The single window of each house was always drafty and seldom worked during the summer months when the residents would want to open it. The doors were all board and batten in style and warped out of shape, making it impossible to seal up the drafts that let in the cold of winter. Most had no floors and had been constructed on bare dirt. Most of these homes also featured an outhouse built at the same time and in the rear area of the building's lot. It was said, often in jest, but true, that the outhouses were better built than the residence.

Those Indians who were fortunate enough to own a horse built shelters, often referred to as a hovel, attached directly to the house. Despite the unsanitary implications of this, it was just the way things were done. The same was so of hastily built chicken coops. It was not uncommon to see them built tightly against the house where the people lived.

There were others, those who had no use at all for the handouts of the reservation officials, who simply dug a deep hole, often even a short tunnel, into the side of a steep hill. They would roof it over and cover the roof with several feet of dirt. As primitive as this was, the dugouts were often the warmest places to be in the winter and the coolest in the summer.

It was up to the agency officials to record and keep track of what was handed out to the Indians. Blankets and warm coats were often misappropriated by the whites and sold for a profit to the many settlers and those traveling through.

Miss Lillie knew for a fact that there was no need for so many Indian deaths. Men, women and children were dying each winter from starvation due to the careless attitudes of their keepers. Disease claimed far too many lives due to the lack of medical care. Many deaths were brought about by acts of outright murder by the white settlers.

The officials ran the reservation with fists of steel and hearts of stone. They protected the white men behind the many acts of violence and cruelty. Greed became a major factor as the Indians were cheated daily with inflated charges and wrongful claims against the government annuity payments that never arrived on time.

The topic of statehood for the Minnesota territory was now being rumored as a certainty as well as talks of another homestead act. It was believed that if Minnesota came into the union as a free state, one where slavery was prohibited, the area would be opened up to even more homesteaders. Good news for them, but bad news for the Indians. Those settlers who had their eyes on more of the reservation lands were especially in favor of this.

Rumors of a civil war between the northern and southern states were starting to spread and grew louder each day.

Chapter Five

Ass Deep

November 1855

    Winter set in early. The first snowfall came the first week of November with five or six inches accumulating on the ground. Several extremely cold days cautioned against what was to come next. A strong wind blew and soon, nearly all of the leaves were gone. The trees were left looking like ominous skeletons reaching silently skyward as if to escape the earth's grip.
    The second snowstorm followed the first by about two weeks. This one had teeth. The ground was already frozen solid. The chill of winter set in and those who had shelter were huddled inside hoping for an early spring. The second week in December was ushered in with a record-breaking blizzard. The temperatures dropped below freezing, often below zero and stayed there for weeks. Many of those in the immediate vicinity of the school sought around the clock shelter with Miss Lillie. The school had an ample stock of firewood and two heavy metal stoves inside to offset the bitter cold of the season.
    Soon, the New Year came and with it, another angry blizzard. The roads had been snowed shut for weeks already and just when it seemed as if the situation could get no worse, it did. Supplies were no

longer available due to the trading post, only nine miles away, being closed and taken over by the horse soldiers. The agency officials had promised that they would make supply deliveries to the settlement, but due to the deep snow, that never happened. It wasn't long until the food supplies were used up. There were far too many mouths to feed. Within the settlement there were many widowed Indian women with small children and many children who were orphans. Even in the best of times, these people lived from hand to mouth. There was never enough food to go around. Usually, these people were housed in makeshift hovels and shanties. Other than Miss Lillie's mission, they had nowhere else to go. The situation was quickly getting desperate.

Mid-January 1856

Red Calf was still very much a part of Miss Lillie's family. He nearly always wintered at the mission and never missed a day of school unless there was reason. His wife, Marion, was now heavy with child. As the deadly winter wore on, Red Calf knew that he had to do something, and soon, for both his pregnant wife and their unborn baby. They had adopted the ways of the whites. He dressed in the style of the white man, usually in farmer bibs, heavy leather boots and a flannel shirt. His hair was cut short in the tradition of the horse soldiers. He was well known as a carpenter and already had worked on several building projects in the Mankato area. His wife liked to wear pretty dresses. Together, he and Marion were looked on as an ideal example of how Indians could be successfully educated and taught a craft. He had cautioned Miss Lillie, early in the winter season that the situation could become severe without the trading post being nearby.

"The stories of my people starving to death each winter are true," he told her. "It happens every year."

The winter conditions worsened and showed no signs of easing up. Red Calf offered to try to get to the main trading post and bring back supplies.

"The main post is over twenty miles away," Miss Lillie said. "In this weather, I won't hear of it."

"It must be done," he replied somberly, "too much is at stake not to try."

"Red Calf," Lillie said, "what are the chances of you making it to the central trading post and then back here?"

Red Calf smiled. It was also his nature to smile a lot. As if they were talking about something trivial, he answered,

"If 'old Winston hasn't gotten too lazy, the chances are good," he said. "We can get there, load him up and get back in two days if I can find a way around the deep drifts."

"Can I go too, Mother?" Colt asked.

Red Calf and Lillie answered in unison, "No."

Lillie smiled at Colt's dejected look.

"Red Calf," she said, "you do know how deep the snow is, don't you?"

He could sense that she was trying to make light of a serious situation.

"Yes, Ma'am," he replied. His answer caused them both to smile as he quoted a reservation official, from whom they had heard the expression on another occasion.

"I believe that the snow is, ass-deep," he paused and added, "To a tall Indian."

"You'll need to take a blanket for Winston," she said softly. "Colt will help you get him ready."

Even though it was nearly dark, Red Calf started on his mission right then. The chill of a brisk wind enhanced the bitter cold. This assured him that there was no sense to wait until tomorrow. He was already wrapped in a heavy blanket. He put on two pairs of mittens that Marion had knit for him, along with a headband to cover his ears. He made sure that he had a supply of sulfur matches in his shirt pocket.

He embraced his wife and patted her protruding belly softly. "I will be back soon," he whispered. He walked outside to the small barn with Colt. He waited as his young friend placed a halter and a lead rope on the horse.

"His blanket is tied pretty tight," Colt said, indicating the tattered material that served as a cloak on the old horse. "It should stay in place for your journey."

"My brother," Red Calf said, "if I am not back in three days you must use up the rest of the horse's feed."

Colt's surprised look caused Red Calf to smile. He pointed at the two remaining sacks of horse feed, "If you boil it long enough, it will keep you," he said. "To starve to death with food this close would be a shame."

"I will do as you say," Colt said. "Even the extra sacks that Mr. Carlton gave us are gone."

Colt watched silently as Red Calf entered the forest leading Winston through the deep snow. The horse had to lunge to get over several drifts as he was led into the tree line where the snow would be more settled. He was surprised to see Red Calf turn and face him. Red Calf raised his right hand in a gesture of good-bye. Then, he turned and disappeared among the trees. Colt shivered. The bitter wind seemed determined to blow right through him. He gazed in the direction that Red Calf had disappeared. He wished that he had thought to offer him the use of his knit cap.

Red Calf knew that the chances of his making it to the central supply post were next to nothing. Winston was winded after going less than a mile. He had to be careful not to overwork the horse. If the horse were to start sweating, he would freeze to death in a matter of minutes. Red Calf knew that death was stalking ever nearer each time they stopped.

He had devised a plan from the start. It was a plan that he dared not mention to Lillie or anyone else. He planned to get close to Carlton's old store, now the army post, with Winston and steal as many sacks of cornmeal and flour as he could tie onto the horse. Then, he would make his way back to the school, providing that he didn't get caught.

It was easy to see where he was going. The moonlight reflected off the snow making it nearly as light as day. He continued on through the cold night, anxious to reach his destination. By full daylight, he was only a short distance from Carlton's old trading post.

He left Winston tethered in a small hollow and closed the remaining distance on foot. He was careful to make his approach to the stable under the shelter of trees. He knew that if someone were to look outside and see his tracks it could mean trouble. He wasn't sure what he was going to do. He was intending to see how the events would unfold.

He made it into the barn with no problems at all. The deep snow near the back provided easy access to a window that had been covered from the inside with some kind of canvas material. He cautiously lifted up one corner and eased himself inside. The surprising warmth of the stable made him wish that he could have brought Winston along. He carefully checked out the area in the dim light as he took in the scents and sounds.

The stable was well stocked with hay and grain. There were over a dozen mounts, each in its own stall. These animals needed to be cared for at least once a day. He knew that sooner or later, a soldier or soldiers would be along to check on the horses and as it turned out, he didn't have long to wait.

The trading post was now being used exclusively as a military outpost and the soldiers had become accustomed to a boring routine. Months had passed and nothing had happened to even stir their curiosity. They whiled away the time playing cards and sipping from a supply of whiskey that never seemed to run out. He could hear two soldiers talking and complaining as they approached the stable from the trading post side. Apparently one of them had a severe cold and was violently coughing as he spoke in short sentences. They entered and began working on the chores necessary to provide for the care of the horses. They were still complaining about this harsh duty station as they returned to the main building. He watched in silence as they entered the trading post through a rear door. He remembered the trading post's layout and doubted if anyone would be in that back storeroom area. Knowing that he was risking it all, he quickly followed in the soldier's footsteps. He paused and listened at the door for a full minute. He cautiously opened the door and went inside.

He could hear men talking through the connecting door to the main part of the trading post. A smile crossed his face as he realized that his mission wasn't going to be as difficult or as dangerous has he had envisioned. He found a well-worn winter coat hanging from a peg on a support column. He put it on over his farmer bibs and concealed himself behind a row of barrels. This large room was filled with sacks of grain, flour, cornmeal, and just about every kind of food store anyone could want. He was smiling as he helped himself to a generous portion of cured ham that hung from a rope. He sliced off several large chunks and returned to his place of concealment. He ate slowly as he patiently waited. Soon, it was late in the afternoon. No one had entered the back room all day and it was doubtful that anyone would. He picked up a sack of cornmeal, placed it over his shoulder, and quickly made his way back to the stable.

He gave four of the army horses' generous helpings of grain. Then, while they were feeding, he made many trips back and forth between the stable and the storeroom. After the first few trips, he stopped being nervous. He doubted that the soldiers would return to the stable until the next day, if then. Darkness was settling in when he saddled the four horses. There were no packsaddles or supply riggings that he could find, so he figured that the military issue saddles would have to do. He started loading them with the many sacks of supplies. When he was finished, he led the tallest horse out through the back door first. The horse reared and lunged forward to plow a path in the deep snow.

He hurriedly led the animal a short distance inside the forest's edge. He tied it to a tree and went back for the others. He smiled at the heavens as he noticed that it was warming up a little and that it was snowing again. The second horse was a little easier to lead as he followed in the broken trail of the first. In a matter of only a few minutes, it was also tied safely within the forest. He led the next two horses outside at the same time. He paused long enough to close the stable door. Finally, after all of his bounty was within the confines of the forest and a safe distance from the trading post, he tethered the horses behind each other. He was smiling from ear to ear as he led the way on foot. The small caravan slowly made its way back to the clearing where Winston waited. The animals were nearly winded by the time they got there. He took the time to feed a measure of grain to Winston. Next, he carefully transferred several excess sacks of goods onto the old horse. This brief pause gave the other horses a chance to rest.

The snow continued to fall all through the night. He had gone several miles, being careful not to cross any of the snowed in main roads or trails. He wanted to be sure that should the lazy horse soldiers attempt to catch him, they would have no fresh sign to follow.

It was nearly daylight when the storm turned into another raging blizzard. He took advantage of this to make his way across a small frozen lake. He took shelter in a hollow that was only about a mile from his destination. The sky, now blackened by the ominous storm clouds, made it nearly pitch dark and impossible to go any farther. He was glad that he knew this area well. He gathered lots of wood and built a huge fire. He waited patiently, wrapped in a blanket near the temporary warmth of the fire, for daylight to come. He dozed off several times, only to be waked up by the cold. Each time, he checked to be sure the animals were secure and tossed more wood on the fire. He awakened as the night sky slowly gave way to full daylight. By noontime, the storm had subsided and the temperature had once again risen. With the promise of a better day, the sun was attempting to break through a hole in the clouds. He left three army mounts tethered in the hollow with their packs on the ground. He circled wide around the base of a hill and arrived at the mission just before dark.

Miss Lillie had been waiting hopefully for Red Calf to return. She cautioned Colt and Marion not to say anything to the others about his being gone. She didn't want anyone to be able to point the finger of guilt towards Red Calf if he was to do what she thought he had in mind when he left. Carlton's old trading post was the only hope. She knew that. If the soldiers caught Red Calf in the act of stealing from them, they would kill him. It was a certainty that they wouldn't hand over any supplies, if he did ask. The soldiers would want to hoard the goods until they were sure of an early spring, or until they were sure that they wouldn't be cut short. She knew the only way to succeed would be for him to steal what he could.

Until this year, food had been plentiful. Nothing even close to this had ever happened. This area had always had an ample supply of food due to being close to Carlton's trading post. Now, Lillie was experiencing what she had heard the Indians talk about for years. She had already talked to Colt about killing and eating Winston if something good didn't happen soon. Now, with the horse gone, she realized that their only hope rested in Red Calf being successful.

It was nearly dark before Lillie realized what day it was. It was Sunday. She announced to those crowded together along the walls and huddled on the benches that it was time for services. Marion sat at the piano and started playing a hymnal softly. It came as no surprise to Lillie when others joined in song. She watched in amazement as these people, more than likely about to starve to death, smiled and joined together in songs of worship. Marion stopped playing as a loud pounding was heard on the door. Several people cheered outright as Red Calf entered carrying a large sack over his shoulder.

He spoke softly to several men closest to the door. They went outside as he crossed the room to join his wife. He embraced Marion and Colt at the same time as Colt rushed to his side. He whispered something in Colt's ear and nodded in the affirmative to Miss Lillie. A fleeting smile crossed his face. A few minutes later, he was stretched out on the floor beside the glowing wood burning stove. In no time at all, he was fast asleep.

Soon, the food pots were full. The smell of cooking meat, baking bread, and corn meal filled the building. Colt smiled as he brought Miss Lillie a plate of food and whispered,

"Don't worry, Mother. This is a stringy old army horse. Winston is safe. Red Calf put him back in the barn."

"Thank God," Lillie said.

"Yes, Mother, we can thank God," he replied with a grin. "And how about if we also thank a really tall Indian?"

"Amen to that," she whispered. "Amen."

The supplies lasted only a short time due to the large number of people that needed to be fed. Lillie knew that they weren't out of the woods yet. As the weeks went slowly by, she heard more stories and rumors about other army horses that were found tied somewhere out in the forest next to large packs of food and miscellaneous dry goods. Although the thought of eating horsemeat was not a welcome one to her, it made no difference to the Indians. The meat was as well received as beef or deer or even as dog meat would have been. They all gave thanks, at each church service, for their meager share.

The men had plenty to do to keep them busy as they rationed out the meat and supplies. Due to the cold weather, there was no worry about the food spoiling. Several young men, including Red Calf, also delivered food to several families who lived in outlying shanties and farms. Shortly before another heavy snowstorm hit, the men made another anxious journey to Carlton's old trading post. Their whispered reports reaffirmed what Red Calf had said. The soldiers were paying little or no attention to the massive stores in the large storeroom attached to their barracks.

Miss Lillie breathed a sigh of relief when she heard the stories that the raid to steal supplies from the trading post had been successful and undetected. This time, they had stolen no horses. The crime of horse stealing carried with it a death penalty if caught. These young men were far more cautious and less desperate than Red Calf had been. She wondered how the soldiers could be so non-vigilant as to allow two successive raids to happen without incident.

Chapter Six

The Fever

The last few days of February were harsh reminders that winter wasn't over yet. More snow fell giving Miss Lillie and those at the mission even more cause to worry. Their spirits rose in celebration as a son was born to Red Calf and Marion. The baby was born during Sunday's church services. Red Calf was at Marion's side the entire time. His face was aglow with pride as the Indian woman acting as a midwife presented him with his son. For a while, they put the harsh times out of their minds as they fussed over this newest addition to the reservation.

The month of March was ushered in by welcomed unseasonably warm winds and several days of rain. Within two weeks, the snow was nearly gone. This was because the warm rains were followed by days of bright sunshine. By the third week in March, Miss Lillie and Red Calf thought that perhaps enough snow had melted off the roads to get a small wagon through to the old trading post. It seemed odd that now with the snow nearly gone, the reservation officials had made no attempts to open the roads and contact the many outlying small settlements and villages. This was the first time they could remember since the new school had been built, that no one at all had stopped by in such a long period of time.

A dozen Indians walked along behind as Miss Lillie and her little man broke the trail with their horse and buckboard. Winston kicked and floundered through the few remaining snowdrifts. They left early in the morning and got to Carlton's old trading post shortly before noon.

Lillie was surprised as they approached. There was a faint trail of smoke coming from the chimney, but no other signs of life. The buildings that lined both sides of this once thriving settlement were all deserted. She was wondering about all that when they pulled up at the front porch. Colt tied the horse to the hitching rail as he had the last time and waited anxiously for his mother to get down.

Meanwhile, Red Calf walked up onto the porch and knocked on the door several times. He exchanged worried looks with Lillie when there was no response from within. Then, one of the women who had come along pointed in through the window of the building next door and shouted, "Miss Lillie, come look!"

Through the window, they could see that the bodies of several soldiers had been laid out on two long tables that had been pushed close together.

"Oh, my God!" Lillie exclaimed.

She hurried onto the porch and opened the door to the trading post. A faint voice from within called, "Mercy. Please, have mercy."

Another voice, also weak, called out, "Plague."

"Oh, my God," Lillie said softly, for a second time. Her eyes were wide in surprise as she took in the scene.

There were a half dozen soldiers lying dead within the interior of the building. Their corpses were scattered about the room. Some were in bunks; others were on the floor where they had fallen. They had started the winter season at this temporary post with over a dozen healthy men. Now, only four soldiers were still alive.

Miss Lillie fought back a panic as she realized the seriousness of the situation. "Keep the others back," she said to Red Calf. "Keep Colt on the wagon."

Colt remained frozen in place in front of the horse. He was still holding onto Winston's reins.

"Mother?" he said, his voice hushed.

"Stay out!" Lillie said, her tone scolding, "Get back on the wagon. I don't want you to come anywhere near."

Colt remained silent as his eyes took in the scene over his mother's shoulder. He climbed up and sat silently in the wagon seat, wondering what was going on.

Lillie designated Red Calf and one other man to drag the bodies outside. They placed them in the building next door on the floor beside the others.

Only Lillie, Red Calf, and an older man named Dove of Day stayed inside with the sick men. Soon, they had placed the surviving soldiers in beds at one end of the building. Red Calf checked out the storeroom and stable. Lillie looked up as Red Calf touched her on the shoulder.

"The horses in the stable," he paused and made eye contact as he broke the news, "they are all dead," he shook his head and added, "Starvation."

"Lord have mercy," Lillie murmured, "The plague must have struck only a short time after you were here."

"Yes," he replied, "that is why the others were not challenged when they came back here to acquire more food. The door to the back was still wide open from where they propped it open that night."

"My God," she murmured.

"There is still plenty of food," Red Calf said, "in the storeroom. We must gather what we can and return to the mission to provide for our people."

Lillie instructed the remaining people to go around the back and gather supplies from within the storage area.

"You must not come in here," she said, "get all you can carry and wait outside." After they had done as instructed, she told them to go into one of the abandoned shacks and build a fire in the fireplace.

"You can spend the night there," she said, "you must leave at first light. Carry what you can and return quickly to the mission."

Noticing a dejected look on Colt's face, she added, "Colt, you must go with them. You must stay away from this place of death. Keep your distance."

Soon, it was dark. Red Calf and Dove of Day were still assisting Lillie. Water was boiling on the stove. The survivors were sipping a hot broth.

Lillie looked at Red Calf and said, "Someone needs to make a journey to the main trading post and let the others know," she said. She looked first at the patients, and then back at Red Calf, "The post doctor needs to be here."

Red Calf didn't hesitate in volunteering, "I will go," he said. He addressed his next remark to Dove of Day,

"We must keep everyone else away from these people." He indicated the soldiers who were suffering from high fevers. "Pray that this disease does not spread."

"All is well, my friend," Dove of Day said. "Miss Lillie and I will be fine."

"I will have to take the horse to go quickly," Red Calf said. Since I must go right past the mission, I will take the buckboard loaded and unhitch Winston there." He indicated several others who were still waiting for instructions. "Have them toss supplies on now, I must leave. In the morning, the others must carry what they can back to our people."

Lillie shook her head in the affirmative. "I've already explained that to them," she said. "Colt will go back too."

Red Calf started on his journey. The road back to the mission was easily traversed. He had considered having Colton ride back with him, but since he knew that he had been exposed to the fever, thought better of it. When he got within sight of the mission, he simply unhitched the buckboard, mounted the horse and rode away. The other roads were still snowed shut in many places. He often had to dismount and lead the horse around, and sometimes through, hard packed snowdrifts. When he got to the main trading post, he was surprised to find that it was also nearly deserted. He pounded on the quartermaster's door shortly after daylight.

The man who opened the door looked familiar. Red Calf could see over the man's shoulder that the room was filled with sick people. Some were in beds and others were laid out on blankets spread on the floor. At first, the man took him to be white due to how he was dressed. Then, realizing that Red Calf was an Indian, he couldn't stop his amazement from showing.

"Come in here," he said.

Red Calf entered the room.

"I know you," the man said. He smiled as a look of recognition crossed Red Calf's face.

"Dr. Morrison?" Red Calf asked.

"Yes." the doctor answered.

"It has been a very long time," Red Calf said as he extended his hand.

The doctor clasped his hand and said, "Several years, at least. It is good to see you."

The doctor seemed to want to visit about anything except the current situation. He tried not to let how tired he was show as he said, "I remember the first time I saw you. I think you were maybe ten years old. It was on the old reservation, up north in what used to be the Colton Township. You were with Miss Lillie and the woman, Sage. Do you remember that?"

"Yes," Red Calf replied. "I need to tell you, it was Miss Lillie who sent me here now. For help."

Doctor Morrison explained that the spotted fever had hit everywhere. White men and Indians were dying every day. He told Red Calf that the situation was dire, with no end in sight. He said now that Red Calf had been exposed, he would have to stay under quarantine along with many others.

"What about Miss Lillie?" Red Calf asked. "She and Dove of Day are alone with more sick soldiers."

"When Lieutenant Harley returns, I'll send you back with his detail. The soldiers are all under quarantine too. They are bringing a medical team here from Fort Ridgley. I don't know how much good they can do. They don't have much experience and the post doctor at Ridgley was one of the first to take ill from this terrible sickness. He may still die of it."

The doctor paused for a minute to let this new information set in with Red Calf. He smiled and added, "You look exhausted. There's food and warmth in the next building. Go there and get something to eat and try to get some sleep. I'll have the lieutenant wake you when it's time to leave."

Red Calf shook the doctor's hand again and smiled warmly. Doctor Morrison was one of the few white people that he or anyone he knew trusted. He was surprised to find that there was food, lots of it, on a long table. He ate his fill and soon was fast asleep wrapped warmly in a blanket by the blazing fireplace.

A rude young lieutenant kicked him awake a few hours later. He was very youthful in appearance and had an obvious mean streak.

"Get the hell up, Indian," he snarled. "Morrison wants you to go along with us."

Red Calf remained silent as he hurried outside. He was relieved to find that Winston was still tied to the hitching post. Someone had tossed a few armfuls of hay down in front of him. He smiled as he noticed this.

The lieutenant led the way at a quick pace followed closely by his seven-man patrol and a military wagon with two army medics wearing white coats.

Red Calf realized that so far the mission area had remained unaffected due to its being isolated from the rest of the people. He knew that it needed to be kept that way. He was nearly overcome with anxiety as he rode bareback bringing up the rear. Doctor Morrison had assured him that the two medics would give instructions to Miss Lillie in how to treat the sickness should it sweep through her mission. He tried to mask his concern as they hurried back to Carlton's trading post. He hoped that it wouldn't be too late to keep the others away from his wife and new son.

Nearly two weeks had gone by and no one from the mission area had come down with the sickness. Miss Lillie was hoping against hope that the exposure time was up and that they would be spared. The weather had turned nice. Most of the snow had melted and springtime was in the air.

It was late in the day when Lieutenant Harley showed up with several soldiers. The lieutenant struggled to remain in the saddle as they stopped in front of the school. Miss Lillie walked outside to see what they wanted. To her surprise, the lieutenant fell from his horse. The soldiers with him were faring no better and dismounted unsteadily. They staggered inside and sat on the school's benches.

"Red Calf," Lillie cried, "come help."

Red Calf had been strangely quiet for the past several days, always seeming to need more sleep. Lillie knew that Marion was worried about him. Despite his urging Marion to take their son somewhere thought to be safer, she had decided to stay with him. He came outside and bent down to help with the lieutenant. As he leaned over he just kept on going until he fell flat on his face. He remained prone on the ground beside the semi-conscious Lieutenant Harley.

Lillie shrieked for Marion.

As if through a fog, Red Calf could see that several people had gathered around. He felt as though he was burning up. He thought he heard Marion calling his name. This was followed by a very long time of silence.

Chapter Seven

The Three R's

Spring 1857

The situation concerning the reservation Indians could well be described as a plight. The treaty of 1845 had been broken and rewritten several times. The latest treaty, only in force for the past few years, had caused the world of the Indian tribes to become very small. They had been herded onto narrow sections of land that bordered both sides of the Minnesota River.

This region consisted of rich bottomland that remained the desire of the white settlers whose numbers grew steadily. They had successfully petitioned the agency officials for access and soon, many sections of the choice farmland had been leased back to the settlers. The payments for these transactions were made directly to the agency officials and supposedly were included back to the Indians in the annuity payments due each year from the federal government.

The reservation was still divided into two separate areas referred to as the upper and lower reservations. The U.S. Army was in control and the Indian wards had little or no say as to what happened to them. The fate of these people and their future was in the hands of the government appointed officials.

The central locale of the Indian agency had rapidly become similar to that of most small towns. It had a main street and a post office. The Indian agency's police force was in a separate building and had a small jail attached to the back. The area had nearly tripled in size in only the past two years. Most of the structures were board and batten construction and several sported tin roofs. There were two livery stables, one on each end of town. The largest building, the trading post, was the center of commerce. The same white traders still operated it and several smaller posts located throughout the reservation. The side streets and many areas behind the more impressive structures were a mismatched collection of shacks and shanties built from just about any material imaginable. Some dwellings were no more than dugouts that were mere pockmarks in the side of the hill on the north side of town. Many of the log huts were covered with roofs made of sod. The signs of abject poverty were everywhere.

The small trading post called Carlton's had been burned to the ground in the hopes of stopping the spread of spotted fever. A newer one was in the process of being built only a mile from the school. As it turned out, the local manager was a white man with a distinct concern and sympathy for the Indian people.

Miss Lillie's church school had been built on a rise in a beautiful area that overlooked a small lake about a half mile away. Several other buildings had sprung up around it making for another small settlement north of the main agency area. The two-room clapboard building served as a school during the week and as a church on Sundays and again on Wednesday evenings. The building was never completely empty or unused. It was a social center and the central gathering place for this growing community located about twenty miles from the town of New Ulm and thirty or so miles from Mankato.

The small shed roof addition attached to the back served as living quarters for Miss Lillie and her foster son. Her role was that of schoolteacher and she also served as the preacher lady. During the epidemic of '56, the school had also served as a hospital and Miss Lillie as a nurse. During the harshest portions of winter, the school building had been used as a shelter for those who were without homes of their own. There were far too many women, their numbers increasing every day, who, like Miss Lillie, were forced to raise their own and orphaned children by themselves.

The local folks, who were mostly Indian, gathered daily after school was dismissed. They discussed current events and offered thanks and prayers to the Lord Jesus. They prayed for deliverance and justice for their people. Their prayers seemed to be doing no good as more and more incidents of injustice and acts of outright cruelty were brought upon them. Utter disregard for their welfare was evident by the calloused actions of their white caretakers.

The settlers, as well as those who operated the trading posts, were never taken to task or held accountable for their hostility. Tales of unfairness and brutality towards the Indian people were commonplace. The horse soldiers stationed at nearby Fort Ridgley provided the advantage they needed to stay in complete control. It was the presence of these soldiers that kept the tribal leaders in check. Often, attempts for justice on behalf of the Indians by the tribal leaders were viewed by the officials as acts of insurrection and were met with instant and harsh penalties.

The government people in charge were restless in the knowledge that they were sitting on a virtual powder keg that could explode at any time. Rumors of a pending uprising were cause for grave concern. The soldiers continued to maintain a firm grip and constant vigil. Anyone suspected of causing unrest was rounded up and severely punished.

The latest rumor was that the population of an entire settlement near the reservation's northern border had been found frozen to death after they had been caught out in the open during a severe snowstorm. The story was that these people had run out of food and had made a desperate attempt to get to another settlement. The agency officials accepted no blame for the incident saying that they had delivered more than enough food and supplies to last those people through the winter. It was incidents like these that caused the feelings of unrest and rebellion to grow. Each year, stories of Indian people starving to death during the long winter months were told. Feelings of hate and distrust spread like a disease among these government wards. The white man's worst fear was that someday a chief would be found to lead the Indian people in a much-anticipated rebellion.

They wouldn't have long to wait.

Sage Elementary School May 1857

The classroom was silent as Miss Lillie offered the Morning Prayer. The children, from five years old to young adult, sat with their heads bowed. When the cue was given they joined with Miss Lillie in reciting the Lord's Prayer aloud. When that was over, she motioned towards the people in the back row.

"We have several guests today," she announced with a bright smile, "I'm sure you all know Red Calf, Marion, and their son, Taylor."

The students smiled and greeted their guests warmly. They were always glad to see them. Red Calf was well known throughout the reservation and Marion and little Taylor were more like extended family than visitors. When they were finished, Lillie turned to young Colton.

She said, "Colt, it's your turn to start the lesson."

Colt knew what to do and met Lillie's stern look with a wide smile. These were the moments she lived for. She loved how his dark face always lit up and how his eyes seemed to shine when he smiled at her. He was fast changing from a boy into a young man.

He lowered his eyes and softly answered,

"Yes, Ma'am."

It was obvious that he was only acting the part of being self-conscious. His reply, calling her Ma'am, caused several of the older students to smile. He was trying hard to impress his role model, Red Calf. His enthusiasm to proceed and start the class was obvious. At twelve years old, he was by far one of the brightest students in the room. Colt stood up and approached the chalkboard. He took a piece of chalk and stretched to reach up very high and wrote a Capitol letter R. Next, he placed another Capitol letter R beneath the first and finally, a third below that.

He faced the students and smiled as he said, "Today's lesson is all about the three R's."

He turned back to the board and quickly starting writing more words. Miss Lillie had moved to take a seat beside Marion and hadn't been paying much attention. She gasped as a ripple of laughter turned her focus back to her son's antics and she read what was written on the board.

Colt stood proudly facing the students with his arms folded across his chest. He was smiling at Red Calf who sat silently in the back row.

There on the chalkboard, in capital letters, he had neatly written the same word three times.

REVENGE
REVENGE
REVENGE

Part Two

This Troubled Land

Chapter Eight

Red Calf the Hunted

Another summer season turned into an early fall. The leaves took on their brilliant colors and soon the snows fell and winter set in. After what seemed like an eternity to most reservation Indians, the spring rains came and once again washed away the snows. This helped to ease the despairs of winter. The budding leaves and the greening land gave a new promise of better times to come.

Red Calf was well known as an honest and persuasive talker. Once the roads and trails were clear of snow he made the rounds visiting with the different tribal chieftains. His attempts at working things out peacefully often put him on the bad side of those angry tribal members who rejected the ways of the whites and derisively referred to him as a 'short hair.' It was still his hope that the problems with the white man could be identified and somehow solved peacefully. He and his band of three friends walked everywhere they went. To own a horse, in these times of such poverty, would have been a great status symbol. Occasionally, an Indian farmer and sometimes even a white settler would offer them a ride on the back of an empty wagon.

Often, they would offer to do a lot of work in exchange for a meal or two and a night's lodging.

It was the second week in July. They were on their way to the area west of Mankato to visit with Son of Tall Man when fate took an unusual twist.

Son of Tall Man was a local tribal chief who at one time had been well respected. He had been a warrior chieftain back during the great Indian wars. Respect for him waned as the years of reservation life took its toll on him personally and on his reputation. It was obvious to most that these years of living under the white man's rule had made him a meek, and now feeble, leader. His main weakness was his love of the white man's whiskey. Anytime they wanted something from him they plied him with whiskey and soon he would agree to almost anything.

It was early afternoon. Red Calf and his friends arrived at Son of Tall Man's cabin just ahead of the soldiers. They exchanged the usual pleasantries and were sitting on the edge of the small porch when the soldiers rode up.

Following closely behind the two columns of soldiers was a wagon driven by a settler. In the back were two other white men and three young Indian women. Lieutenant Harley was in the lead. The soldiers, about a dozen in number, reined to a stop across the dirt road from the cabin. The wagon came to a stop only a few yards away.

The men on the porch stood up as the lieutenant reined close to the porch with one of his soldiers, a young private. He ignored Red Calf and his friends and made no attempts at protocol as he addressed Son of Tall Man,

"These squaws have asked for your consent to come with these men," he said. "We need your permission to take them from the reservation."

Son of Tall Man stood gazing at the young women and made no reply. It was obvious that he was embarrassed that the soldiers had shown up while he had company.

"Chief," the lieutenant said with a disrespectful sneer, "I said, they asked to go," he twisted partway around in his saddle and nodded his head in the direction of the white men as he added, "with these men."

He turned and motioned towards the wagon. The two settlers had positioned two of the woman between them, facing the chief. The man holding the reins now stood with one leg in the wagon bed and one knee on the seat. He was smiling a nearly toothless smile as he placed his hand on the shoulder of one of the young Indian girls.

"They will bring them back unharmed," the lieutenant said, his tone still disrespectful.

Red Calf stood silently, waiting for a response from Son of Tall Man to the lieutenant. When none came, and the chief remained silent, it was he, who broke the silence, "What is this all about, Lieutenant Harley," he asked in perfect English.

"What business is it of yours?" the lieutenant replied in a cross tone of voice. It was obvious that he recognized Red Calf and had no use or respect for him. "This matter is between the chief and me and does not concern you."

Red Calf lowered his eyes and remained silent out of respect for the chief.

The chief said, "Pay your tribute and leave." His English was quite good. He motioned towards the women and acting as if he was laying down some rules he added, "They can serve you for one week, no more. Then, return them to here to their rightful places with their people."

The private dismounted and walked over to the wagon. A man in the wagon bed passed a canvas sack to him. He returned to the porch and handed it to the chief.

The lieutenant smiled as Son of Tall Man took the sack and looked inside.

"Three bottles," he said. "One for each squaw, it is our finest whiskey."

The lieutenant waited as the private climbed back into his saddle. He commanded the troops to prepare to move out. The young women on the back of the wagon had made no sounds. They watched the young Indian men, standing on the porch beside the old chief, out of the corner of their eyes. They dared make no eye contact with them as they hung their heads with looks of shame.

Red Calf exchanged knowing glances with the others in his party. He knew that the lieutenant was making a mockery of a tribal rule in asking permission to take the women from the reservation. He stepped forward, out into the dirt street, and stood in front of the settler's wagon. He raised his right hand to show that he had no weapon and spoke in the native tongue to the women.

"Is this so?" he asked, his voice commanding, "Did you ask to be taken to the white man's lair?"

All three young women silently shook their heads to answer. 'No.'

"Hey, Injun!" the settler driving the wagon shouted. "Move the hell out of the way!" He was still standing with one leg in the wagon bed, leaning forward and balanced with one knee on the wagon's seat. He reined the team hard as he shouted causing the wagon to lurch ahead.

Red Calf was knocked violently to one side as the horse struck him with its shoulder. The team and wagon thundered ahead. He rolled on the ground and scooped up a rock in his hand as he sprang to his feet. As he came back to an upright position, he drew back and threw it with all his might as the wagon thundered past. It was a good throw. The rock hit the white man who was driving the team in the side of his head. This caused him to twist abruptly and fall awkwardly from the wagon's seat. The rear wheel rolled over the man's throat and shoulder when he hit the ground and bounced back beneath the wagon. His neck was crushed and death was instant.

Several soldiers had been watching. They saw Red Calf throw the rock and watched as the man fell to his death. They reined their horses around. One of the other white men in the wagon had grabbed onto the reins and brought the wagon to a stop only fifty feet beyond where the man lay.

Red Calf stood defiantly in the center of the road. He watched in awe as the events unfolded. His was an attitude of curiosity and surprise as he realized what had happened and that the white man was dead. The bugged eyed stare from the dead man's face told all. He knew that he was in some deep trouble. He backed up slowly to the porch of Son of Tall Man's shack. In a matter of only a few seconds he found himself surrounded by excited soldiers all with their weapons drawn and pointed at him.

One of his companions, called Winter Rain, cried out in broken English to the soldiers, "Stop! It was an accident. He meant no harm."

In a flurry of motion, with adrenaline flowing and emotions raging, one of the green horn soldiers pointed his Sharps rifle at Winter Rain. He started to shout something. His shrill voice was instantly obliterated by the report of the rifle as it went off accidentally.

The force of the muzzle flash and bullet, fired an arm's length from Winter Rain's chest, caused his body to propel violently backwards and hit with a sickening thud on the steps leading up to the chief's cabin. The bullet went completely though the unfortunate man's body and shattered a clay pitcher filled with water that sat innately by the side of the door. For a moment, there was silence. Everyone remained frozen in place. The soldiers seemed fixated at the sight of the two dead bodies as they switched their glances from one to the other.

The white man lay in the center of the street, his body spread out in a grotesque fashion. The Indian boy was positioned, almost as if resting, on the cabin steps. If not for the blood soaked front of his shirt and the wide-eyed look of amazement on his dead face one could have suspected that he was merely relaxing in the coolness of the shade.

No one paid them any mind as the three young women in the rear of the wagon silently climbed out the opposite side. Like ghosts, they disappeared silently into the thick underbrush that bordered the clearing.

The two white men still remained standing in the bed of the wagon. They were both staring slack jawed at their fallen friend whose body lay a scant fifty feet away in the center of the dirt road. The blood from the dead man's mouth was soaking into the ground. One of them exclaimed, in a hysterical tone, "Oh my God! Oh my

God!"

Nearly a full minute of awkward silence followed. Then, several things occurred simultaneously. Red Calf dashed across the front of the porch. His mind was panicked with thoughts of escape as he scrambled quickly around to the side of the cabin. He disappeared a few moments later into the surrounding woods.

Lieutenant Harley was also in a panic. He had drawn his military issue revolver. He emptied it hurriedly at Red Calf as he was making his escape. Tufts of dirt and chunks of wood from gunshot impacts with the ground and the side of the cabin were explosive in motion as he missed his target with all six shots. Through the gun smoke put out by the revolver and several soldiers who also fired their rifles, chief Son of Tall Man had somehow received a mortal wound to his stomach. The force of the shot caused him to jerk back against the wall of his cabin. He stood stiffly with one hand covering the wound, the other still holding tightly onto the sack with the whiskey. A look of disbelief came over him as he slowly slid down to a sitting position.

Another of Red Calf's companions, whose Christian name was Joseph Ladd, also panicked and attempted to make an escape by running directly down the dirt road. He was nearly seventy-five yards away, almost to the bend in the road, when a soldier's bullet struck him squarely between his shoulder blades. The force of the bullet knocked him straight to the ground where he laid quivering for a few minutes. The remaining Indian, Brown Tooth, was knocked unconscious by a blow to his head from a rifle stock. In the moments that followed, it seemed as if everyone was moving in slow motion. A lot of things were still happening at once.

Brown Tooth had been knocked senseless to the ground. Several soldiers immediately set upon him and his hands were bound securely behind his back. The lieutenant slowly turned to face his men. His command, 'Get him!' sounded as if he spoke in slow motion as he pointed wide-eyed at the area of forest behind the cabin where Red Calf had disappeared. Chief Son of Tall Man remained slumped in a sitting position leaning against his cabin wall.

The confusion lasted for several minutes as the soldiers tried to get their mounts under control. An old woman, who had been inside the cabin, ran screaming onto the porch. She was sobbing hysterically as she grabbed onto Son of Tall Man and attempted to drag him inside. Another soldier had also panicked. In the heat of the moment, he killed the woman instantly with a single rifle shot to the side of her head fired from only a few inches away. It was a horrifying moment for the soldier when he was instantly splattered with blood and brain matter as half of her head disintegrated from the impact of the bullet. Her body came to rest violently against the top porch rail. Her remaining eye stared vacantly skyward.

The lieutenant was frantic as he fumbled to reload his revolver. A few minutes later, after some semblance of order was restored, he stayed with his prisoners and the wagon while a detail of soldiers set out in hot pursuit of Red Calf.

The bodies of the woman, Winter Rain, and Joseph Ladd were left where they had fallen. Chief Son of Tall Man was thrown unceremoniously into the back of the wagon along with the captured Indian youth and the dead white man. Lieutenant Harley's smile was morbid as he picked up the sack containing three bottles of whiskey from the porch. He took the time to tie it securely to his saddle's pommel before mounting up. They made haste back to Fort Ridgley. When they got there, they discovered that the chief had died along the way. The captured Indian, Brown Tooth, was placed in the stockade to await charges.

This incident had gotten completely out of control. Now, the Indian agents and the military personnel assigned to protect them were faced with the task of rounding up the escaped Indian, Red Calf. Before the week was out, Brown Tooth was to be tried on charges of taking part in what was now called an uprising attempt. As the story grew, it became common knowledge that it was his acts of violence that had led to the murder of a white settler and the deaths of four Indians. Brown Tooth was declared to be guilty at the start. His sentence was already predetermined to be death by hanging.

The renegade Indian, Red Calf, was now a hunted man with a price on his head. His focus in life had turned on the events of a single day. It was a day that had dawned with those who knew him believing him to be a chosen one. One whose wisdom and knowledge of the white man's ways would help to free their people from the bondages of poverty imposed on them by these so-called guardians. Before the sun had gone down, his reputation had changed. He was now, and forever would be, an insurrection leader and a murderer of white men.

There was much that the soldiers didn't realize to be significant at the time. One thing of importance was the fact that Red Calf was very well educated and schooled in all of the white man's ways. He could read, write, and speak English better than most white settlers. He knew his way around the reservation and had influence with most of the tribal leaders, including his brother, Tall Cloud.

The second most important thing they should have noticed about him was his fierce loyalty to his people. They didn't know it yet, but this included the condemned Indian, Brown Tooth, whom he viewed as his Indian brother.

To Red Calf, there was no stronger bond than that which he felt towards his people.

No one seemed to notice that the fuse had been lit. The first of many powder kegs was about to blow sky high.

Chapter Nine

Kegs of Powder

July 1857

It appeared as if all hell was about to break loose in both the upper and lower reservations. Reports of isolated attacks on white settlers and soldiers were the buzz of the town. Evidence of unrest was everywhere. Stories and rumors of the insurrection and predictions of the pending trial and execution spread like wildfire. Settlers were flocking to Mankato by the dozens to witness the public hanging of the murderous Indian said to be responsible for it all. Several newspapers, one from as far back east as Chicago, had sent reporters and even a photographer to the area to chronicle the event.

A cash reward of one hundred dollars had been posted for the capture, dead or alive, of the Indian outlaw Red Calf. His likeness had been drawn on a reward poster and copies were put up everywhere. Anyone caught harboring this most wanted man would be subject to harsh punishment, including hanging, if their efforts to shelter him in any way led to more grief or harm brought upon the white settlers.

Army patrols were stepped up. Lieutenant Harley was put in charge of bringing Red Calf to justice. His intentions were simple. He planned to hang Red Calf on the same gallows alongside Brown Tooth.

It was mid-morning when the army patrol, under the command of Lieutenant Harley, slowly wound its way along a back trail that traced a route around a small lake north of New Ulm. Their scout, cautiously leading the way, was a Sioux Indian whose Christian name was John the Baptist. He reined to a stop and leaned forward on his army mount, precariously, as he focused his attention on the fresh footprints made in the trail only hours before. He twisted around in his saddle and motioned for Harley to come alongside. He looked first at the lieutenant, and then up at the cloudy sky as the lieutenant reined up alongside.

He said, "It rained here early this morning, Lieutenant. These tracks are no more than two or three hours old." His English was nearly flawless. It was obvious that the white man had educated him. His face was expressionless as he motioned at the tracks.

The lieutenant gazed for a moment at the fresh prints in the soft soil. He turned his attention back to the scout, "Are you sure?" he asked in a low tone, "How many?"

The scout met his look and held up three fingers as he replied, "Three men. Two are moccasins tracks, Sioux. They were in no hurry."

"The third set?" the lieutenant asked.

"White man boots, like yours," the scout answered.

Lieutenant Harley was obviously excited as he asked, "Is it Red Calf?"

The scout shrugged, "Could be."

The lieutenant followed close behind as the scout led the way. His heart was racing as he drew his service revolver and held his thumb on the hammer as if to cock it to a firing position. He was expecting an ambush at any time. His eyes were constantly scanning the surrounding trees and bushes as they moved slowly following the lead of John the Baptist. The trail snaked through a series of sharp hills and ravines covered with layers of thick underbrush and tall trees. Soon, its course dipped to the shores of the small lake known to the natives as 'Lake of Blue.'

They could smell the wood smoke from a long ways off. The trail wound though a clearing and meandered towards the lake until it followed the edges of a sandy beachfront. It was obvious that the campfire was only a short distance away. The scout reined his horse around to face the rest of the patrol. Lieutenant Harley held up his hand as a signal for everyone to stop. He indicated that they dismount. They did so as silently as they could. The scout, still mounted, motioned that they were to follow him.

It was obvious that Lieutenant Harley didn't want his Indian guide along on this phase of the patrol. It was his intention to approach the campfire on foot and engage those rogue outlaws. It wasn't in his plans to share the credit for victory with anyone, let alone an Indian scout.

The lieutenant motioned for John the Baptist to dismount. "You remain in the rear and help hold the horses," he said. He paid no mind to the scout's stone-faced expression as he softly instructed Private Moore to stay behind as well.

"Keep the horses quiet," he said. "If you hear firing, we'll need you to come as fast as you can."

Private Moore was a young man, barely eighteen years old. He was a raw recruit. His youthful features seemed out of place for a frontline Calvary unit.

"Yes, Sir." he answered.

"And keep a close eye on the Indian," the lieutenant cautioned in a low tone of voice. "Never turn your back on a damned red skin."

"Yes, Sir."

"Is that clear, Private?" the lieutenant insisted.

"Yes, Sir," the private answered for a second time. "Perfectly clear." He came to attention and offered a salute.

The corporal cut in. Speaking in a loud whisper, he said, "Sir, perhaps we should take the scout with us and leave another soldier with Private Moore."

"What?" the lieutenant said. His tone was instantly angry. He bristled at the thought that his authority was being questioned. "I'll give the orders, Corporal Benning."

"Then maybe we should leave at least two men behind, sir." the corporal insisted. "We don't know what to expect up ahead and we may end up needing more than a one man reinforcement."

A cold look from Harley ended any more suggestions from the corporal.

"Follow me," he commanded softly as he turned to lead the way. The others joined in and they set out in single file, walking lightly along the trail.

Red Calf and two others, More Boy and Wild Fisher, were watching the scene from a place of concealment near the top of a small ridge. They had a clear view of the beach area and the trail on which the soldiers had been riding. A wide grin crossed his face as he watched the soldiers. They were approaching cautiously on foot with their rifles in the ready position. They followed the lieutenant as he walked slowly along the trail in the direction of the decoy campfire. He was pleased to notice that the scout had been left behind.

The soldier's course caused them to pass within fifty feet of their position. Even if they were to look directly at them, there was no danger of discovery. Their camouflage was such that it was doubtful that even another Sioux would have been able to spot them. They watched and waited patiently until the soldiers had disappeared around a bend in the trail. The last thing they wanted to do was engage the soldiers in battle. With only one rifle between them the outcome would be predetermined.

Red Calf looked towards where the soldiers had left their horses and noticed that the scout and the soldier had disappeared from view. He motioned to the others and they cautiously made their way back in that direction. It only took a few minutes to get there. Red Calf smiled as they approached. The scout was proudly astride a mount waiting for them. The army private was lying on the ground. He was twitching and convulsing. His chocking and gagging sounds had reached them long before they came into the clearing. The scout's hatred and bitterness towards the white soldiers was made apparent in how he was dispatching of the private. Death was slow in coming. The soldier was prone on the ground with his hands secured behind his back. A length of rawhide also secured his feet. He was face down, gasping and choking in his own blood. His tongue had been cut completely out. The scout had threaded a piece of rawhide though the tongue and tied it securely around the doomed man's neck. The private's eyes were wide in disbelief; his body was twitching wildly against his bonds as he fought a death that was imminent. Red Calf and the others seemed to pay no attention to him as they hurriedly climbed onto the army mounts.

The scout waited until Red Calf was mounted before speaking. "What about the other soldiers?" he asked. He motioned in the direction that the patrol had disappeared. "Do we stay and fight?"

Red Calf glanced at the dying soldier, then at the scout. "No. We must hurry. Our brother waits," he said.

The scout held the private's rifle to his shoulder and aimed it in the direction the soldiers had gone. "I can get at least two," he said.

"Now that you have killed a white soldier," Red Calf replied, "they will come for you. You can never live in peace again. It is certain that more will come."

"More?" The scout shrugged his shoulders and added, "How many more must come before it makes no difference?"

Red Calf nodded his head in agreement.

The scout said, "Today is truly a day of shame for Lieutenant Harley."

Red Calf acknowledged his remark. "You speak the truth, John the Baptist. Every day is a day of shame for him."

"His scalp," John the Baptist said. He motioned towards the fallen soldier. "To take it will strike fear into the hearts of the whites. This I save for you, Red Calf."

Red Calf shrugged his shoulders and replied, "The honor is all yours."

As the former scout slid out of the saddle and knelt by the dying soldier, Wild Fisher said, "We must hurry." He raised his voice to be heard as a series of loud squeals and gasps of misery came from the soldier, "Our brother, Brown Tooth, is counting on us."

John the Baptist took his time with his knife. When he was finished, he stood up quickly. He was holding the soldier's scalp in one hand and his rifle high in the air with the other. He kicked the prone and still writhing body and quickly climbed back into the saddle. He raised his rifle high and fired a shot. His intense voice followed the shattered silence as he let out a loud war whoop.

Red Calf quickly reined his horse around. He joined in with John's war whoop. The others chorused in. He also fired a round into the air.

"The soldiers will surely be coming back now!" Wild Fisher yelled.

"We go," Red Calf said. "They are many and we have only two rifles." He indicated the dead soldier now lying still in a pool of blood. His somber expression turned into a wide grin as he added, "You will never scout for the army again; you who are called John the Baptist."

The former scout returned his smile. He quickly reined his horse around to lead the way. In a matter of moments, he was racing at a breakneck pace back along the trail. Red Calf and the others followed closely. It had been a good day for them. They now had over a dozen good mounts and one more rifle. They believed that soon, others would join them and they would get even more rifles. Red Calf realized that they would have to act soon. Brown Tooth was due to be hanged in two days. He was already formulating a plan as he rode along quickly bringing up the rear.

Lieutenant Harley led the way as they slowly closed the distance towards the location of the campfire smoke. He was fully expecting to find several worthless Indians asleep around a comfortable fire. In his mind, he envisioned an easy capture. His pulse quickened as they got close enough to actually see the campfire. He was certain that it was only a matter of minutes until he had Red Calf and his cohorts in custody. The soldiers hastily formed a skirmish line as they made the final approach with their rifles shouldered and ready to fire. When they were about fifty feet from the smoldering campfire Lieutenant Harley anxiously leaped ahead of the rest. He had his revolver cocked back to the firing position as he rushed brazenly into the small clearing. He immediately stopped and turned around in complete circles several times, looking for their quarry. There was no mistaking the look of disbelief on his face.

"Where in the hell did they go?" he said softly, his voice incredulous.

Another soldier dropped to one knee and leveled his rifle expectantly at a thicket on the far side of the clearing. His eyes were wide in fright.

"Damn, stinking Indians," he murmured.

The other soldiers immediately turned to level their rifles away from the campfire towards the surrounding forest. Fearing an ambush, they expected to receive hostile fire at any moment. Their eyes looked everywhere in an attempt to see where their intended prey could have disappeared.

Then, from the direction back along the trail where they had left the horses, a shot was heard. The distinct sound of an army issue Sharps rifle being fired was instantly followed by a war whoop and then another shot was heard. A chorus of many war whoops followed this.

Lieutenant Harley froze in place for a moment. He exchanged surprised looks with his corporal.

"Damn it, sir, it's a trick!" the corporal shouted.

"We gotta get to the horses!" another voice echoed.

The eleven soldiers turned and retraced their steps, still in single file. This time, Corporal Benning was in the lead as he raced back at a dead run.

Lieutenant Harley's mind was in a spin. He offered no further commands and simply tried to keep up with the others. As they crossed the open area where the trail skirted the sandy beach, he thought that perhaps they should slow down. After all, it was an excellent location for an ambush. A scant few seconds later they were all standing surrounding the fallen soldier's body. The corporal was first on the scene. He was obviously upset. His voice was trembling and filled with rage as he turned to his commanding officer,

"I damn well tried to warn you against this, Sir!" he exclaimed. "Take a good look at Private Moore."

Lieutenant Harley tried to avert his eyes from the sight of the dead soldier. He attempted to suppress an involuntary shudder. The corporal's voice was strangely calm as he spoke while cutting the bonds that held the private's hands and feet secured behind his back, "He was still alive only a minute or so ago, Sir." He made eye contact with Lieutenant Harley as he added, "They did all this while he was alive."

It was about then that the harsh reality of it all hit the lieutenant. His eyes took in the macabre position of the body. It registered in his mind just what it was that was tied around the dead man's throat. A large portion of the dead man's scalp was missing. He turned and rushed a few steps away. He stood with both hands on his knees, bent forward, gasping for breath as he retched and threw up uncontrollably. Several other soldiers were doing the same thing.

By the time he regained some of his composure, Corporal Benning had dragged the private's body off to the side of the trail. He had removed the dead man's coat and now used it to cover the remains.

"If you're ready, Lieutenant," he said softly, "we need to get started back. It's going to be a long walk."

Lieutenant Harley met his look with one still filled with surprise and fright.

"What about Moore?" he asked, his voice shaky.

"I think it best that we send a patrol back for him, sir." the corporal answered. "We'll need to take a few minutes to cover the body with rocks."

"Whatever you say, Corporal," the lieutenant stammered, "whatever you say." He moved to the side of the trail and sat on a large boulder waiting impatiently. It was obvious that he was deeply shaken.

Corporal Benning supervised as the others covered the body with a small mound of stones. Then, he quickly positioned the troops a column of twos with he and the lieutenant in the lead. He heard a soldier somewhere near the back of the line remark sarcastically,

"Can someone tell me again just how stupid these damned heathen Indians are?"

It seemed ironic that he would smile at such a comment, but he couldn't suppress himself as he grinned. His voice was clear and confident as he called over his shoulder, "You make a good point, soldier."

The corporal led the way, this time at a fast march. Every man walked quickly with his rifle in the ready position expecting more trouble at each twist and turn of the trail.

Red Calf's older brother, Chief Tall Cloud, had been rounded up and questioned the second day after the incident at Son of Tall Man's shack. The soldiers didn't have to search hard to find him. He had been locked up in the army stockade near Mankato since the day the incident occurred. Despite this knowledge, it was rumored that Tall Cloud had played an important part in what the army now referred to as an attempted Indian insurrection.

At the actual time of the killings at Son of Tall Man's, Tall Cloud had been in the middle of a shouting match at the main trading post. He had tried to use his influence as a tribal chief to get justice from the traders. To no avail, he openly accused the whites of stealing from the Indians and holding back their supplies. The accusations were reversed when the white trader accused Tall Cloud of stealing from his store.

Tall Cloud had no choice except to go peacefully when the post officials showed up and placed him under arrest. Four days later, on the same day that Lieutenant Harley's patrol was ambushed, the newly appointed Indian agent had already intervened on Tall Cloud's behalf and he was released from jail. It was a vain effort by the agent to help ease tensions. Tall Cloud, on the advice of his longtime friend and mentor, Chief Little Crow, wisely disappeared from sight as details of the new events unfolded.

The white trader declared that he was content to know that Tall Cloud had been publicly humiliated as a common thief. He decided not to pursue the matter any further when word of Lieutenant

Harley's battle with the chief's brother, Red Calf, reached them. As the story grew it was rumored that Red Calf now led a band of at least a hundred warriors. This rumor, combined with the pending trial and execution of Brown Tooth, was all that anyone talked about. It was rumored that even the great white father in Washington knew of Red Calf's name and was watching the situation with great interest.

Due to all the unrest on the lower reservation, Brown Tooth had been taken from the stockade at Fort Ridgley and transferred to the jail at Mankato. This area was more or less the center of activity for the reservation lands. The local courthouse and its jail facility were going to be used to house the now famous Indian murderer. The trial and execution were scheduled to start at noon the next Saturday. The trial was to be in the form of a military tribunal even though it was being conducted in a civilian court. The actual proceedings were expected to last for no more than an hour, two at the most. Everyone was aware of the volatile relationships between the whites and the Indians. For this reason, the tribal council was left out of any proceedings. For the duration of the trial and execution, Indians were forbidden to be within the town limits.

Several events were shaping up at once. A hanging scaffold was being built in the town's square for Saturday's show. The carpenters involved in the construction were having a hard time building it with any degree of accuracy due to being drunk most of the time. It seemed that every passerby in town had a desire to stop and offer advice and share a drink or two. The entire town was engulfed in a festive atmosphere.

The acting territorial governor had ordered a force of one hundred militiamen to the area to reinforce the soldiers from Fort Ridgley. His concerns were more political than anything else. It was expected that very soon, Minnesota would be granted statehood. The last thing he wanted was for an Indian uprising to jeopardize that event. To refer to this group of men as a military militia was stretching it at best. Most of the members of this rag-tag bunch were disgruntled settlers. It was common knowledge that they wanted more land and hated the Indians with a passion. They were poorly trained and supervised. Straight away, they started to run roughshod over the immediate area causing even more hard feelings and unrest.

Tall Cloud and his younger brother, Red Calf, were nowhere to be found. Rumor had it they had been seen together, with their families, heading north towards Canada. This rumor only lasted a short while as the reservation officials continued to try to pin something on Tall Cloud.

A cash reward of one hundred dollars was offered for the capture, dead or alive, of the rogue Indian scout known as John the Baptist. The truth about the incident at the Lake of Blue was the last thing the army wanted known to the public. The army claimed that he had attacked a soldier and stolen a horse.

The military trial and public hanging of Brown Tooth was set for Saturday, two days hence.

Even a blind man could have seen that the fuse had been lit.

Chapter Ten

The Little Colored Boy

Friday evening

The town of Mankato had nearly doubled in population in only the last two days. People were coming in from everywhere to witness the execution of the Indian murderer, Brown Tooth. The saloons were bustling with business and whiskey was flowing. The soldiers in charge of the jail were having a good time as well. Any settler who wanted to get a look at the Indian could do so for a small fee. One settler had paid with a jug of corn whiskey. It wasn't long before the sergeant and the two soldiers assigned to nighttime guard duty were half drunk themselves.

It was shortly before midnight when a young colored boy showed up at the front door of the jail carrying a covered basket. The sergeant saw him through the window, as he stood bashfully on the boardwalk in the dim light cast from the kerosene lamp attached to the front wall of the jail. He grinned as the boy sheepishly approached and knocked softly. Knowing that the boy was about to knock, the sergeant tore the door open. With a boisterous laugh he shouted, "Boo!" He and the soldier behind the desk roared with laughter as the boy reacted with a start and nearly dropped the basket. He stood there staring up at this giant of a man, his eyes wide in fright.

"Hey, you!" The sergeant boomed, "What have you got there, boy?"

The boy lowered his eyes and stammered, "A basket of food and drink complements of Miss Gloria at the Raven." He turned and pointed down the street at the sign that read 'Raven Saloon' several doors down.

"Well, bring it on in here," the sergeant boomed. His voice was loud and filled with mirth at the boy's apparent fright. "We ain't gonna bite you."

"Yes, sir," the boy murmured. He entered slowly and carefully placed the basket on the desk. "Miss Gloria says I have to come back and get the basket when you all are through," he said. He lowered his eyes again and added, "If it be all right with you, sirs."

"Of course it's all right," the sergeant said. He lifted the lid. His eyes went wide in surprise at the sight of fresh baked rolls, fried chicken, a bottle of store bought whiskey and two bottles of wine. He grinned at the boy and added, "You tell Miss Gloria, whoever she is, that I thank her and I said that you can come back for the basket in about an hour."

From deep within the cellblock area a voice called, "Who's out there, Sarge?"

"No one important, just a little colored boy," the sergeant answered, "he's fetched us something to eat."

The boy's eyes opened wide in an expression of surprise as he gasped, "Is that him, sir?" he asked, pointing to the door that led to the rear of the jail. "Is that the nasty, murdering Indian we been hearing about?"

"Hell, boy, that ain't no Indian talking, that there is Corporal Burns."

"I ain't never seen no killer Indian," the boy said, "What does he look like?"

"How old are you, boy?" the sergeant asked, "Are you sure you're old enough to be looking at a no good murderous Indian like we got locked up back there?"

"I'm twelve, sir," the boy said bashfully. He lowered his eyes and fixed his gaze at his feet as he added, "I'll be thirteen come next month."

"Go ahead and take a look for yourself," the sergeant said. "Here, take this with you." He passed a couple rolls and a bottle of wine from the basket to the boy, "Give this to Corporal Burns while you're back there."

He unlocked the door and opened it. "Chow's coming," he yelled. "You be nice to this boy."

The short hallway led past a row of three cells. A kerosene lamp was dimly burning on a shelf at the end of the corridor. Below the shelf, the shadowy figure of a guard could be seen. The soldier sat in a chair holding a double barrel shotgun across his knees. As the boy walked slowly towards him, the corporal got up and eagerly approached. He took the food and drink and sat back down.

"Go ahead, boy. Take a good long look," he said, indicating the center cell. "That's one dead Indian come noontime tomorrow, so get your eyes full."

In the dim light cast from a kerosene lamp, he could see the rogue Indian. Brown Tooth had been stretched out on the thin mattress on the single cot in the small cell. His face was expressionless as he sat up and swung his legs over the edge of the bed frame. He met the boy's stare. The boy seemed to be frightened. He gasped and turned and ran back to the front of the jail.

"Don't forget to come back for your basket," the sergeant shouted after him as he tore out through the front door. He turned to the other soldier and added, "Have you ever seen such a young darkie move that quick before?"

They laughed at that comment and allowed that they hoped the boy would remember to come back for his basket. They continued to enjoy the lunch and liquor.

"Are you sure, Colton?" Red Calf asked. "There are only three soldiers inside?"

"Yes," Colton answered, "two are in the front room and the other is in the cellblock. I saw Brown Tooth with my own eyes."

"He is well?"

"As well as can be expected," Colton responded. He was sounding like someone years older as he added, "They beat him pretty badly."

"We must act quickly," Red Calf said.

"The horse soldiers will be drunk soon," John the Baptist said. "They will open the door for our little friend."

They continued their conversation in hushed tones as they watched the front of the jail from across the street. Red Calf and John the Baptist were both dressed in fresh looking army uniforms. They had both gotten close military style haircuts just for this occasion. The other two, Wild Fisher and More Boy, wore civilian clothes and had their long hair tucked up under their hats.

"John and I will go inside," Red Calf said as he formulated their final plan. "When the door opens, we will hurry inside and free Brown Tooth." He glanced at Colton, "Did you see where they keep the key for the second door?"

"Yes. It is fastened with a string to the sergeant's suspender," he answered. He placed his thumb where his own suspender attached to the front to his britches indicating where he had seen the key when the sergeant used it to open the door.

"When we go inside," Red Calf said to Wild Fisher, "you two start to slowly walk across the street leading the horses." He pointed to the narrow alley on one side of the jail, "You must be there and ready when we come out. We may need to move fast."

A few minutes later, Red Calf, John the Baptist, and Colton crossed the street. The two men positioned themselves out of sight around the corner on the alley side of the building. Colton walked up to the front door alone. As he had done before, he knocked softly.

This time, the other soldier opened the door. He greeted Colton with a broad grin.

"Come on in, boy," he said. "Everyone else is asleep so be quiet, okay?"

"Yes Sir." Colton answered. He had to leap out of the way as Red

Calf slammed his body into the door violently knocking the soldier backwards into the room. The soldier's attempt to shout a warning was cut short as Red Calf's long knife was driven viciously up under his chin and straight into his brain. At the same time, John the Baptist rushed into the room. The sergeant had been passed out with his head resting on his arms folded on top of the desk. He raised his head slightly and opened his eyes at the sounds of the disturbance. He gasped and struggled briefly as John the Baptist slammed his head onto the desktop and cut his throat from ear to ear.

Colton watched the events unfold wide-eyed and silent. He remembered to close the door behind them and watched with bated breath as Red Calf got the key and opened the door to the rear of the cellblock.

The corporal, still on guard in the cellblock, never woke from his slumber. His throat was cut from ear to ear by John the Baptist in the same manner as the sergeant's had been. Red Calf opened the door and greeted Brown Tooth with a strong embrace.

"We must hurry," he said.

They went back to the front part of the jail. Colton was still standing silently by the door with an expression of amazement on his young face. For some reason a chill went all the way up and down Red Calf's spine as Colton's expression turned to a solemn smile.

"You have blood all over yourself," he whispered as he eyed Red Calf up and down, "only once before have I seen you like this." The sight of Red Calf in this condition instantly brought back memories and emotions that he had experienced that day long ago when they had caught up the men who had raped and murdered his best friend, Ruth.

"This I regret, little one," Red Calf said, "We must hurry and get you back to your mother."

"Here," John's voice was intense as he passed several rifles and handguns to Red Calf and Brown Tooth. He slung several more over his shoulder and started to fill a sack with boxes of cartridges, shot and gunpowder charges. "We must take all we can carry."

The others showed up in the alley leading the horses. They quietly walked out the front door and mounted up. No one paid them any mind as they rode slowly down the alley and disappeared into the night. If anyone had noticed they would have seen two soldiers, three settlers, and a small boy riding unhurriedly in the darkness. Once they had put a little distance between themselves and town they urged their horses to almost breakneck speeds as they raced through the night. The moon provided ample light to see the road as they thundered past shanties and through the centers of several small communities on their way back to the heart of the reservation. They dropped Colton off at the school building shortly before dawn. Miss Lillie was still sleeping soundly when he cautiously climbed back in through the window of his bedroom. She never did find out about this adventure with Red Calf. He was certain that if she had known, it would have been curtains for both he and his friend.

Brown Tooth picked out several rifles and filled a sack with ammunition and supplies. He and John the Baptist decided to join forces. They immediately headed deeper into the reservation lands. They made many stops speaking of war with the white man and recruiting more followers as they went. Red Calf, Wild Fisher, and More Boy, went in another direction with plans of doing the same.

The escape was discovered shortly before dawn by the relief guards assigned to the jail from Fort Ridgley. When they saw what had happened they immediately called the rest of the soldiers to full alert. The post commander, who was present for the trial, kept a tight lid on what had happened. All anyone ever knew for sure was that Brown Tooth had escaped. He saw no need to give the Indians more reason to celebrate. He was certain that to admit to the murders of three of his soldiers would have been a mistake.

The lead Indian agent, the military officials, and the acting territorial governor all agreed that the less that was known about the details of the escape the better. The rumors that were spreading were giving way to more trouble than was needed already. They all believed that the main powder keg was about to blow sky high. They were hoping that the arrival of a large supply of food and goods for the Indians would serve to pacify them and help to defuse the situation.

The Indian agent, and even the local traders, made many assurances. They promised that all of the supplies due were indeed on their way. Food was soon to be plentiful. The causes for unrest would undoubtedly be addressed. They promised that soon, the instability would die down.

This weak and false attempt at pacification actually worked for a while. The long awaited supplies and part of the annuity payments finally arrived. Food became plentiful and things did calm down.

Time passed and with each tick of the clock statehood for the Minnesota territory loomed nearer. Even those on the tribal council believed that the situation would improve once the area had a real governor and a new state government. These hopes were destined to last for only a short time. The corrupt bunch in charge didn't care. Nothing ever changed with them.

It was common knowledge that Indians were much easier to control during the winter months when their movements and activities were slowed down by the harsh weather. The pacification plan was simple. Give them food and supplies for now; keep the unrest and trouble to a minimum.

The constant onslaught of settlers assured that there would be plenty of new money to be made. The territory was growing by leaps and bounds. The rich bottomlands were still in limited supply and there were many new arrivals that were willing to pay top dollar for lifetime leases of that land. Those who granted the leases and transfers of ownership were growing fat off the misery and suffering of the Indian people.

There was talk that the railroad would soon connect Mankato and St. Paul. Everyone knew that statehood was just around the corner. The rumors of an imminent war between the northern and southern states echoed even louder each day.

The three most famous rogue Indians, Red Calf, Brown Tooth, and John the Baptist remained as shadows, always just beyond the reach of a determined Lieutenant Harley and his horse soldiers.

A series of small powder kegs had gone off. Even so, no one in authority had the wisdom to put out the fuse that was still slowly burning. It was only a matter of time until it reached the largest powder keg of all.

Chapter Eleven

The Beginning of the End

Lower Reservation, May, 1859

It was a time of mourning in this part of the Indian nation. Those who wished to pay their final respects to Miss Lillie lined up outside the clapboard building that served as both schoolhouse and church mission. Word had spread quickly about her tragic accident the day before. The immediate area was filled with people from all walks of life.

Today was one year to the day since Minnesota had become the thirty-second state to enter the union. Miss Lillie had been on her way to Fort Ridgley, the day before, to participate in a celebration of this first anniversary of statehood. Apparently something had spooked her horse only a quarter mile from the school causing the unfortunate accident.

Dr. Morrison explained that despite his best efforts there was no way to repair the internal injuries suffered by Miss Lillie. The carriage accident had broken nearly all of her ribs and it was only a matter of time, perhaps hours, until she died. The soldiers who were assigned the duty of patrolling the roads and back trails of this outlying settlement had stopped to pay their respects also. There was an unspoken truce between those in uniform and the rogue groups of Indians whom they pursued. For now, for these few hours and perhaps days, their concern for Miss Lillie was a common bond that caused each side to respect this undeclared truce.

When the proper time came to pay their respects, Red Calf and Lieutenant Harley stood silently at her bedside. Her eyes told them that she appreciated their being there in this rare show of unity. In her weakened and drugged state, they could only hope that the words of thanks they spoke to her were being heard and understood. Both knew it had always been her wish that Harley and Red Calf could make peace. They hoped that their show of harmony would make her feel at ease. Those who knew Lieutenant Harley were very surprised by his action. It was out of character for him to show this kind of respect.

Her tireless efforts, during times of crisis, not so long ago, would be long remembered. The onset of spotted fever had taken the lives of many soldiers and Indians. Even the post doctor at Fort Ridgley had succumbed to the dreaded disease and had almost died from it. The fever had nearly claimed the life of Lieutenant Harley who now stood in temporary solidarity with Red Calf, his sworn enemy. It was Miss Lillie who had tended to them both when fever and death had stalked them. It was she who had seen their ordeals through. They weren't about to forget that.

Dr. Morrison had sedated her heavily. As the hours wore on and the medicine took effect, he felt sure that she was in no pain. Towards the end, it was uncertain if she even knew where she was or who was with her. Miss Lillie's foster son, Colton, now fifteen years old, never left her side. He was dressed in his Sunday suit and his hair was neatly combed. He was nearly overwhelmed with a feeling of guilt. He believed that if he had been with her, instead of with Red Calf, the accident wouldn't have occurred. He was holding her hand, rubbing it gently, when the powerful tremor of death came over her. With her last breath, and in a questioning tone that sounded like one of recognition, she called his name. "Colton?"

"I am here, Mother," Colton whispered. His voice was trembling and he made no attempt to hide his tears.

With a final shudder, and a sigh that seemed to last for a long time, her body relaxed as death took her spirit away. Colton remained kneeling at her side holding her hand. Dr. Morrison, who was in the next room, had heard Miss Lillie and hurried back into the room.

He softly pronounced her dead and pulled the bed sheet up over her face. He turned, looking curiously about, expecting to see the boy. He raised his eyebrows in an expression of surprise as he bent to look out the open window. Colton was already astride a horse riding double behind the outlaw Indian, Red Calf. He exchanged glances with Lieutenant Harley who stood silently beside the open doorway and then left the room to rejoin his wife.

As Mrs. Morrison embraced him, a mutual feeling of dread swept over both of them. She, too, had looked out the window in time to see the black Indian boy. Colton looked out of place in his Sunday suit. His short wavy hair was neatly combed. He was nearly man grown now and looked years older. As he met her gaze he held his right hand, palm first, in her direction. His somber expression was one that she would never forget.

It just didn't seem right to see him riding off like that. He was holding on to one of the most notorious and wanted warriors in the Indian Nation.

"Oh, my God," Mrs. Morrison murmured, as she watched out the window.

Dr. Morrison remained standing silently at her side. They watched as a long line of young Indians, all on foot, followed Red Calf and Colton as they slowly disappeared around a bend in the road. Dr. Morrison was astounded at how quickly the boy had disappeared from the room to join those on the outside.

"This is so strange," he murmured to his wife.

"What do you mean?" she asked, as she remained looking out the window.

"The boy's natural mother, the Indian woman named Sage," Dr. Morrison said softly, "all those years ago."

Mrs. Morrison turned to face him and tearfully asked, "What about her?"

"Her dying words," he said softly, "Or perhaps I should say, word. It was the same as Miss Lillie's last word."

Mrs. Morrison gave him a questioning look. She felt a chill overcome her; she had also heard Miss Lillie.

"Colton?" she whispered.

He nodded his head somberly and replied, "Yes."

She watched through the window, almost in awe, as several soldiers went outside with Lieutenant Harley. The soldier who had remained with the horses stood up and came to attention. She continued watching with a sense of dread as the Lieutenant returned the soldier's salute and motioned in the direction the Indians had disappeared. She breathed a sigh of relief when the soldiers mounted up and rode off slowly in the opposite direction.

Then, she realized what it all meant. She knew that after today, the truce would be ended. These same men, Indian and white, would resume their routines of killing and cruelty towards each other.

She could feel the color draining from her face as she stood gazing out the window with both hands clutched to her chest. Her heart seemed to skip a beat. She whispered, "Miss Lillie, Miss Lillie, what have you done?"

Chapter Twelve

Training Camp

Following the death of his foster mother, Colton became as a shadow to Red Calf. He believed that no lasting peace with the white man would ever be realized. He was determined to master the art of war. Around campfires and all throughout the reservations, stories of past battles and great victories won by the courage and cunning of Chief Tall Cloud were told. Red Calf, now one of the most wanted rogue Indians in the Nations was also one who was viewed as being larger than life. Since his rescue of Brown Tooth from the white man's jail, only a short time ago, his was a reputation was very similar. Colton was determined to learn all he could from both.

Although Red Calf was one of the most wanted and notorious Indian outlaws in the territories, it was nearly unbelievable how free he and his family lived. He and Marion had built a very nice log cabin on a small bluff overlooking the Minnesota River. Their cabin was mixed in with about a dozen others, some mere shacks and blended in with the hundreds of outlying Indian settlements that were scattered all throughout both the upper and lower reservation lands. Their water was pure and plenty from a small spring that bubbled ice cold water year around. They used water from this spring to cultivate and maintain a large garden planted into the side of the bluff close to their cabin. As a result, their winter stores often meant the difference between a very harsh winter and one of plenty for themselves and the others in the area. A large chicken coop was located in the back next to the outhouse. With fresh eggs, and lots of poultry as needed, theirs was a nice setup.

The rough and winding road on this side of the river wound its way to within a quarter mile of them at the base of the bluff. On many occasions they had watched in silence, the movement of the horse soldiers and a never ending stream of wagons.

Colton had been amazed and learned a valuable lesson the day an army patrol stopped in front of a cabin that he and Red Calf were visiting, not far from theirs. They were working together with an Indian whose Christian name was Robert, putting up a supply of firewood to see them through the winter. Colton remained out of sight but he had a clear view and was close enough to hear what was happening. At first he wondered why Red Calf had remained in the open and had not attempted to run as the soldiers reined their mounts up the hill and came to a stop in front of the cabin. Then, he realized that had Red Calf, or Robert for that matter, made any kind of move that appeared to be trying to escape or not to be seen, it would have instantly brought out suspicions from the soldiers. A corporal was in charge and seemed friendly enough.

"Hello there." He said as he reined his horse to a stop.

The Indian named Robert turned and called in the native tongue to his wife who was inside. She came out and addressed the soldiers in broken English, "My man Robert does not speak English." She said. Then she smiled and asked, "What is it that you want?"

The corporal replied, "Just a routine patrol." He directed his next remark to Red Calf who had stopped what he was doing and was watching the soldiers with a curious expression. "What kind of hair cut is that for an Indian?" he asked, noticing Red Calf's short hair.

Red Calf's face took on a look of confusion. He looked at the woman and asked in the native tongue, "What does he say?"

The troop's scout and translator caught up with them at about the same time. He interrupted before the woman could reply and told the corporal, "He doesn't speak English, Sir." Then he directed his question to Red Calf, "Why do you have a white man's hair cut?"

Red Calf shrugged and answered, "We are trying to become as they in order to live in peace."

The scout translated for the corporal who smiled and said, "That's a hell of an idea." Then, his voice commanding, he said, "Let's move out."

As the soldiers disappeared from sight, Colton came from his place of concealment and stood silently beside Red Calf. "What if the scout had been someone who could recognize you?" he asked.

Red Calf's smile was faint as he answered, "He did. His name is Black Limb. He is a brother to Winter Rain."

Colton now understood. He also had known Winter Rain, the young Indian shot dead on the front porch of Son of Tall Man's shack the day Red Calf became a wanted man. Although many hated and disrespected scouts and Indians who worked for the soldiers, it was now apparent that everything is not always as it appeared. It was now Colton's turn to smile.

A small victory

There was an almost jubilant air of excitement spreading among the Indians in the lower reservation. A young Indian man had been rescued from a beating committed by three soldiers in a barn near the main trading post. He had been falsely accused of stealing. This time there had been only the three soldiers present. A group of a half dozen Indians happened upon the scene even as they were pummeling their victim. This time the soldiers didn't get away with it. The Indian men had forgotten their places and sought immediate reprisal. This resulted in the tables being turned. All three soldiers were nearly beaten to death themselves.

The Indians then disappeared without a trace taking with them the soldiers' weapons and ammunition. They had also stripped the three soldiers of their uniforms and boots and stole those as well.

They did this before any whites could come to their assistance. To add insult to injury, they also quietly led the soldier's horses away. Moving slowly, in broad daylight, they drew no attention to themselves. Once out of sight, it is said that they mounted the horses and riding double, 'rode like hell' as they made their getaway. The whites inside the trading post had been unaware of any trouble until one of the severely beaten soldiers staggered from the barn area. He was bruised and bloody wearing only his long handle underwear. He stood unsteadily at the bottom of the stairs leading up to the back porch pleading for help.

In an effort to ward off further trouble, a reinforced troop was dispatched to the lower agency from Fort Ridgley with orders to set some examples.

They arrived only to find the place deserted of all Indians except for women and children and a few Indian men who worked for them. They had no idea where everyone had gone and despite several scouting expeditions and angry questioning of some of the women and children, they found no sign of any Indians who could have perpetrated the injustice upon the soldiers.

Tall Cloud showed up at the main store about noontime the day after the incident. Little Crow and several other Indian leaders happened to be there at the same time. Tall Cloud was still a designated spokesman for his band and tried in vain to offer some kind of solution that would cause the soldiers to go away. They were really upset and determined to get the stolen rifles back. His meeting with the white traders ended as usual with harsh words, shouting and threats.

There were many Indians, including Little Crow, who thought it funny that the soldiers had been left only the dignity of their underwear after the attack. He also was challenged about the incident. The whites believed without a doubt that he knew exactly what happened and who was responsible.

"One of these days, Little Crow," the white trader said bitterly, "you and that heathen Tall Cloud will wish you had been more helpful. Those bastards stole rifles and horses this time. That makes this a serious, hanging offense."

"I cannot tell you what I do not know," Little Crow said. He quickly exited through the front door hoping his smirk wouldn't be seen.

Advice from Tall Cloud

It was a welcomed feeling of relief to Tall Cloud when he got back to his cabin and found Red Calf and Colton waiting to see him. He still didn't have the whole story about what had actually happened with the three soldiers and wouldn't be surprised to find that they had been in on the mischief. Although happy to see them, his first reaction was one of near panic. He knew the soldiers were combing the area and could show up here, at his house, anytime.

"It is too dangerous for you to be here." he cautioned; "You must go. I will come to you. We must try to find an answer to all the madness."

"Yes," Red Calf said, "but I must tell you, I now believe that there is no answer that involves justice for us. No solution and no hope for lasting peace."

Colton had remained silent. When Tall Cloud gave him a questioning look, he said, "Mother always taught us," he paused for a moment and looked at Red Calf, "that peace was something that we can and must achieve. Through all our years of schooling and times together, this was her belief."

"She often mentioned you," Red Calf said to Tall Cloud, "as an example of how we should always strive for a peaceful solution."

Colton said, "Red Calf and I want you to show us the ways of the warrior in case we do have to go to war with the whites."

"This I will do," Tall Cloud said, "but not here, not now. Go. Meet me in three days at the Lake of Many Birds." His voice turned stone cold serious as he added, "I also ask that you bring several others; those who have proven to be leaders. I will inform More Boy and Dove of Day who are nearby. If you will listen to our words, there will be hope."

"So it shall be," Red Calf replied, "There must be hope."

They left quickly exiting through the front door and then moving quickly around the back of the cabin to disappear into the forest. As they distanced themselves, they could hear the sounds of horses on the main road and wondered if perhaps they had left Tall Cloud just in time.

One of many small and isolated lakes in the forested territories north of New Ulm, the Lake of Many Birds, was one known to the natives as a place of plenty. Small game; rabbits, birds and deer were almost always there for the hunt. The fish in the lake were also plentiful. There was a series of stick weirs and water traps at the inlet and outlet of the lake that the Indians had used and kept in continuous use since anyone could remember. The maze created by the handmade weirs led the fish to a place where they could not escape. Due to the isolation and rough territory, it was as safe a place as any for them to meet. The lake was about a mile long and maybe a half mile wide at its widest point.

In all, there were seven men who arrived with Red Calf and Colton to learn from Tall Cloud. Accompanying Tall Cloud was Dove of Day. He was an older man. Colton remembered him from his many visits to Miss Lillie's mission and his unselfish help during the time of the great fever. More Boy was another he knew to be a friend. It was he and another present, Wild Fisher, who were also instrumental in helping to break Brown Tooth out of Jail. The Indian named Robert and two others had accompanied Colton and Red Calf.

There were several nearly dilapidated cabins on a small rise a short distance from the lake that readily served to house them. With just a little attention, each was soon a comfortable place of refuge. Each evening a campfire was used to keep the mosquitoes and other vicious insects at bay. A low fire with fresh evergreen boughs placed on it repeatedly created a thick smoke referred to as a 'smudge', and generally did the trick.

For three days, they asked many questions of Tall Cloud. His answers were sometimes such that they could only guess at the meaning. One thing that they clearly understood was the need to have a plan for victory; a way to stay one step ahead of the white man.

"Just the sheer strength of their overwhelming numbers and superior weapons will always result in defeat for us," Tall Cloud cautioned. "Unless," he added, "unless you have the winning strategy."

"Some of your battles were lost," Dove of Day observed. His voice lowered as he added, "Tall Cloud, many of your battles were lost."

"Yes." Tall Cloud replied, "Through victory and defeat, we were as one." His gaze went from Colton to Red Calf and to the others as he directed his next remark to them, "You would do well to also listen to the words of Dove of Day. He was there, older and wiser than either I or even Little Crow at the time. Heed his words as well. Listen to him now as I did all those years ago."

"It is easy to remember and talk about the victories," Dove of Day added, "We must never forget the defeats and always try to reason why."

Red Calf said, "It is true the whites believe that we are just a bunch of savages, unorganized, uneducated and ignorant in the art of war. It is their belief that we can easily be defeated at any given time. Unfortunately, they are usually right." He paused and added, "When we defeated Harley at the Lake of Blue, not far from here, we did so because we devised a strategy as Tall Cloud advises. We had a carefully crafted plan and we stuck with it. Had we chosen at the last moment to remain and fight, surely some of us would have died. As it turned out, we gained many horses, another rifle, and a warrior story proud to tell."

"Another thing you must do," Tall Cloud said, "you must practice always. You must practice fighting each other, practice running through thick brush to escape, practice the ways of the night warriors to remain undetected as you watch and listen to the whites even in their presence." He paused, "Do this; do this and your chances for victory will be great. If others will follow your example, if you will teach them, we will have a chance. If we only offer a fight to the enemy, our days will be numbered."

Dove of Day added, "And know this," he paused and looked at Red Calf, "know that you could not have rescued our brother, Brown Tooth had you not thought and planned each move in advance as you did. This is the real lesson, the one which you must teach others."

It was all clear to Colton. He had been there when the infamous rescue of Brown Tooth took place. He remembered as clear as day how Red Calf and John the Baptist had gone over the plan again and again. They had rehearsed him in his part as well. If not for the coaching from Red Calf, he may not have even thought to look where the key to the cell block had been kept, let alone trick the soldiers into letting him see the captive. Nor would he have remembered to give credit for the whiskey wine and rolls to someone named 'Gloria' at the Raven saloon. Yes, success was tied to having a good strategy.

Tall Cloud left to return to the lower reservation the morning of the third day. Dove of Day remained and continued to surprise them with his vast knowledge and experience. Until this meeting, those who knew him thought him to be a meek and average Indian. They had no idea, until this meeting, that at one time he was a mentor and equal to both Tall Cloud and Little Crow during the great Indian wars. They were surprised to learn that it was he who had convinced them that to show compassion and spare the life of an enemy from time to time. This actually served to make ones reputation even more fierce and respected.

It was only an hour after sunrise the fourth morning that they were first surprised, and then amazed as they greeted the arrival of many young Indian men. These men wanted to learn to fight, to win, and were ready to rebel against the whites on a moment's notice. Colton and Red Calf, were both to some extent, schooled in the ways of the white soldiers and wasted no time in organizing these young men into smaller groups. When they had five groups of six to seven men, they appointed one in each group to be a leader. Before the end of the fifth day, there were over forty young men in training.

With this many men, came other immediate problems. The logistics in managing them were all new to Red Calf and Colton. They all had to be fed and they needed shelter and weapons to practice with. To make it all happen, they divided one group into two teams of four men and assigned them the task of providing food for that day. They immediately started training with the others in hand to hand combat.

Most of the young men had shown up with some kind of weapon. Nearly a dozen had arrived carrying old and somewhat outdated rifles. As long as they were still functional, they were welcomed. Those who had recently stolen rifles and horses from the soldiers were there and were welcomed as heroes. The stolen rifles were the new Sharps carbine that fired cartridges making it much faster to reload and fire again.

They knew that in a battle, even the most basic weapon like a club, or a handmade spear, could be used with success. They devised a method of cross training with any weapon imaginable that caused the warriors to feel a sense of pride unfelt until now.

In the evenings, around the campfires, Colton and Red Calf insisted that each man learn new words in the English language. Colton asked, "How can you spy on the whites and report what was said if you have no knowledge of their words?"

Red Calf offered, "When you get back to your villages, those of you who can, must get as close to the whites as possible. Offer to work for them for little, then listen, observe and learn."

This first training camp was as real and functional as anything the army had to offer its troops. For over three weeks it continued, always with new people showing up unannounced and insisting that they be included. It turned out to be a great moral builder and seeded hope in the hearts and minds of all who attended.

Colton and Red Calf were both very aware of the enormous responsibility for the lives and safety of those young men and that it rested with them. Tall Cloud had been insistent that they understand this.

"Dove of Day says we must not give false hope," Colton said to Red Calf. "We cannot let a warrior have a sense of victory until it is earned and real."

"Yes," Red Calf agreed, "and that includes us. For this reason, we must train even harder."

There was no Indian who could keep up with Colton in a foot race. For this reason, he was the one who ran the new warriors in groups of sometimes a dozen at a time. As he led them through a reed marsh, as was the tactic, Red Calf and many others would be waiting to spring an ambush. Soon, most had mastered the art of surprise. Knowing that there would be times when mounted soldiers would be chasing them, they trained relentlessly in how to escape on foot by sprinting and racing headlong into thickets and areas where soldiers mounted on horses could not go.

Several Indians had brought horses. Most were older farm animals, not the sturdy type of mounts used by the soldiers. Still, they served well for training. The horses that were considered fit for a warrior were ridden hard and pushed to the limit as they were often urged to breakneck speeds even in the thick of the forest. Before long, nearly all the warriors in training were riding and maneuvering the horses at an expert level. More often than not, they rode without a saddle or a bridle. Even using a simple halter, the Indians learned art of horseback warfare.

Another strategy that needed to be taught was how to steal supplies. This included food, weapons and even horses. There was only one way to do this. Red Calf and Colton led a group of nearly two dozen young warriors off the reservation to get real world experience. This was better than bringing grief down on their people by causing trouble at home.

Their raids and exploits were very real. In the course of what they considered training, in a period of only three weeks, six Indians in their group were killed and several severely wounded. Their gain was many horses, rifles and lots of ammunition. Other prizes included cash money from several small trading posts.

They were welcomed north of the border in Canada by other Sioux Indians from closely related tribes. Having a northern refuge was another excellent idea. During the long and confining months of winter, they didn't have to worry about being caught by surprise and attacked by the horse soldiers. Several dozen young braves took wives and stayed in the North Country nearly all the time.

Since the area was nearly all French Canadian, the second language there for the Indians was French. They thought it very unfair that the government of the nation of Canada had no reasons to treat the Indians with contempt as the government troops back home did. For this reason, talk of a civil war was welcome. In fact, they hoped that a war would break out and the whites could spend time killing each other.

Chapter Thirteen

White Man's Way

November 7th 1860

The thriving town of Mankato remained the hub of activity for settlers desiring to file claim to the lands near the Indian reservation. The telegraph office which was now the center of interest connected this remote area with the rest of the country. It was mid-afternoon. A small crowd had gathered. They were anticipating receiving word over the wire any time about the presidential election.

"I sure hope this information is right," the telegraph operator exclaimed as he listened to the clicking, "It seems a little early to know for certain, but they're saying that Abraham Lincoln won the election." He twisted on his stool to face the open doorway as someone repeated his words, shouting to the others, "Lincoln won!"

A cheer went up. The operator said, "They're telling me that we now have a new president-elect."

"How can they have had time to count all the votes?" a woman asked. "How can it be? It's only been one day?"

"They say he's got most of the electoral votes," the operator said as he finished writing down the message, "There ain't no question about it. Lincoln won."

"Does this mean that 'old Buchanan is gone?" a man on the sidewalk asked.

The telegraph operator rolled his eyes back in his head as a ripple of laughter went through the crowd. He sarcastically said, "Buchanan had better be on his way out. If he ain't, it means we're going to have us two presidents."

A frown crossed the operator's face as someone near the back of the crowd reply angrily, "We're bound to have two presidents, and soon, if those southern states hold true to all those threats and secede from the union!"

"That's such a crock," a man wearing a white shirt and bright red suspenders said, "This election should make the issue final. You would think that they could see that."

"I'll drink to that!" a voice shouted.

For the next few days, they laughed and drank to all kinds of things. A festive mood spread through the area. Minnesota was a free state, meaning that slavery wasn't allowed, and had been a welcome addition to the union only a few short years ago.

The next few weeks went by quickly. Those who had voted for President Lincoln still talked about how anxious they were to see if he could keep the states united. Their worst thoughts were realized the third week in December, when word reached them that South Carolina had seceded from the Union. Before Lincoln was sworn in as the sixteenth president on March 4th, 1861, the Confederate States of America was already formed. A West Point graduate and former U.S. Army officer named Jefferson Davis was elected president.

The telegraph wires were alive with reports that Mississippi, Florida, Alabama, Georgia, Louisiana and Texas had all followed suit and seceded from the union. Many people believed that the country was about to go through one of the most difficult times in its short history. Those in the know braced themselves for some bitter times ahead. Most believed that all hell was about to break loose and as it turned out, they didn't know the half of it.

At first, all this talk of politics and war made little or no difference to the reservation Indians. Soon, it became apparent that their world was about to be affected in a very serious way.

The newly elected president appointed a close friend and confidant as the new Indian agent. It was said that he was a political appointment and had never been in the western states. It was soon believed by many that he had no experience for this position. It was believed that he took advice and counsel only from those whites in the area that were used to having things done their way. The story goes that his 'second' in command, a man named Hiram Jackson, was, for all intents and purposes, the actual Indian agent. Other than an initial meeting it is said that Jackson was the only one from Indian affairs that spent any time at the Indian affairs office on reservation land. He operated with impunity, and even the military leaders, most of whom dealt only with Jackson, often wondered just who, and where, his boss was.

For a short while, many Indian leaders were hopeful for a better relationship with the new people in charge of their affairs. The tribal council made a series of good faith attempts to work with the new administration on behalf of their people. It was only a matter of time until that brief glimmer of hope faded away. Soon, it was extinguished altogether and placed with the memories of better times along with the rest of the white man's broken promises.

Spring 1861

Another long winter was behind them. The customary, isolated, reports of starvation filtered in from various parts of the reservation. The tribal elders, as usual, were upset over the way things were being handled by the whites. By now, their authority was so limited that even to complain often resulted in false accusations against them. This often led to arrests and vicious beatings at the hands of the horse soldiers.

Tall Cloud and Little Crow both tried to reason with the government agent Jackson at their first meeting. He and several other tribal representatives were gathered on the large covered porch that surrounded the agency building. This was one of those rare times when food was plentiful. Jackson had instructed his people to provide lots of food on several long tables.

"When our meeting is over," he said, "all may eat."

Tall Cloud nodded politely at his remark and began, "Everyone knows," he said, "that in the summer months, it is a certainty that the far-away rumble of thunder, and flashes of lightning in the distant clouds, warn of an approaching storm." He motioned at the council members, dressed in their finest traditions, seated cross-legged on the floor of the porch and added, "The tribal elders see these same types of signs in the white man's actions towards us. It started, again, early in the spring. It continues even now."

Jackson assured Tall Cloud that his ways of doing things were in the best interest of the Indians. He was aware of the alliance between Tall Cloud and Chief Little Crow and spoke with authority.

"The great white father in Washington has personally asked us to care for all of you." he said, "All this talk of gathering storm clouds must stop."

Tall Cloud was careful in his choice of words, "The talk of unrest will stop when our people are no longer suffering from hunger. It will stop when our people no longer die of simple colds and disease for which you say medicine is available. It will stop when we know that you, Jackson, can be trusted to keep your word."

Although nothing specific was agreed on at this meeting, Jackson gave assurances to Tall Cloud and the others that the problems with the delayed payments and supply deliveries would be less now that he was in charge.

The rumblings grew louder even as the whites talked to them of better times. Two young Indian men from the upper reservation had been rounded up by the soldiers and placed under arrest. The two men were carted off the reservation and taken to the jail in Mankato. Witnesses against them said that they had been trying to stir up trouble and recruit Indians to fight against the soldiers. They were charged and found guilty of attempted insurrection. Rumor was that they had been taken to a prison somewhere in Kansas. Other rumors claimed that both men had been hanged. No one knew for sure. The tribal leaders who tried to get details were told that the rumors were false. No records of any such event existed. The agency officials had no obligation or need to give out any information to the Indians.

The rumblings of trouble sounded again, this time louder, when another young Indian from the upper reservation was found beaten to death. His body had been found in a ditch within sight of Fort Ridgley. Stories were spreading that he was one who had been educated by a missionary in the North Country. The rumor was that he had gone to the post seeking food and relief for his people.

Despite all the bad things that did happen, the winter months had been relatively mild. Many of the reservation Indians made it through the long winter season in better shape than usual. This was notwithstanding the fact that the prior year's crops had been poor and supplies promised from the white man never arrived.

There were those who believed that the unseasonably warm winter had shown them a touch of mercy; more mercy than their caretakers had ever shown. This warmer season combined with the good fortune of several well-known Indian farmers is what really made the difference. A growing number of young Indian farmers now lived in houses and had developed their properties in a similar manner as the whites. Many of these farms were complete with barns, chicken coops and pigsties. There were many who took pride in their work. They never revealed the true nature of their crops to the agency officials. Despite the poor harvest, a portion had been held back, in secret, to help themselves and others through the harder times.

The hollow words and promises of the whites were never believed. As the days, weeks, and months went by, more and more stories of hardship and injustice spread. It was as if storm clouds had settled overhead and nothing could take them away. They became more infuriated each time more of their land was taken away. The spring and summer of 1861 were to be remembered as times of darkness.

The winter snows were barely gone and the leaves were new on the trees. Rumors were spreading about a new treaty that had been proposed by the government. This one would require them to move to an area even closer to the Minnesota River. It was understood that all land on the north side of the river was to be signed over to the whites. There were many young Indians who were ready to rebel over this.

Friend

The Sioux word 'Dakota' is said to have several meanings depending on how it is spoken. It can also translate to mean 'friend' in the English language. This was the chosen name of a young Indian from one of the original Sioux bands. He was becoming very successful in his farming activities. Friend's farm was the envy of many. During the long winter months it had been his supplies and generosity towards his people that had kept many from facing a slow death by starvation.

He had adopted many of the white man's ways. He and his Christian wife, Lisa, were raising three children, two girls and a boy. Their farm was located on the opposite shore of the small lake that was only a half-mile away from Miss Lillie's old mission and school. The school had been shut down after the death of Miss Lillie. It now served as a military outpost. It often annoyed him to gaze across the expanse of the lake and see the horse soldiers on the other side. The actual school building garrisoned a troop of several dozen soldiers. This was another insult, a slap in the faces of those Indians who had subscribed to Miss Lillie's teachings and desired to be educated. Still, Friend and Lisa remained silent and complained to no one. Their girls, who were now twelve and fourteen years old, had learned to read and write when Miss Lillie had run the school. His young son had been barely old enough to walk when the tragic buckboard accident had taken Miss Lillie's life.

Lisa was worried when the outlaw Indian, Red Calf, and the young black Indian, Colton, showed up at their farm in late spring. She knew them both well. She and Friend had sat through many classes together with Red Calf and Colton. It had been Red Calf's act of bravery that had kept their family from starving to death only a few short winters ago. Red Calf and his wife, Marion, had taken refuge in a remote area in the upper reservation. The horse soldiers seldom went there, and even if they did, the chances that either would be recognized were slim. It was well known that anyone caught sheltering Red Calf would be hanged as an example. It was this fact that had Lisa frightened as Red Calf, Colton, and her husband, discussed a meeting that was about to take place.

"If you are caught with Red Calf, they will brand you in the same way and you can never live in peace again." Lisa said, her voice intense. "I beg you, my husband, do not go away with them."

"I must go." Friend answered, "There is much unrest. If it is true that we are to be moved off our land we will have no choice except to fight."

"They are many," Lisa said softly, "you are few."

"We are many, if we unite now." Red Calf said, "Lisa, it is only a matter of time until they have us all dead."

"There must be other ways," she replied.

"None that I can see. Our choices are few." Friend said, "I know you are frightened, as am I. If we are moved closer to the river, the soldiers will have us all in an area small enough to control our every move."

"It is so, Lisa," young Colton said, "their control tightens with each Indian death and each broken treaty. Even Miss Lillie never would have stood by silently while being forced off her property in this manner."

"Your mother is missed by many," Lisa said, "as are you. We got word that the white lieutenant, Harley, has tried to get papers on you."

"Papers?" Colton asked, "What does that mean, papers?" he exchanged glances with Red Calf.

"You are known to associate with Red Calf," she answered, "if the lieutenant had his way, there would also be a money reward for your capture."

Friend cut in, "It is only due to the full tribal council, that Harley does not get his way. They still have a little influence with the whites in some matters."

"This is so," Colton said, "It will be a wise thing to remember never to trust Lieutenant Harley."

"Yes," Red Calf said, "we must agree, he honored the truce during the time of mourning for your mother. I will always wonder why."

"I am sure that there was a reason, other than honor, for that." Colton said.

"He still takes advantage of any opportunity to abuse our women," Lisa said in a matter of fact tone. "The agency officials have never raised a hand against him or any white man for their many acts of mistreatment."

"All the more reason to get involved now," Colton said, "It is true that even your husband, even you or any one of us, can be accused of anything and taken away anytime."

Lisa smiled weakly. She knew that their plight was nearly hopeless. She had great respect for the black Indian boy, now grown into a man. She said, almost hopefully, "The tribal elders. Did they not negotiate this new treaty? The one that is rumored?"

Friend and Red Calf exchanged glances. Friend knew, as did everyone else, that Red Calf's older brother, Tall Cloud, was one who served on the tribal council and had signed off on many of the treaties that were only to be broken later. He was perceived to be weak as he gave in more and more to the whites.

"It is a truth of life," Colton said, "that negotiations, even with the most honorable intentions, are only as binding as those with whom they are made."

Lisa was amazed at the young man's apparent wisdom as he continued, "I fear that Tall Cloud tries too hard to trust those who cannot be trusted."

"This is why I must go to this meeting," Friend said. "The rendezvous will be over in less than a week. We can finish planting when I return. I must have a say."

Colton said, "We have been long in training, Lisa. Many of our braves are now well armed with rifles and pistols. We will take good care of Friend."

"All this talk of war," Lisa replied, "even when I was a little girl, when our people fought a long lasting fight, the talk of war never ceased. Even after the whites imposed their peace, our people suffer, and still, we talk of war."

"It is not our wish," Colton said softly.

"What is your wish?" Lisa asked.

"Only for the chance to live in peace and with dignity," he answered, "only that."

Lisa remained silent. A chill swept over her. She had a premonition that something was going to go wrong.

"I will talk with the council and with Tall Cloud," Friend said. He placed his arm around Lisa's shoulder and looked around slowly. He motioned towards the area where the children were supposed to be sleeping in the next room and said, "Our children must have some kind of hope."

"Please be careful. Speak your piece and return quickly, my husband," Lisa said.

She smiled as Friend's face lit up with delight as his daughters and small son came into the room. They somberly gave their father a farewell embrace.

Chapter Fourteen

White Man's Law

Fort Ridgley, May 1861

The post commander's expression was grave as he called his officer's meeting to order. He tried to mask his anxiety as he introduced the major who had arrived only the day before with a small detachment of men.

"Gentlemen; I ask that you give the major your full attention," he said. "He is replacing me as post commander, effective immediately." He paused for a moment at their surprised looks and added, "We have some important changes that are taking place. I want you to hear the details from him."

The major wasted no time with small talk, "Thank you, Colonel. I assume that this is everyone?" he asked. "Five commissioned officers?"

"Yes, Major," the colonel answered, "we are, as you know, a small post."

"Hmm," the major mused, "four lieutenants and a captain," he paused for a moment and referring to the captain added, "and a doctor at that."

"That's about the sum of it, Major," the colonel said. "Even Fort

Abercrombie, to the North, is shorthanded."

"How many non-commissioned officers do we have?" the major asked.

"We have eight, total, spread out over the reservation. We can have them here in short order. For now, I thought it necessary to bring in only the officers."

"Very good," the major said.

"We are hoping that you can bring us up to date on what is happening, Major," the colonel said, "I'm sure you know that rumors are a dime a dozen these days."

"Very well," the major said as his eyes swept the room. "You are all, I am sure, aware of what happened two weeks ago back in South Carolina, at Fort Sumter," he paused as he made eye contact with each officer.

"Yes, we heard." the colonel answered on behalf of everyone present.

"It would appear that we are now at war," the major stated. "President Lincoln has requested that we conduct a massive enlistment campaign."

So far, the officers were already aware of what the major was explaining to them. Then, he got into the real news, "I am to take over command of this post. The colonel has been ordered back east. He will take half of the troops with him to fight against the Confederacy. This includes officers and enlisted men and they all will serve in the regular army. They will be escorting several hundred raw recruits by rail back East for training."

The major paused and made eye contact with several officers. He said, "I'm sure the Indians in our care will require less manpower to control them once they are moved to the narrow strip of land along the south side of the river." A wry grin crossed his face as he noted a sour expression from the colonel.

"Easy to control?" the colonel said softly. He hesitated and said, almost resignedly, "You need to keep in mind that we are the ones who are surrounded."

"Point taken, Colonel," the major said. "If we have to, we will make a couple examples." He extended his hand, palm first in the colonel's direction and added, "I am well aware if that becomes necessary we will have to exercise extreme caution. The Bureau of Indian Affairs have received far too many complaints from this area."

"Now that we have Jackson broken in a little," the colonel said hesitantly, "there shouldn't be any problems."

"Jackson?" the major questioned. "I haven't met him yet. What ever happened to his boss?"

"Haven't seen or heard from him in months," the colonel answered, "could be he is back in Washington living the good life."

"I hope that you are right about having Jackson broken in. The last thing the president wants is more insurrections. But, enough talk of trouble with Indians. Let's discuss more general things."

"Such as?" the colonel asked,

"Well, for one thing, it's good to know that we aren't alone in this. All of the frontier posts are being whittled down to a skeleton staff."

"All of them?" the colonel asked. He raised an eyebrow in a questioning expression.

"Yes, Sir, all." The major's tone was serious as he added; "we need to be careful not to underestimate the strength of the Confederacy. We may be in for one long, awful war."

The colonel shrugged. His tone was scoffing as he said, "It shouldn't take more than a couple months to whip a bunch of misfit confederates. They have no army and no navy, at least none that have any training or experience."

The major shrugged at the colonel's comments.

"The governor will be assigning some militia units to reinforce the regular soldiers," he continued. "They will perform some of the more routine tasks and patrols."

"Militia?" the colonel asked.

"Yes," the major replied, "we need them, now, more than ever. The confederate side has offered to reward any Indian tribe who will fight against us, and by God, we need to make sure that doesn't happen here."

"Not much to worry about with this bunch," the colonel assured him, meaning the Sioux tribes. "What we have here is a bunch of dime-store Indians. Give them a sack of grain and an occasional bottle of whiskey, and they become like little puppy dogs, meek and easy to control."

"Whiskey? I thought that was illegal," the major said. He smiled as a ripple of laughter went through the room.

"It sure is, Sir," a young lieutenant stated.

"I hope to hell you are right about easy to control," the major said. "Meek and easy to control they had better be. I doubt that anyone will be sending reinforcement troops back here from the eastern battlefields."

The meeting was opened for discussion. The officers were all excited to get the opportunity to go back east and fight in a real war. As soon as the meeting was adjourned, the colonel and the major teamed up to make the selections as to who was to go and who was to stay.

Lieutenant Harley was extremely upset when he found out that he was to remain at the fort.

Two days after the meeting at Fort Ridgley, the colonel marched off seeking fame in a real war against a real enemy. He led the way on horseback surrounded by a cadre of flag bearers, drummers, and soldiers. They were followed closely by a rag-tag group of local recruits.

Word had spread and there was no doubt that the Indians now had knowledge of the army's weakened state. A company of militia, over forty men strong, arrived two days after the soldiers departed. These men were assigned to several different regions. It was anticipated that the impending plan to shrink the reservation boundaries again would cause more unrest. The new post commander had been briefed on the relocation plan even before he started his journey to the area. He wasn't worried. He was confident that fear and brute force would suffice to keep the local Indians in their place.

The major named Lieutenant Harley as his acting executive officer. He believed that Harley had the necessary coldness to fill this position. It was with his approval that one of the lieutenant's first acts was to assign part of the militia reinforcements to be housed in the old mission-school building. The major also agreed that these rough-cut civilian recruits shouldn't be left unsupervised. He readily approved Lieutenant Harley's request to assign Corporal Benning to provide assistance to the militia lieutenant. He was aware of rumors of bad blood between the lieutenant and the corporal but never became privy to that information. He was confident that Corporal Benning would serve well in his role as the regular army's agent and advisor.

By the end of the first week, the militiamen were already restless. They were assembled daily in the former classroom of the old elementary school. They talked among themselves as they were seated on the rows of benches awaiting orders.

Surprisingly, there was room enough inside this former classroom to accommodate all of them. This area of the building also doubled as a dining hall. The next room, which was equally as large, and had once served as a church, now served as a sleeping area. The two small rooms attached to the main building were utilized as officers' quarters.

Corporal Benning had pinned a large map of the immediate area on the wall. He had shown them which roads to patrol. Over the course of the last week, he had attempted to whip them into some semblance of a military unit by conducting daily drills and military maneuver exercises. It became obvious by the end of the first week that it was going to take much more than a few drills and practice exercises to get this group into shape.

"As soon as the local Indians are relocated from this area," the corporal said, he paused and indicated the area on his map that took in the farmland on the far side of the small lake, "the regular army personnel will be leaving and relocating closer to the river."

"What's going to happen here?" the militia leader, a lieutenant asked.

"Well, Sir," the corporal answered, "your forces will more than likely be assigned to provide local security. Can't say how long I'll be here, since I'm top on Harley's shit list."

The lieutenant chuckled, Benning continued, "This area has already been spoken for, paid for, and divided up. It will be re-settled within a few weeks."

"How about those places," the lieutenant asked. He pointed out the window, across the expanse of the nearby lake, at several small farms on the other side.

"Those places will have white people on them by the end of the second day," the corporal said with a smirk. "That's what they call choice property."

"Who lives over there now?" another man asked. "It doesn't seem right that Indians would live in regular farm houses like that."

"That farm," the corporal said, "is currently held by a buck that calls himself Friend." He chuckled unmistakably as he added, "He's got two of the best looking young squaws you've ever seen. His wife ain't half-bad either."

Word came down from the main agency office that the entire Sioux tribe was to be relocated to a narrow strip of land on the southern bank of the Minnesota River. The whites gave their word that just compensation would be paid to the Indians for giving up more land and to offset their inability to grow crops. The tribal leaders, now powerless, had no choice but to go along with these new promises.

One of the worst aspects of the new treaty was that those Indians who lived on the north side of the river were all to be relocated to the south side. This wasn't going to be an easy task to accomplish. When the time came the regular army personnel would be assigned to that area to maintain control.

Chief Tall Cloud was doing everything he could to gain assurance from the agency officials that the agreed on annuity payments would arrive in time to help his people through the next winter. It was said that the new treaty would go into effect within a month. He knew that timing was essential if they were to buy the much-needed supplies necessary to see them through. All of these changes were expected to amount to no more than another string of broken promises. It would surprise no one if those supplies and payments never arrived.

Another troublesome factor was that the Indians were allowed to meet only with the approval of those who managed the agency. They were told that any non-approved meetings or gatherings would be viewed as attempts at insurrection. The penalty would be harsh. These rules made for an awkward situation. Under the watchful eye of the horse soldiers, those who wanted to speak their minds were forced to remain silent.

The third week in May, word got back to the reservation officials about a secret tribal meeting. Rumors said that an unauthorized meeting was being held somewhere up north, perhaps as far away as Canada. A roll was held and many of the Indian chieftains, including Tall Cloud and Little Crow, were unaccounted for. This led to some hasty decisions by Jackson and his bunch.

Central Agency

"Where do you suppose all them damned Indians have disappeared to?" Jackson asked. He was sitting comfortably behind his desk in the Indian affairs' office. His large frame, plunked comfortably in the oversize chair, dwarfed the small desk. His question was addressed to the new post commander, a tall man of medium build who sat opposite him.

"We don't know yet," the major said. "We've got patrols out looking. Maybe we'll find out something soon."

"Is there any meaning to all this?" Jackson asked. "Why would the leaders just up and disappear like that?"

"There's never any rhyme nor reason to what a damned redskin will do," the major answered. "If you're worried about it, you're the only one. It's a safe bet that they will do nothing. Since the upper and lower reservations were formed, they've always made a lot of noise, but there has never been any real action on their behalf."

"What about the stories I've been hearing about that one really bad-ass Indian called Red Calf?" Jackson raised his thick eyebrows in an expression of curiosity, "The whispers say that he and some buck named Brown Tooth slaughtered three of the colonel's own men. Is that right Major? Over in Mankato at the city jail?"

The major was obviously taken aback by this line of questioning. His voice was seething with anger, as he said, "It doesn't matter what to hell you heard." He emphasized the word, 'you', referring to Jackson, "The only thing that matters is that the army will catch that slippery heathen. You can bet real money we will."

"The three dead soldiers were said to have died in the same wagon accident." Jackson shook his head. "You and I will need to come up with better stories than that."

"Meaning?" the major responded, inquisitively.

"Keep in mind, Major," Jackson said, his voice low and intense, "you only have to deal with the locals on this end of the reservation, I have to answer to my boss and keep an eye on the entire Sioux population. This includes not only your own Chief Tall Cloud, but others who think themselves to be real warriors."

Jackson insisted, "Keeping a lid on things is one thing, Making up bullshit stories is another." He stared long and hard at the major as he sipped his nearly empty cup of coffee and added, "There's also a story going around about a deceased soldier, Private Moore." He put his cup down and looked expectantly over the major's shoulder at the closed office door. "Hey, woman!" he shouted rudely. "Bring more coffee!"

The major shrugged, "What about Private Moore?"

"I doubt that he fell from his horse and died of a broken neck," Jackson said. "That is the official incident report. Right?"

"Yes, I've read it."

"Maybe, he accidentally scalped himself when his body hit against a sharp rock on the ground."

"Enough of this! Damn it," the major exclaimed, "what's your point?"

"I didn't mean to be offensive," Jackson said. "I just want to be clear. Your army post has a dead-or-alive warrant out on another buck. 'John the Baptist,' of all people." He grinned inwardly, aware that he had struck a raw nerve with the major, "I'm sure that he did more than beat up a soldier and steal an army horse."

The major met his stare and said, "I guess you do get around, after all."

Jackson said, "It would be a grave mistake to underestimate this office, Major." He smiled again and said, "It's just that, well, everything I just mentioned happened before you got here. Right?"

The major shrugged as he answered, "Yes."

"What we have here is a chance to help each other, a chance for a fresh start. What we don't need is an Indian uprising. The president has his hands full with other matters. He's got a real war to run. The last thing we want is for rumors of trouble, here, to reach Washington."

"Let me worry about rumors and trouble," the major said flatly. "I'm sure we can come up with a way of shutting down rumor mills."

"I hope so," Jackson murmured. He looked up as the door opened and an Indian woman wearing a red-checkered dress entered. She was carrying a tray with a silver pot and two cups. "About time," he muttered. He motioned for her to come closer. He asked the major, "Would you care for coffee?"

"Yes, thank you."

"Back to the subject of the missing chiefs. Is there any credence to those stories that the Indians are having some kind of a secret pow-wow, somewhere up north?" Jackson asked as he scooted back in his chair to be out of the woman's way.

He waited until both his and the major's cups had been poured. The woman set the tray and coffee pot on one corner of the desk and turned to exit the room. Jackson questioningly asked, "Sugar?"

"Please," the major said, "two."

Jackson scooted his chair closer to the table. He leaned forward and spoke in an intense whisper, "Those redskins need to be found. I don't want to know the details of how you do it," he said. "You are the military, it's your job. However you keep the peace is okay with me."

"We'll do our best," the major murmured.

"I hope to hell so," Jackson said. "It seems as if things are getting out of hand. We've even heard rumors about a nigger Indian stirring up the locals."

"I hadn't heard that," the major said.

"Maybe, we need to keep in closer contact and share information," Jackson said.

"What did you mean about a 'nigger' Indian?" the major asked. "I thought us northerners were supposed to call them 'colored' or something like that."

"I guess you will find out over time," Jackson replied. "Just never underestimate this one. What makes him so dangerous is that the Indians look up to him."

The major offered no response and sipped on his coffee. He smiled brightly when the Indian woman returned carrying a tray of cakes and cookies. She set the tray on the table beside the coffee pot and once again left the room.

The small band of rogue Indians grew larger each time an injustice was served up by the whites. Red Calf, and most of these who had been labeled as outlaws, made camp two hills to the north of the north shore of the Lake of the Woods. This was near another Indian reservation's boundary. The area was only a day's hard ride to the Canadian border. Many of the braves now wintered in Canada. They had left their women and children there to return to fight against the whites with their brothers. Many spoke French, instead of English, as a second language due to the area being an expanded French settlement.

This area of northern Minnesota was still somewhat wild and uninhabited. It gave those Sioux who remembered what it was like in the old days, a small taste of freedom. The hunting and fishing was good everywhere. The many lakes and rough terrain made for excellent hiding places in the event of military pursuit should the soldiers come.

John the Baptist and Brown Tooth had both taken wives and wintered in Canada. Word of the spring rendezvous reached them even before the snows had melted. They were anxious to come. They had picked up a following of nearly two-dozen young braves. They were well mounted, well-armed, and itching for a fight.

The actual meeting was held a full day's ride to the north of the reservation lands in the Many Lakes area. The meadows along the banks of the Bon River had long been a place of rendezvous. The meeting place and time had been kept secret. If the horse soldiers got word, they would surely come and attack. Red Calf and his band were among the first to arrive. He was pleased to introduce the Indian farmer, Friend. Those who spoke in the native tongue called him Dakota. Several others from the lower reservation had also accompanied them. It was with great joy, the next day that he greeted his older brother, Tall Cloud.

There were many meetings, some long and often intense. It was with great restraint that those who viewed Tall Cloud as a weak leader kept their opinions to themselves. His explanation, that his only options were to trust the white men and try to barter for better conditions sounded frail at best and were met with great doubts.

Little Crow understood the losing battle that Tall Cloud fought almost daily trying to negotiate terms with the whites. He did his best to back his friend in all ways.

"I was once a warrior chieftain," Little Crow said to them. "I fought side by side with Tall Cloud. I too wanted war, war without end with the white man. We must understand that often he has had no real choices and believe that he has always tried to make life better for our tribes."

Tall Cloud stood and motioned with his arm in a slow sweeping motion towards the East. "No matter how many we kill, no matter how hard we fight, still they will come. Their numbers are greater than the grains of sand along the riverbanks, greater even than the stars in the sky."

John the Baptist sprang to his feet and shouted, "Then we must kill more of them than they us, and faster." He shook his fist at Tall Cloud, "I have killed the white eyes. Long have we been in training with Red Calf. The soldiers have gone to the East to fight among themselves. I say that now is the time."

Brown Tooth also stood up. His self-control was more apparent as he said, "I, too, have killed the white soldier. John the Baptist is right. The soldiers are weak as they fight their own war. Now is the time for us to strike."

Tall Cloud said, "You all know," he paused as he looked from face to face, "you all know that I am not afraid of the whites. I am not afraid to fight, or to die." He shook his head sadly, "I try to reason with the enemy to bring peace because I have seen war. The spirits of our people, from all of the tribes, cry out for vengeance. This I know."

There was silence around the campfire. Tall Cloud knew his words were falling on deaf ears with most of the warriors. He was seething with anger as he stood up. "Do what you will," he said, "I will continue to bargain for peace." He threw his blanket wrap down and quickly walked away.

For what seemed like a very long time, there was an unnerving quiet. As Tall Cloud's shadow disappeared among the tents and teepees, a feeling of unrest swept over the gathering as heat lightning lit up the sky in silent flickers of brilliant light. It was Red Calf who broke the silence.

"Many years ago, in another time of war, Tall Cloud did fight. He fought with great honor. I, of all people, can never forget. It was he who found the small boy beneath the body of his dead mother. It was he who took the boy in as family, made him his brother, and taught him the ways of the ancients." Red Calf paused. An eerie stillness settled around the campfire. In the flickering firelight, his shadow was cast tall and ominous against the rising smoke. "My brother has guided me since those times of darkness. Always he has been right in his approach," Red Calf seemed to stand taller as he added, "His ways are right and honorable. It is not him, but the white man who brings dishonor to everything that he and the tribal elders have tried to do."

"You are right." Colton said. His voice, spoken in a low tone, carried for all to hear. He stood up. Those gathered seemed to watch in awe as he spoke,

"The white man has many ways of subduing our people. In their eyes, we are less than human. They call me Nigger; they call you, my brothers, Prairie Niggers. They do all they can to make us less than they."

He paused for a moment as if awaiting a response. When none came, he continued, "I remember, as a child, seeing my best friend, a young girl, lying dead in Red Calf's cabin. White men, evil men, had their way with her." Again, he paused. It was obvious that most of the Indians present knew precisely what he was talking about. "Yet the white man did nothing. I remember standing, watching in silence as my people brought those accountable to justice. It was our people, not the white man's law that settled the score with those responsible. To this day, if the white man knew which of us exacted justice, we would be rounded up and hanged as they tried to do to our brother Brown Tooth."

"What Colton says is true," Red Calf said. "I now agree with John the Baptist and Brown Tooth. We need to acquire more weapons. The only way to do that is to raid and plunder from all of the white settlers who violate our land. We must strike before they lay claim to anymore. We must strike even as they try to pass through."

Friend had been sitting listening intently as the events unfolded. Colton asked, "How do you see it, Friend?"

Friend was stirred up. This was the first time he had agreed with those opposed to Tall Cloud's methods.

"Give me a rifle," he said. "Give me a horse. If none are available, I will steal my own." He stood up in solidarity with Red Calf and Colton. "I am with you, my brothers."

Brown Tooth said, "There are many rifles, only a day's ride from here on a wagon train heading west. We saw them pass two days ago."

"We can also get many weapons from the army patrols." the young black Indian said, "We have followed them and watched them as prey. They are soft and unsuspecting."

A loud cheer followed by a chorus of war whoops went up as the braves realized a sense of unity. They were ready to fight. They only needed a leader and there were several to choose from. That same night, just before dawn, a rider tore into the camp bringing bad news.

Many things were about to happen at once. They were awakened in the pre-dawn light to the news that the homes they had left behind were all burning. The reservation authorities hadn't waited to make arrangements with the tribal leaders. Their people were being rounded up and herded to the south bank of the river. The Indians who were forced to go were leaving nothing to the whites. They were burning everything they had to leave behind. This news ended the rendezvous as everyone hurried back to the reservation.

Colton rode hard with Friend as they headed back to the lower reservation. His only plan, for now, was to return to his band with the horse that Friend had borrowed, after Friend got home. Everything changed just before dark the next day when they arrived to find the farm in ashes.

The sun was setting over the horizon as they approached a gruesome scene. Friend reined in his horse as they neared where his two milk cows lay dead in the field. He exchanged glances with Colton as he noticed that both animals had been shot. Colton's expression was one of disbelief.

"We left here only four days ago," he murmured.

"Who would do such a thing?" Friend asked. "My Lisa could not have shot these animals in preference to leaving them to the whites. We have no guns."

Colton offered no reply as they approached the smoking ruins. His heart was heavy with sorrow as he took in the scene. He whispered aloud, almost as if praying, "Let it be Lisa who set fire to this place."

Friend walked his horse slowly towards where the house and barn were still smoldering. Only one corner wall of the cabin was still standing. For a moment, he froze in place as he stood staring in disbelief.

Through the wisps of smoke and shimmering heat waves, he saw them. His wife and daughters were lying dead just outside the smoldering house. Their bodies were naked. It was plain to see that they had been raped and brutalized. The oldest girl had been stabbed and slashed by a knife several times in the chest. The other's neck was bent to one side at an odd angle.

Colton sat silently in his saddle. His expression was incredulous as Friend dismounted and approached the scene. He felt as if the look of amazement was etched on his face as he watched. He noticed, but thought nothing of, a gunnysack that was tied to the hitching rail. Hundreds of angry flies were buzzing around it. He expected Friend to cry out in grief. Instead, Friend fell to his knees, silent, between his daughters' lifeless bodies. His face showed no emotion as he attempted to close their eyes with the palm his hand. They had been dead for some time and that didn't work. He was obviously in shock as he stood up slowly and looked around. He focused on the maimed body of his wife. Lisa had been disemboweled. Friend stood staring down at what was left of her. Her lifeless eyes seemed to stare back at him, pleading.

Colton watched in awe. A powerful shudder came over him. He felt as though he could see Friend's soul leave his body as his eyes took in the devastation.

Colton somehow became more aware, aware that he was surprised with himself, surprised that he could be so calm over all of this. Then, something dawned on him. He realized that he was an Indian too. What it meant hit him right between the eyes. It struck with much more impact than he had felt when he first realized what it meant to be black in a white man's world. He felt bitterness boiling within. It was a type of bitterness that he had never experienced before. He was sure that after this day, there would be no more peace.

Colton wasn't aware that he had dismounted until he realized that he had moved the mangled body of Lisa and placed it near that of the oldest girl. Next, he carefully dragged the youngest girl nearer. Then, he used his blanket roll to cover the remains. The eerie silence was broken by a loud, heart-wrenching moan from Friend. He had discovered his son's headless body. It was charred and burned beyond recognition in the still smoldering ruins of the cabin.

Colton moved close and stood staring in disbelief over Friend's shoulder. Then, it dawned on him what it was in the fly covered sack that was hanging from the hitching post rail. He had overlooked it at first. Now, he nearly staggered as he walked back to the rail. His hand was shaking as he reached to untie the small grain sack. He was lightheaded as he untied the knot. He felt as if his spirit had been separated from his body. An eerie feeling of weightlessness overcame him. He was amazed that he could view himself from above. He gasped as he saw the expression on his own face. He watched the scene with horror as he watched himself open the sack. The boy's lifeless eyes, wide in surprise in the severed head, stared back at him. It was at that moment when he realized that, only minutes before, he truly had witnessed Friend's soul leave his body. A moment later he was back as before. He was gasping for breath as he stood on the ground, holding the sack open for Friend to see what was inside. A short time later, he felt no shame as he retched uncontrollably after watching Friend slowly tie the knot back in the sack and place it carefully by the boy's mother.

The sun was gone from the sky. A faint glow of pink in the western horizon was all that was left of this day. As the moon started to show its face, Colton found a long handled shovel leaning against the rail of the pigsty fence. He dug one large grave a few feet from the bodies.

Friend had spoken no words. He stood silently with his gaze fixed somewhere far away across the lake. His silhouette was unmoving in the flickering light of the flames that still danced along the one corner of the remaining wall.

Colton buried the remains in the dim light cast from the still flickering fire and that of a half moon. Daylight was breaking as he fashioned a small wooden cross to mark the spot. Friend hadn't moved all night. His sorrow was over-powering as he remained sitting with his back resting against a fence post and watched the sun rise over the treetops.

Over a dozen sets of shod hoof tracks, leading from the garrison across the lake, gave sign as to who was responsible.

Colton's voice was soft as he placed a hand on his friend's shoulder.

"We must go, Dakota," he said in the native tongue.

"Where?" Friend responded. "There is no place else."

"My friend," Colton said, "it will not end here. We must go back and join with Red Calf. To engage the soldiers here, with no weapons, would be foolish." Friend offered no reply. He mounted up and silently followed Colton. He was dazed and without emotion as they rode on.

As the story goes:

With little thought to the timing, the agency officials had announced that the Indians had but two days to gather their belongings and be ready for the move to the south banks of the Minnesota River. The soldiers from Fort Ridgley and several groups of militia were assigned to escort them to the new location. This announcement did not go over well. By this time, many young farmers had already planted their fields. Word spread that they would not be allowed to take their livestock, only what they could bring on their wagons or carry on their backs. This proved to be the last straw. Discontent over the imminent actions by the soldiers spread. It was talked about throughout all of the Indian settlements. They bitterly agreed that anything of value to the white man should be destroyed. It was rumored that white settlers were already bickering over some of the more choice farmlands. The black columns of smoke from the fires, as they torched their homes, could be seen for miles. They felt as if there was no recourse except to allow nothing of value to remain other than the land itself.

Those white settlers who laid first claim to the lands were extremely upset when they arrived at the different farm locations. Many were furious to find that the Indians had butchered what was left of their livestock and left the carcasses to rot. This included cattle, pigs, chickens and anything living that had to be left behind.

The soldiers attempted to round up and punish those who had set fire to their homes. This task proved impossible since none of the Indians had ever been given any kind of deed or title. The situation also provided cover for several heinous acts perpetrated on the Indians by the white soldiers. The attack on Friend's farm was only one act of many that were covered up by the agency officials and the militiamen.

One Indian man was killed after he viciously attacked a member of the militia with an axe handle. It had been a futile attempt to protect his young wife. He was immediately overpowered, tied up and gagged. They kept him in the same one-room cabin, so he could watch, as the soldiers took turns raping and humiliating his wife. Later, as a jug was passed around, the Indian was castrated while his wife was forced to watch. Then, he was dragged outside. A rope was tied around his neck and tossed over the limb of a tree. The executioners simply pulled on the rope until his feet were raised a few inches above the ground. His body, bloody and naked from the waist down, was left dangling from the tree in plain sight. This was intended as a message to others. The tree was located near a well-traveled road that many would have to pass by on the way to the south bank of the river. When the Indian woman wouldn't stop screaming, a gag was placed in her mouth to shut her up. She was thrown to the ground a few feet from her husband where she slowly choked to death. The last things she saw and heard was the body of her husband hanging from the rope and the disgusting sounds of laughter coming from the drunken white men.

The next morning, several soldiers were ordered to remain near the hanging tree. They were left there so that no one would cut down the body. They said nothing as a passerby stopped and placed a blanket over the dead woman. It was a gruesome reminder that worked for a while. With very few weapons at hand, the Indians were forced back into an enduring patience.

The agency officials were made even more furious as reports of the Indians destroying their own homes and butchering their own livestock came in. They threatened death by hanging to anyone who would damage reservation property. As with most decrees, this one also got out of hand in a hurry.

The newspapers were too busy with stories of the War Between the States to pay much attention to unsubstantiated rumors coming from deep within the Indian territories. The saloons and houses of ill repute missed the constant stream of business from the soldiers as they were moved either back east to fight in the war, or closer to the

river to watch over their Indian wards.
    No more lit fuses.
    No more powder kegs.
    It was war.

Part Three

Black Bat from Hell

Chapter Fifteen

The Red Man's War

June 1861

The wagon train slowly made its way West around the base of the low ridge. Like a slow, cumbersome serpent, it followed in the tracks and wheel ruts of those pioneers who had gone before. The settlers were amazed at the desolate change of landscape as the forested hills of the troubled Minnesota territories were left behind. The wagons slowly entered the sparsely treed and rolling hills. They could see in the distance, the barren plains that would eventually take them into the Dakota territories. The bright sun reflecting off the distant sagebrush gave it an eerie purplish color.

This was a small procession made up of only seven wagons. As they journeyed deeper into the plains area, the settlers were totally unaware that their every move was being watched day and night. A small band of warriors had paralleled their course for the past five days, waiting for the right opportunity to attack.

Led by Red Calf, the group included John the Baptist, Brown Tooth, Colton, Friend, and several others who had been with them since the trouble started. This included Wild Fisher, More Boy, and several of their friends. They were a dozen strong. They had revenge in mind as they patiently learned the routines of the white man's camp. Only half of those in the raiding party were armed with rifles and two rode double as they followed their prey. They knew that soon, if they were successful, they would all be well mounted and well-armed. They knew that much was at stake. If all went well, soon, they would have enough horses and guns to recruit and arm many more braves.

After the attack, their plan was to split into three groups and then they would travel the high country to different reservations in their efforts to recruit warriors. They believed that if they could provide rifles and ammunition, the odds would change and be in their favor. The timing was important. They wanted to have an armed camp, ready to strike, long before the horse soldiers returned from the east. They were possessed with a sense of urgency as they waited with a forced patience for the situation with the wagon train to be just right. They were certain that it wouldn't be long now. Red Calf and Colton, as they had been taught by Tall Cloud, had carefully planned every move that was to come.

The driver of the lead wagon squinted into the bright sun that was slowly sinking over the top of the next hill. A rider could be seen, silhouetted against the sun, as he rode back towards the wagons. He recognized the incoming rider as their scout and pulled his wagon to a stop. He stood on his wagon's seat for a better view. He waved at the rider and shouted something to the wagon behind his. Several men who had been riding on horseback beside the second wagon hurried on ahead to meet the scout.

The returning scout led the way in a more southerly direction for about another half mile until they reached their next campsite. They stopped when they came to a large open area that was sufficient for the trailing wagons to come up alongside those that were in the lead. Soon, the wagons were arranged in two rows. This made for a good defensive position in which to spend the night. There was a small stream a short distance away. The horses were unhitched and led to water. The lush grass at the stream's edge would be a perfect area to picket the animals for the night. This wagon train had been on the trail since the snows had melted. After nearly three weeks of boredom, a false feeling of security had settled in. With over a dozen armed men in their party, they believed that no enemy, Indian or bandit, would be foolish enough to take them on.

Other than an occasional night owl or coyote howl, the journey thus far and been peaceful and serene. As darkness descended, a feeling of false harmony and calm settled in. Everything that happened was routine. The usual sentry was posted. The women cooked the meals over two common fires. Conversations and laughter drifted in the still air.

As darkness descended, two dogs barked furiously and raced off into the night. The dogs had done this for the last three or four nights in a row and the settlers paid them no mind. Soon, their barking stopped and they returned, as usual, a few minutes later. No one was aware that even the barking of the dogs and their racing off into the night only to return a short while later had become a routine. They had no way of knowing that death was stalking as they settled in for the night.

The usual single lantern had been left burning on a small table that had been set up near one of the fire pits. The sentry had settled into a chair next to the table. He was wrapped comfortably in a warm blanket to offset the chill of another long night. It was a routine to which he had become accustomed. It was just before dawn when he twisted around in his seat to reach for the coffee pot, still simmering in the coals of the fire. He became a little anxious when he saw a man standing only a few feet away.

"Hey," he said softly, "you startled me."

"Quiet," the man whispered. He quietly walked behind and around the man's chair as he said, "we don't want to disturb the others."

"Who are you?" the sentry asked his voice still soft as he twisted back around to see.

"I am Friend." These were the last words the sentry heard as his head was brutally split open by a small hand axe. These brief sounds of disturbance were followed by a long period of silence, interrupted only by the routine of the chirping crickets and croaking frogs from down on the stream bank. A few minutes later, the deadly silent attacks of Red Calf and the others were interrupted by a woman's shrill scream. This was followed by several gunshots. Then, all hell broke loose.

Daylight dawned on a great victory for those in the raiding party. Most of the rifles captured were the new cartridge fed Spencer repeating lever action models. Several were Sharps rifles that also used cartridges. There was a lot of ammunition.

All but two of the white men were dead. One was the scoutmaster, a young man who had previously led several wagon trains successfully through this territory. Although it did no good, he hadn't given up without a fight. The other survivor was a man who had nearly slept through the entire battle. He was a heavyset man in his late forties. He had rolled out from under the wagon and sat up to the sounds of shouts and screaming. Although too late, this had made him instantly wide-awake. He had been clubbed in the back of the head. His hands had been bound behind his back and he was roughly herded to the center of the campsite.

The Indians had suffered no casualties or serious injuries. Also surviving were three women and a small boy.

In an effort to be more like Tall Cloud had been all those years ago, Colton and Red Calf insisted on a good will gesture and loaded the women and the boy in one of the smaller wagons. Later, they traded them to serve as slaves to several prominent Frenchmen traders in a northern border settlement. Both were pleased that they had done this. The 'civilized' side of them thought it the right thing to do and when they got several good rifles and boxes of ammunition in the trade, they were glad they had spared those poor souls.

The horrible things that were done by the others to the two men remaining can only be imagined.

July 1861

Tall Cloud had given up on any chances for a peaceful solution to the problems faced by his people. He realized the white man's most serious mistake soon after they were all herded onto the lands near the south bank of the Minnesota River. The mistake was in placing so many Indians in a small area. When they had been spread out over many hamlets and settlements, the soldiers had appeared to be many and the Indian numbers few; all that was reversed now. The soldiers seemed to realize this and for a while, the incidents of violence towards the Indians seemed to decline.

The agency officials supplied them with lots of lumber and building supplies. The white traders were acting very generous in passing them out. Although this was a good surprise, it was merely a temporary effort of pacification on behalf of the Indian agent, Jackson. Much needed supplies were delivered and unloaded as promised. Food and even medicine became plentiful. Routines settled in and the sense of immediate danger was minimized.

Tall Cloud was amazed at how quickly the supplies were now being handed out. Each week, a number of beef were slaughtered and delivered promptly by wagons to different distribution points on the lower reservation. Word spread that the same good things were happening for the people on the upper reservation as well.

As time went by, Tall Cloud devoted his efforts to insuring that adequate housing would be available for his people before the winter months set in. The area was a flurry of new construction as the small buildings went up. There was still the matter of the tin roofing and metal wood burning stoves being made available. For some reason, he actually believed the new agent, Jackson, when he was once again assured that the much needed necessities would be arriving and dispensed to the Indian people in a very short time.

The whites were already talking about offering yet another treaty, one that would increase the payments of hard cash and guarantee more food and supplies. Tall Cloud shuddered at the thought of another treaty. In his mind, he knew that his people would have no more of the white man's false promises and guarantees. His hope was that things, as bad as they were, would stay much the same.

Word of the successful raid against a wagon train reached Tall Cloud long before the whites were aware that it had happened. Several weeks went by before an army patrol stumbled across the remains of the wagons and settlers. More reports followed. There were reports of bold raids on army supply trains as far away as the Dakota Territory. The reports always ended with the news that their warriors were growing stronger and greater in number each day.

It was also said that the black Indian, Colton, had been seen near the Canadian border. The story was that he and another had traded several white captives for guns and ammunition at a French settlement. When Tall Cloud repeated this news to Little Crow, they both smiled.

Chapter Sixteen

No More Chances

January 1862

The winter was not that much different from the last one. Still, it seemed to be unusually long and harsh. The Indian people had no place to go. They had nothing to do other than endure and await the handouts from the whites. The spirits of many young people, male and female, were broken daily as their plight wore on.

In these times of hardship, many injustices on both sides of the issue were never reported. The Indians had no one to report injustice to other than to those who were committing the very acts. The white settlers still filed many false reports. Reporting the truth was never considered. The last thing the government agents wanted was for those in power in the eastern region to lose faith in their judgment. This would have meant the end of some lucrative moneymaking opportunities. It didn't matter what the story was. The officials discounted anything not favorable towards them as false rumors. Their claim was that these stories were being made up to spread unrest. The well-armed soldiers had quickly put down any attempts at reprisal for the cruelty shown by the whites during the events of the last spring and summer. No one dared to question the authority of the agency and the local traders. Problems with the trading posts often ended with more false accusations, usually against young Indian men. The soldiers always settled the disagreements in favor of the whites.

The small houses that had been hastily erected did little to off-set the misery of winter. The sheets of tin roofing never arrived and as a result most of the roofs leaked. The wood burning stoves that had been promised never arrived. When the authorities were challenged about this by Tall Cloud, he was nearly arrested and threatened with jail if he continued to try to upset the locals. Makeshift fireplaces were common and many shacks were abandoned in preference to shelters dug into the sides of steep hills. These were roofed with a layer of boards and several feet of dirt. These new conditions made it difficult for the people to adjust.

The river was a natural barrier that would limit where anyone could flee should the soldiers decide to attack. A single road wound through the area on its way to the upper reservation. No one felt at ease, no one felt safe. Many of those young men who wanted to be warriors and had been motivated to fight earlier in the summer were now missing. According to Tall Cloud's roll, which he never shared with the white officials, over one hundred young men were absent. He knew that they were all holed up somewhere away from the watchful eyes of the whites. They were undoubtedly waiting for the timing to be right before returning. They were camped in remote parts of the upper reservation or perhaps as far north as Canada. Word was that they were in training. Tall Cloud knew that they were the same ones who were doing the raiding, killing, and stealing so often reported. It was rumored that they were collecting many weapons for a vengeful return to the reservation.

For a short time, the new agent, Jackson, had kept his word and food had been plentiful. For this reason, it had been forbidden for any member of the tribe to put up winter stores. The Indian agents decreed that hoarding food was another prohibited act.

"There is no need to hoard food." Jackson had assured Tall Cloud and several tribal leaders. "Now that your people have been moved closer together, you will receive your supplies on a regular schedule."

Many did not listen and it was a good thing that they did not. It was their hidden supplies of beef jerky and stored ears of corn that was to carry them through the long winter months. These lessons had been learned the hard way.

Never trust the whites.

A whooping cough epidemic spread through the lower and upper reservations in early February and lasted until early spring. Many children and many adults died as a result. Medical attention, although promised, was never made available. As the wails of grief-stricken parents pierced the silence of the night, so did the cold realization of what was in fact going on.

The agency officials, taken in by the lure of fast money from a never-ending flow of settlers, wanted them all gone. Only with the extermination of the Indian people could the lands be divided up. Only then could the area be developed in the manner desired by the white settlers.

Right or wrong, this was the belief.

Sandiyohi

The Indian tribes, for countless generations, had been a near nomadic people. They had lived in areas that they returned to each year after the great seasonal hunts. They had also grown and stored many crops and times had been good.

Since ancient times, the Sandiyohi area had been spoken of as a land of plenty. It was thought to be only two day's journey north from the upper reservation. The elders often spoke of good times as they told the stories and explained the traditions of this area and of their past heritage. These stories were passed down from generation to generation. Now that the white man had taken over their lives and moved them from one confined area to the next, it was only a guess where the real sacred valley was to be found. Many years had passed since the last gathering. Only a few tribal elders were thought to be old enough to know the way. One was a man too old to make the journey. It was said that he gave the directions to the sacred valley to a holy man named Spirit Keeper only moments before he died. Spirit Keeper was a common name, or perhaps a title, that was given to many religious leaders.

Spirit Keeper believed that the Sandiyohi area was a spiritual site and that the sacred valley was a real place. It was a place of prosperity that had seen many great encampments somewhere along the banks of the Shakopee River. In times past, many tribes would come together there. They organized great buffalo hunts. They would mingle and exchange items of trade. Young men would offer much of value to the fathers of young girls from the neighboring tribes. It was an area and a place of memory that the legends talked about proudly. They had been a simple people in those days. The spirits had always guided them.

The January thaws came early along with unseasonably warm temperatures. In only a week, nearly all the snow melted away. Spirit Keeper told of a vision. In his vision he saw teepees in such numbers that they could not be counted. As far as the eye could see, on both sides of the sacred valley, campfires burned. He began talk of making a journey to the Sandiyohi sites. The answers from the spirits, he said, could be found there.

Nearly a dozen people decided to make the journey with Spirit Keeper. The white man's law forbade them to leave the reservation without permission. Spirit Keeper went through the proper channels with the tribal leaders in an attempt to get it. It came as no surprise when those in authority at the agency turned down his request to make the pilgrimage to the sacred valley. They decided to go anyway. Somehow, word of their plan got back to the militia soldiers.

The federal soldiers were spread thin. The militiamen assigned to back them up had no desire to ride regular patrols. Many had simply gone home for the winter months. This left the area open to unauthorized movements on behalf of the Indians. The soldiers knew this and were determined to make an example of the Indian medicine man should he be bold enough to lead others off the reservation.

The lands north and west of the upper reservation were an expanse of rolling hills. It was a wide-open area dotted with occasional scrub pine trees and sagebrush. The upper fork of a small tributary of the Shakopee River wound its way though. This provided for a good trail to follow. It was believed that this trail led all the way to the sacred valley that the holy man had seen in his vision. The fork of the stream was nearly a day's journey from the upper reservation. Once there, it provided for an excellent campsite. It was also visible from many miles away. Spirit Keeper and his small band made camp. So far, it had been an excellent trip. They took it as a good sign when they were able to catch many fish from a small pool the high waters of the small stream had created.

They were unaware that an army scout had spotted them. The scout returned hastily to report their movements to the militia station still operating out of the former schoolhouse. The next morning, the officer in charge quickly assembled his men. He led the way, unencumbered by federal troops, as they left in the predawn light. They rode hard, thundering through the upper reservation shortly after sunrise. They came upon the unfortunate pilgrimage shortly after noon.

At dawn, the Indians had resumed their trek. One woman, a wife to Spirit Keeper, fell behind due to having a sprained ankle. Her sister, whose Christian name was Dora, remained with her. As they continued their journey, they dropped further and further behind the others. They had sat down to rest on the side of a small ravine when the horses of the soldiers could be heard thundering by on the other side of a nearby rise. They made their way to the top of the rise in time to see the last few soldiers disappearing from sight along the stream bank. They were riding hard in the same direction that the band had gone. The women exchanged worried looks and hurried along their way. After several hours of hard travel, they found the bodies.

No one had been spared. Most of the bodies were in a small group. The soldiers had herded them together and bound their hands and feet. They had wasted no bullets. It was plain that only knives, axes and clubs had been used to kill the seven men and three women.

The body of Spirit Keeper lay grotesquely with a small wooden club positioned near his head. Dora picked up the club and stood staring at the bloodstains. She stopped breathing as her eyes took in the rest of the heinous sights. The women, friends that they had spoken to only hours before, were lying dead. It was obvious that the soldiers had taken their pleasure before killing them. One had been clubbed to death. Her body was separate from the others, draped face down over a rock that protruded waist high from the ground. The others had their throats gruesomely cut from ear to ear and were still spread out on their blankets.

Both women were weeping bitterly, huddled together near the bodies, when they heard the soldier's horses. They hurried a short distance away and concealed themselves in a shallow depression behind a growth of scrub pine. They watched silently as the soldiers returned.

Apparently, the soldiers had experienced a change of conscience. They tied ropes around each body and dragged it downhill to the stream that was flowing hard with the runoff from the melting snow. The bodies were unceremoniously thrown into the swirling rapids and quickly swept away. The women watched, horrified, as the events unfolded. Their hearts sank when a young soldier rode directly to their location. He reined to a stop and stood tall in his saddle stirrups looking directly at them.

Private Orrin was a young farm boy who had joined the militia with visions of action and adventure. At the time, he had signed on for a one-year hitch after which he planned on joining the regular army. His year would be up come spring. It wasn't what he had thought it would be. He was sick and tired of how the militia was being run and had put in for an early release. His request had been denied and he was reassigned to this militia unit that was based out of the former mission and school north of New Ulm.

Private Orrin had just turned eighteen. His light blonde hair and thin face made him appear to be years younger. It was due to his innocent look and boyish features that he constantly had to prove himself with the older soldiers. He had been fed up with that since the beginning. This was his first real mission with his new unit. He had been re-assigned here only a week ago to finish out his enlistment. With only a short time left to serve, he was anxiously counting the days until he could leave this bunch behind.

They had ridden hard in the pre-dawn light and nearly all morning to catch up to these wandering men and women. At first, it had appeared as if they were merely going to turn the Indians around and herd them back to the reservation. The situation got ugly in a hurry.

"A couple of them squaws are looking pretty good." A soldier remarked.

"Not bad," another agreed. He looked at their leader and asked, "What about it, Lieutenant? It's been a long time since we had us a squaw."

The lieutenant ordered the Indian men to sit in a small circle. His soldiers quickly bound their hands behind their backs. Next, they bound their feet together. Even before they were finished, several soldiers were already in the process of stripping one of the women.

Private Orrin was aghast as he realized that it was Sergeant Collier who was assaulting the woman.

"Quit struggling, whore!" the sergeant shouted.

In the blink of an eye, all three women were being molested. Two soldiers set upon each of them. The captured Indian men shouted in protest.

"Shut them the hell up!" the lieutenant ordered, his voice loud and tense.

"Sir!" Private Orrin shouted. "This ain't right."

"What ain't right?" Sergeant Collier asked, mockingly. He stood over a captive who was prone on the ground. "Didn't you hear the lieutenant?" He made eye contact with Private Orrin as he drew back with a hatchet. He sunk it violently in the man's head, killing him instantly. His voice was gleeful as he re-established eye contact with Orrin. He drew back his arm to strike another as he asked, "Do you mean this?"

The three women had been knocked to the ground and hastily bound. The soldier's attention sidetracked back to the captive men. For a moment there was silence. The soldiers got out their long knives and began the killing in earnest.

Private Orrin stood watching the displays of savagery in disbelief. He was startled out of his initial shock as the lieutenant motioned towards him and shouted to one of the men, "Save something for the new trooper, Orrin."

"What the hell are you doing?" Orrin gasped.

He took a step back as a soldier clubbed a victim with the butt of his rifle.

"We need to know, Private," the lieutenant asked, "are you with us or against us?" The lieutenant was a heavy-set man in his mid-thirties. He wore a long scraggly beard. It nearly sickened Private Orrin to watch him as he used his long knife to cut a struggling man's throat with a slow back and forth sawing motion.

"My God, Sir," Orrin stammered, "what the hell is going on here?"

The lieutenant stood straddling his victim and drew his service revolver. The madness in his eyes was clear to see as he cocked the revolver and aimed it at Orrin's head. He said, his voice loud and intense, "Are you with us or against us?"

The activity stopped. The soldiers stood up and formed a half circle around the steaming corpses. Blood was still pumping from several slashed throats. Several of the victim's bodies were still quivering. The soldiers were now focused on the lieutenant and the private as they watched expectantly.

"Sergeant Collier," the lieutenant said, "help assure me that the private joins us."

A moment later, a rifle was placed against Orrin's back. "He means it," Collier said from behind. "So do I."

The remaining live Indian was an old man. He was dazed from several blows to his head. Orrin's mind was swimming with amazement as he realized what the lieutenant wanted. He knew that he needed to be a part of the group or he would soon join the Indians in their fate. He knew what he was doing was wrong as he drew his long knife. He was shaking with fear and excitement as he stepped forward towards the unfortunate Indian. He plunged the blade straight into the old man's chest. A feeling of disgust swept over him as the man's body jerked and stiffened slightly before relaxing in death.

"See," Collier said as he put his rifle back in its scabbard, "that wasn't so hard."

The soldiers laughed and turned their attention back to taking their pleasures with the women. Orrin got on his horse and moved to wait a short distance away.

The soldiers were finished and the women dead about an hour later. They were a jovial bunch as they mounted up and thundered off. Orrin brought up the rear. Even though he felt like retching, somehow, he wasn't too bothered by the whole incident. He tried to rationalize the situation in his mind as he reasoned that had the situation been reversed, the Indians would have done the same to all of them. They had only gone a half-mile or so when the lieutenant and Sergeant Collier came to the decision that it would be best if the Indian's bodies were never found. It was Sergeant Collier's idea to return to the scene and drag the bodies a short distance down the hill to the swollen stream and toss them into the swirling current.

"Hey! Wasn't there a club by this one?" the lieutenant shouted as he fastened the rope around his pommel in a half hitch. "Dead Indians can't move clubs." He urged his horse in a downhill direction. "Did one of you men take it?"

No one paid much attention to what the lieutenant was saying as they watched what he was doing. The Indian's lifeless body was dragged behind the horse, twisting and turning over the rough ground.

A short distance away, two women were ducked down into a small depression surrounded by a thicket of scrub pine and a tangled layer of underbrush. From his position, Orrin could see them as clear as day when one of them moved. Several other soldiers, including Sergeant Collier, had also caught the movement out of the corner of their eyes.

"What was that?" Collier shouted, indicating the clump of scrub pines.

Orrin whirled his horse around. "I see it too," he shouted. "I think it was a damned old porcupine." He spurred his horse towards the thicket.

He reined his horse around hard, keeping himself between the thicket and the others. He stood tall in the stirrups as he got to where he could see down into the small depression. The two Indian women stared back, their eyes wide in fear.

"Damn," he murmured. His mind was in a spin. It was certain that they were as good as dead.

Their faces were frozen in fright. The younger woman was holding the missing club clutched to her chest with both hands as she remained on her knees. Her breath could be seen coming in short gasps in the cold air.

His pulse was pounding in his ears as he stared into the woman's eyes. He knew that their only chance for survival was to remain undetected by the others. A cold shiver went up and down his spine. The lieutenant wasn't here and neither was Collier close enough to put another gun to his back. He nearly panicked as he realized that both Collier and Kelly were about to come over.

"Well?" Collier shouted questioningly. He and Kelly reined their horses in Orrin's direction. "What the hell is it?"

"Hell, I don't know, ground squirrel or something." Orrin shouted.

"You sure?"

Orrin made no reply. Instead, he stood upright in his saddle stirrups and unbuttoned his trousers.

"Damn!" Collier said to Kelly as he reined his horse to a stop. "Will you look at that stupid son-of-a-bitch? He's going to do it again. What that disgusting fool does is enough to make a grown man want to puke."

Kelly had also reined his horse to a stop beside Collier. He leaned to one side to spit. He wiped his mouth with the back of his hand and said, "Hell, he's just a kid."

"I'm telling you, it ain't proper for no white man to stay in the saddle and go piss like that." Collier said. He turned quickly to avert his eyes as they viewed a thick yellow stream of urine arc over the horse's neck.

"Let's get back to dragging," Kelly said in a disgusted tone. "Those bodies ain't gonna throw themselves in the river."

They spurred their horses back to where only one body remained. The other soldiers had already dragged the rest down to the stream.

"Hurry the hell up, Orrin. You ill-mannered bastard," Collier yelled. "We don't got all day and want to get back to the schoolhouse by dark."

"Yes, Sir," Orrin called. He smiled as he finished buttoning his trousers. He was pleased that his disgusting diversion had worked and had caused the others to keep their distance. He settled back down in his saddle.

He exchanged looks with the women. A feeling of dizziness swept over him as he realized that they were certain to view him in the same light as the white animals he rode with. Even as he murmured, "God speed to you," he wondered if either could understand English. He spurred his horse and hurried to join up with his unit of militiamen.

Private Orrin was bringing up the rear as the last body was dragged to the stream's edge. Kelly reined back and paced his horse slow enough for Orrin to come alongside. He eyed Orrin's horse and shook his head in disgust at the wet marks on the animal's neck left by the soldier's urine.

"It really bothers Collier when you piss over your horse like that," he said.

"What's he gonna do?" Orrin retorted, "Put another gun to my back?" Kelly was about to respond when he added, "Hell, I'm a part of this man's army too. What he and the lieutenant did to me back there wasn't right."

"Maybe not," Kelly said, "but at least now they know that you've got as much to lose as the rest of us over this deal should anyone of importance find out." He leaned to spit again. "It'll keep you from squealing on any of us." He wiped his mouth with the back of his gloved hand. This caused Orrin to grin. Kelly's action merely served to spread the black tobacco stains from the corner of his lips to the side of his face.

"After what you and the others just did and what you saw happen with these people, do you really think it proper to gripe about seeing me piss while I'm a horseback?" Orrin said, "Damnation if that's all that bothers you..."

Kelly retorted, "It ain't right for a white man to do that. Just don't forget that it's Collier and the lieutenant that you need to pay mind to."

"Damnation," Orrin said, his voice nearly normal.

"You weren't here when we moved them dirty red-skin squatters from across the lake back there at our barracks," Kelly said. "These here squaws today were let off easy compared to what we done to them others."

"What do you mean?" Orrin asked.

"Hell," Kelly replied proudly, "there were sixteen of us that day and we only had two of them Indian whores to go around. The older one, well, she only got to pleasure the lieutenant. That bunch all spoke damned good English. The old whore put up such a fuss that the lieutenant felt the need to shut her up early on." He paused to spit again.

Orrin was nearly sickened as Kelly finished his story. "He cut that whore's guts right out. You should have seen it." He was obviously proud as he grinned, "That filthy whore crawled screaming halfway out the door while her guts strung right out across the floor behind her. Talk about stink! Man, did that whore stink."

Kelly paused for a moment and grinned at the startled look on Orrin's face. "Hell. Like I was saying," he said, "today there are only nine of us, not counting you, and we had three squaws to share." He paused to spit again. "If the others sense that you're going to be worried over a few dead red-skins, you've got more trouble in your future."

"Damn," Orrin muttered. His confused expression caused Kelly to grin.

"Don't be so serious about it, boy," Kelly said. "They were just Indians."

"Would Collier or the lieutenant really have shot me," Orrin asked, his voice an intense whisper, "if I hadn't stabbed that man?"

"No doubt in my mind," Kelly answered.

"Son of a bitch," Orrin murmured.

"You had better believe that those filthy redskins would have done the same thing to any of us," Kelly said, defensively. "Don't doubt that for a minute."

"I don't doubt anything," Orrin said.

Changing the subject, Kelly said, "I remember the first time you stood and pissed out of your saddle like that. It was due to a bet you had with Miller. Right?"

When Orrin didn't respond, he added, "The rest of us wouldn't mind at all if you didn't do it no more."

"Damn," Orrin said, again. "Is that really all that bothers you guys?"

"It just ain't natural for a white man to do that," Kelly insisted, so don't do it anymore, okay?"

"Okay," Orrin said. "Hell, my enlistment is up come spring and I'm not going to sign on for another hitch with this bunch."

"Ain't no one gonna miss you," Kelly said.

He ignored the private's answer as Orrin mumbled, "Nor will I miss you."

The stories of brutalities brought on these people by the militia soldiers spread rapidly. Government officials never recorded these accounts as well as many other stories. They were merely discounted as more attempts to stir discontent with the Indian people.

The militia soldiers said that the part of the tale about two surviving witnesses, both Indian women, only added to how false the story really was. After all, they had been there. They were laughing inwardly. They all knew for sure that no one could have survived.

Chapter Seventeen

The Dare

French Crossing, July 1862

French Crossing was a settlement that had been in existence for as long as anyone could remember. French fur traders had originally established it. This area of the Minnesota River was wide and shallow. It had a firm sand and gravel base that made for a stable river crossing. The crossing was a main thoroughfare on the trail west due to its being a central point where several trails merged. Now, it seemed as if someone, somewhere, had opened a floodgate releasing a steady flow of white settlers to and through the reservation lands. This was one of the more noticeable side effects of the new Homestead Act. This act, which offered 160 acres of free land to just about anyone who wanted it, was signed into law by President Lincoln in May, 1862. Now, only a couple months later, the world of the Indian tribes was about to change in a most violent and permanent way as more land was ceded back to the government.

The settlement's population had more than doubled in only the past year because the government had recently opened up all these millions of acres of land to homesteaders. Much of this was land that had been negotiated away from the Indians in the last treaty. As a result, dozens of merchants had set up shop hoping to make money off the endless stream of settlers.

The infamous treaty of 1851 had been signed not far from this location at a similar river crossing area only a few miles upstream. Over the next few years, the government officials had escalated their acts of aggression and used several clauses in the agreement to go back on the terms. This treaty had gained the government millions or acres of land and relegated the Indian nation to an area that consisted of two narrow strips of land, each approximately twenty miles wide and seventy miles long. These reservation lands bordered both sides of the Minnesota River. The latest agreement, the treaty of 1858, had eliminated the area on the north side of the river. Tall Cloud had also been involved in the negotiations of this accord that ceded another million plus acres back to the government. He was extremely upset over all of these doings but like so many others, he had no real bargaining power. The government's "take it or leave it" philosophy was backed up by a very powerful military.

Incidents of violence, killing and destruction were occurring more frequently and more openly that ever. The Indian people had been herded into the remaining small reservation area. Many had lost all hope. It was believed by nearly everyone that it would take another war with the white man to set things right. It was these constant rumors that gave hope to many. Word had it that the outlaw Indian, Red Calf and his band would soon be coming down from the North Country with vengeance in mind. It was said that when they did, any Indian brave who was willing to learn to fight and to kill would be welcome. It was certain that the war to defeat the white man wasn't far away. There was no shortage of young men eager to unite. It was the subject of countless talks around campfires and meeting places. All they needed was a sign. They believed that the spirits guided Red Calf. They also believed that his destiny was in part due to his relationship with another young Indian, a young man whose reputation was growing each day.

It was said that the black Indian, Colton, nearly eighteen years old, was by far the most cunning warrior the Indian nations had ever seen. The stories spread and he became larger than life in the tales that were told and retold throughout the reservations. Many believed in his invulnerability. It was whispered that the spirits guided him and that he could do no wrong. Even the whites believed some of the stories. As a result, Colton, like Red Calf, now had a large reward offered by the government for his capture.

There was also talk that the Indian bands led by John the Baptist and Brown Tooth were uniting for an assault. It was known that these warriors were responsible for countless attacks and coups against the endless stream of white settlers who dishonored their land. Those in the know told that these braves would soon be coming down from the distant North Country like proverbial bats out of Hell.

Word spread that the outlaw Indian, Red Calf, and the black Indian, Colton, were expected to be in the area soon. Anytime there was talk among the Indians that Colton was going to be present, they came in great numbers to listen to his words. He spoke with conviction in a calm tone of voice that was heard as thunder. It was said that when he went into battle, Hell and all of its fury went with him. It was rumored that an Indian brave had been heard bragging that French Crossing was where the Indian people would get together and there they would sign their own declaration, a declaration of war.

The Upper Store

More trouble was brewing on the upper reservation. There was no question about it. The trading post known as The Upper Store was filled to an overflow capacity with food and supplies. The outside wooden platform at the rear of the store was an area whose floor was the same level as the beds of the large wagons that brought in the goods. This outside loading dock was stacked high with merchandise. Boxes and sacks of food and medical supplies were piled high beneath the lean-to roof. There was no arguing that food was plentiful. The overflow was such that a barn on the edge of town had also been filled to capacity with dry goods. More wagonloads of supplies arrived each day. These huge freight wagons were fulfilling long overdue orders from the reservation officials. Despite the overabundance of supplies, the traders were determined not to let a single grain of food be distributed until they had their money from the government. There was talk of a huge shipment of gold that was supposed to arrive from St. Paul any day to settle these issues. Until the gold arrived, the traders weren't about to give up a thing to the Indians. They didn't care. No matter what, they held the upper hand.

It was very late at night when two desperate and nearly hysterical Indian women summoned Tall Cloud from his house. He and his wife had been sound asleep when the piercing wails and loud banging on their door woke them.

"Tall Cloud!" A woman's voice shouted, "Tall Cloud, wake up!"

His wife got up and lit a lamp. She threw on a robe and went to the door.

"Who is there?" she shouted. "Who would wake us at this time of night?"

"It is I," a voice wailed tearfully, "the one called Laura-Lee. Tall Cloud's brother, Red Calf, is married to my cousin, Marion."

The light cast from the lamp illuminated the porch in a faint glow as the door was opened. The woman called Laura-Lee had fallen to both knees in an expression of supplication. The older woman who accompanied her had done likewise.

"Please. We need to speak to Tall Cloud." Laura-Lee said, her voice begging.

Tall Cloud, awakened and alert from the disturbance, spoke from within.

"Let them in, wife." he said; his voice was soft and calm as he added, "At this time of night, whatever brings them must be very important."

As they entered, his voice was filled with recognition as he looked at the younger woman and said, "I know you. You are wife to Cardinal the Carpenter."

"It is so!" Laura-Lee exclaimed. "This is my mother-in-law, her name is Best of Two. My man, Cardinal, is in trouble. We beg you to help us."

The older woman followed Laura-Lee into the room and assumed a kneeling position with her back against the closed door. "Have mercy," she stammered.

"The trouble is with my husband," Laura-Lee said beseechingly. "Those white men at the store have captured and beaten him. All he did was try to get food for us and our children."

Tall Cloud exchanged worried looks with his wife. He was fully aware that food was plentiful and that it was being denied distribution to their people until the money for its payment arrived from St. Paul.

The old woman said, "I beg you, Tall Cloud. Come quickly and save my son. He is a good boy. His only intent was to feed his family."

"What did he do?" Tall Cloud asked.

"He and another were caught trying to take sacks of cornmeal from the back of the store. It was the armed soldiers who caught them." Her voice broke as she added; "They beat them both nearly to death and have them tied up on the platform steps. The soldiers and several whites are now getting drunk and kicking them and talking of killing them."

"Even as we speak?" Tall Cloud asked.

"Yes. We hurried here to seek your help."

A few minutes later, Tall Cloud was walking rapidly in the darkness with the two women. It was several miles to the upper store. The darkness was occasionally lit up in an eerie manner from a series of heat and chain lightning flashes that danced across the heavens on this hot and humid night. His mind was in a whirl. This was something he had feared would happen. With food this close, it wasn't right for the whites not to allow distribution. He had been replaced as spokesman for the lower bands a short time ago and only hoped that whatever influence he did have would help in the release of the two men. They got to the store as the eastern sky was getting bright with the promise of another sunny day. The store was lit up from kerosene lamps. Loud voices and laughter could be heard from within as they approached on the main street.

"Wait here," Tall Cloud said softly to the women. "I will go to the door alone."

The women waited, one on either side of the wide set of wooden steps that led up to the covered porch. Laura-Lee stood with her hand on the rail as if expecting to climb up and help her man at any time. Her mother-in-law remained at her side standing with her arms folded across her chest.

Tall Cloud knocked on the door.

"Who the hell is it?" a voice shouted from within.

Tall Cloud remained silent and knocked on the door again, this time louder.

"See who the hell that is!" A voice shouted. Other grumbling voices could be heard as the loud banging on the door irritated those inside.

A large white man with an unkempt bushy beard opened the door. He was obviously very drunk as he looked at Tall Cloud through bloodshot eyes. He shouted back over his shoulder, "Nothing to worry about. It's just a damned old Indian. Probably come for them two in the back."

The man standing behind him recognized Tall Cloud.

"Hey!" he shouted for all to hear. "We've got us one of them Indian Chiefs right here! Take a look. It's that worthless Injun they call Tall Cloud."

The man who had opened the door paused to spit. He hawked a gob of tobacco directly onto Tall Cloud's moccasin.

"What the hell do you want, Injun?" he growled.

Trying his best to ignore the man's obvious disrespect, Tall Cloud answered, "I have come to find out what has happened to two of my people..."

He was cut off by another voice from inside the store.

"I'll bet this fool is after them two good Indians. You know, the two that are hanging around on the back porch."

From within, men were laughing in a boisterous way. "Two damn good Injuns, says I!" someone exclaimed.

Five or six men came to the door and walked outside. Several were armed with rifles, several with handguns. One was carrying a double-barrel shotgun.

"You say you come for a couple of thieving Injuns?" A man asked. He was a tall man wearing a pair of bright red suspenders and an eastern-style derby hat. He glanced at the women and added, "Are both of these whores with you? I heard you had four or five wives, you damned heathen." Without warning, he nailed Tall Cloud in the face with the stock of his rifle. Tall Cloud was knocked backwards from the force of the blow. He tumbled unceremoniously down the stairs and came to an abrupt stop, flat on his back, on the ground. He sat up, dazed, and wiped blood from the corner of his mouth with the back of his hand. He sat silently waiting as the man shouted, "Hell, if you came for them two thieving Injuns, you can have 'em. They are both out back. Go get 'em and take 'em the hell away from here." He paused to spit, hitting the older woman on her shoulder with a filthy gob of tobacco juice. "Just get the hell away from here. Don't you have the sense to know Injuns ain't allowed in this area during the hours of darkness?"

He and the others retreated inside.

Laura-Lee and her mother-in-law hurried around to the rear of the store. Tall Cloud was close behind. He was off balance after his humiliating treatment. As he rounded the back corner, he heard Laura-Lee shriek. More screaming and wailing, this time from the older woman followed.

It was now full daylight. The sun was starting to peek over the tops of the trees as his eyes took in the scene.

The two Indian men were indeed 'hanging around' on the back porch. They had been hung from the main support rafter that held up the roof over the wide stairs. Their lifeless bodies were twirling slowly in the gentle early morning breeze. Their faces were ashen in death, their eyes staring blankly.

Tall Cloud stood and stared in amazement. The women had both fallen to their knees. He was seething with anger as several white men came onto the loading dock from within the supply store. The same one who had viciously struck him with his rifle stock was the first to speak,

"Take these thieving redskins away from here," he said. His voice was raised and angry as he added, "Now!" He reached up and sawed through the ropes with his knife. First one, then the other dead man fell to the ground. The second man's arms caught up in the space between two of the steps. This caused him to remain as if sitting naturally in the shadows cast from the rising sun. The two women remained silent, in shock, watching.

"Did you hear me?" the man shouted, obviously angry, "I mean you, Injun. Get 'em the hell out of here."

There was no response from Tall Cloud.

"Hey, you. Indian," the man insisted. "You had better wake the hell up."

Tall Cloud remained frozen in place. As hardened as he was, this was a scene that sickened him. As he stood staring at the dead men, his mind was flooded with memories. He had fought against the white man, long ago, in the Indian wars. He had surrendered with honor when the white soldiers had proven their superiority. Since then, he had always done his best to seek a peace with honor for his people. The white man shouting at him from the loading dock laughed with the others and turned to join them as they walked back inside. He called over his shoulder, "It ain't like there's a damned thing you can do about it. You don't have the guts."

Tall Cloud and the women untied the remaining ropes from the bodies and slowly dragged them a short distance away from the platform. The women waited, weeping, as Tall Cloud left them to go to the livery stable to borrow a wagon. He returned shortly with three other Indian men. They silently loaded the two dead men on the wagon. The women climbed into the wagon bed, still sobbing softly and sat beside the bodies. Tall Cloud glared at the supply store with a look of unmistakable hatred as he prepared to leave. One of the other Indian men climbed onto the seat beside him. Tall Cloud snapped the reins gently and drove off.

Several white men from the supply store had once again walked outside and were watching from the loading dock as the wagon disappeared from sight. Each held a steaming cup of coffee as they continued with their attitudes of indifference.

"Do you 'recon that's the last we'll see of them dirty redskins?" one asked.

Another man, this one noticeably more sober than the others replied, "You had better hope the hell those heathens go away and stay away."

"Hell, Charlie," another man asked, "what'd you mean saying he don't have the guts? That sounds like a dare to me. Why'd you go and smack that Injun with your rifle stock anyway? He was just here to get them others."

Charlie smiled and adjusted his derby. "Hell, it doesn't mean much to dare a stinking Indian." He cocked his hat to one side as he sipped his coffee, "I always wanted to knock one of them bastards." He winked at the others and added, "I guess it is true, those damned redskins do bounce."

"No doubt," another man said, nearly shouting, "that fool bounced at least twice while I was watching."

A ripple of laughter followed this remark.

"Aw, don't make a big deal out of it." Charlie said, "They ain't nothing but low down, stinking Indians. Our people will take care of everything."

"For sure," was the reply; "No doubt about it."

Two soldiers joined them. One was a lieutenant. He also held a steaming cup of coffee. The other soldier, a sergeant, was too hung over to say much.

"Lieutenant Harley," one of the men said, "that damned chief, Tall Cloud," his tone was questioning as he asked, "who in the hell is he, anyhow?"

The lieutenant, obviously suffering from a hangover, grinned and said, "He's one of those want-to-be warrior chieftains like you read about in the five cent novels. He thinks that he was a big deal, years ago, when he thought they could fight against us and win. He's just another dime store Indian, a lackey to Little Crow and the others. Hell, his own people just replaced him as their designated spokesman.

"Hey there, Charlie," another man said, "you ain't going to lose any sleep over what went on here. Are you?"

Charlie shrugged. "You mean over waiting for him to get even or something?"

"Someone said that the other Injuns look up to him because he has 'charisma,' whatever the hell that means."

"Didn't see much of that," Charlie retorted, "Hell, all that means is that someone thinks that the other Injuns listen to him. Don't matter, they're all worthless."

"Don't be too bothered by of any of this," the lieutenant said. "A couple bottles of whiskey and he'll forget everything that happened here."

"Eh?" a man asked, "What? Did something happen?"

Lieutenant Harley shrugged his shoulders and said, "Like I said, there's next to nothing to worry about. These reservation Indians are useless."

As they went back inside the sergeant asked, "Sir, how about some breakfast?"

The lieutenant sounded interested in that thought as he answered, "Sounds good to me, Sergeant."

Tall Cloud wasted no time in driving the borrowed wagon to the main agency building in the lower reservation. He reined the team to an abrupt halt in front of the agency director's office. This same building housed the agency's Indian police unit. The women waited in the back of the wagon, still crying softly, as Tall Cloud took the stairs two at a time. The Indian man, named Wide Hail, who had accompanied them, remained sitting on the wagon seat awaiting the outcome. His was a more than curious interest in how things would turn out. Just last spring his wife had been missing for several weeks before her body was discovered on a narrow trail about a mile from the east entrance to Fort Ridgley. She had been brutally raped and murdered. His pleas for justice had also fallen on deaf ears. Tall Cloud had also tried to help him. Now, he was doing what he could to help Tall Cloud.

The reservation police division was made up of Indian men who had been trained by the army to perform routine duties to be expected of police officers anywhere. Everyone knew that they were merely a token force. The government officials employed and referred to them as examples of the government's goodwill. No one took them seriously and if they had, it would have made no difference. It was common knowledge that the government people still called the shots.

Two Indian police officers rushed outside moments after Tall Cloud burst into their office. They ran down the stairs and immediately checked the back of the wagon. The first man, wearing corporal stripes on his sleeve, slowly shook his head as he examined the corpses. There was no question that the dead men had been hanged. He and the second Indian police officer exchanged glances. In a low tone, the corporal said, "Let us hope that we can keep this to ourselves." He paused and twisted around to watch as Tall Cloud slowly walked down the steps, his face expressionless. The man accompanying him was their sergeant. He was a white man who had been hired only a few weeks before.

Both Indian policemen hung their heads in shame as their sergeant made no secret of the fact that he was trying to sweep the whole incident away.

"Bring me a witness," he told Tall Cloud, "and I will file papers against those whom you claim are responsible."

"Will you not send someone to the upper store and ask questions?" Tall Cloud said. "This is all I expect."

"I will see what I can do," the sergeant said, "for now, get them planted in the ground before they get to stinking any worse than they already do."

The two Indian officers exchanged knowing glances and said nothing as Tall Cloud climbed wearily back on the wagon. The man on the seat beside him gently snapped the reins and drove down the street. They turned a corner and soon were out of sight.

"There will be no justice, Tall Cloud," Wild Hail said. "As sure as the sun rises, you know this."

When Tall Cloud offered no reply he continued, "We all know of the dark time that comes. The whites will not be satisfied until they have driven the entire tribe off the lands and have everything that is rightfully ours. Can you not see this?"

Tall Cloud answered in an almost defeated tone, "What you speak of, yes, it is coming. I remember from the days of the great Indian wars what follows. This I will try to avoid, my friend. Not that long ago, our numbers were almost three times what they are now. Yes, my friend, I truly know what is coming. I swear that I will try to find peace until I am sure that none can be had." He snapped the reins to urge the horse to a faster pace as he added; "Only as a last resort will I ask my people to die and become extinct."

Wild Hail nodded silent agreement.

Chapter Eighteen

Stirring the Hornet's Nest

Two days after the incident at the upper store, Tall Cloud was still trying to get some form of satisfaction from the agency officials. The facts were out and the grumbling from his people could not be ignored. Young men were talking of revenge and turned to him for some kind of justice. Caution was thrown to the wind as the Indian people protested in various ways. There was an incident where a soldier patrol, passing through a small village, was set upon by an unarmed and very angry crowd. The young Indian men and women hurled handfuls of fresh horse manure and rocks as the soldiers passed through. At first, it appeared as if the soldiers would gain the upper hand as they kept control of their horses and drew their weapons. It was the size of the mob and the intensity of what was happening that swayed them from firing a single shot. They spurred their horses and hurriedly left the area. This was considered a small victory for the Indian people and taken as a good sign.

Tall Cloud explained to any official he could get to listen that the army had taken an active part in the hanging of two Indian men. In the same manner of the Indian police, they also chose to ignore him.

He made his last try for diplomacy at the agency headquarters. Jackson had refused to meet with him and his options were few. He stood with two other tribal leaders in front of the desk of the agency director's assistant. The man behind the desk was a young man who wore thick eyeglasses. He looked at Tall Cloud and the two tribal leaders who were with him. He shrugged his shoulders in an indifferent manner and said, "How can we bring charges against anyone when we cannot prove that what you say is true?"

"The agency's Indian police have seen the bodies," Tall Cloud insisted.

"We can find no one from the upper store who will confirm your story." The man said. He was sweating profusely as he wiped his forehead with a handkerchief.

"They murdered our people!" Tall Cloud exclaimed. "What more proof do you need?" It was rare for him to lose his composure. He did so now as he leaned forward and pounded his clenched fist on the table. He said, his voice as cold as steel, "I need to talk to Jackson. This cannot go unchallenged."

"I will see what I can do," the man said. He appeared to be even more apprehensive as he got up. He added, "Just be sure that you don't try to start another insurrection. After what you have said to me, I would have to testify that you are indeed trying to stir things up." He turned as he added, "Good day to you, gentlemen," and left the room.

Tall Cloud stormed angrily outside followed closely by the other tribal leaders. He knew that word of this incident had spread and that it was only a matter of time before real talk of insurrection would be heard. He pitied whomever the soldiers would come after. The white man's philosophy was simple; make an example and crush them at the start of any disturbance; put them in their places before they could grow strong. He knew that a drastic change was needed, and now. He hoped that the bloodshed that was sure to come would be over quickly. He was at home, with these thoughts on his mind, when he had some unexpected company.

Tall Cloud was sitting on his front porch when two riders, each leading an extra horse, appeared on the trail from the main road that led past his house. There was something familiar about the one in the lead. His face lit up with a wide smile as he recognized his adopted brother, Red Calf. That same smile was made even larger as he recognized the young black Indian, Colton. "Hello, my brothers!" he exclaimed as they reined to a stop at his porch.

As Red Calf slid down from his mount he said, "For you." He motioned with his hand indicating the two extra horses. He embraced Tall Cloud and added, "They are unmarked. Let us hope we don't have to eat either one of them for a while."

Colton untied a large sack from his saddle pommel and passed it to Tall Cloud's wife who had also greeted them with a hug and a big smile.

"We don't mean to impose," he said with a grin as she took the sack of food. Her relieved look was unmistakable as she went inside to prepare dinner.

"Now I am sure that you are indeed crazy," Tall Cloud said to Red Calf, "riding on a well-traveled road, out in the open like that."

Red Calf smiled. "Crazy maybe, but not stupid. The army patrol won't be back until late tomorrow."

Tall Clouds' inquisitive look caused him to add, "As you have taught us, we know the routine of the white man." He paused as he saw a look of pride on Tall Cloud's face. He continued, "Tonight the horse soldiers will camp on the trail by the pond near the white settlement we call Enfield. They will have a support wagon and a cook. They will pitch tents and will post two guards. The guards will be relieved every two hours. The soldiers all will be complaining that they are to sleep in tents when they could have easily returned to the warm, comfortable barracks back at the fort. You see, my brother, their every move is predictable."

Tall Cloud was impressed. He asked Colton, "Did you two watch to know their routine?"

"No," Colton answered, "we only had to ask Dove of Day, he knows nearly everything."

Tall Cloud smiled, "Your raids and news of your success has long been known, what you did with the captive women and the white boy was wise."

"Thank you," Colton said, acknowledging the complement. "Your brother was as much a part of it as was I."

They had heard about the humiliating treatment towards Tall Cloud by those at the central agency. Red Calf and Colton both assured Tall Cloud that they thought he had done the right thing in how he had handled the situation.

"It is my fear," Red Calf said softly, "that someday we will hear that you have been killed. This, my brother, would be the worst possible news I could hear."

Tall Cloud's wife interrupted the conversation as she called a single word from within the cabin, "Dinner."

Fort Ridgley, first week in August 1862

The post commander was seething mad. Another of his patrols had been attacked by a group of unarmed young Indian men and women. This time it had happened right on Main Street in front of the agency headquarters. A troop of six men had been assaulted with hurled stones and horse manure, mostly horse manure. It was a clear message of disrespect. He was venting at several of his officers even as their separate troops were assembled and waiting for orders outside. Lieutenant Harley was doing his best to conceal his grin as the major unloaded on a replacement officer, Lieutenant Jennings.

"These acts of deliberate insurrection will stop!" he said, his voice angry. "Lieutenant, you had damn well better know that I am serious about this."

"Sir, what could we do?" Lieutenant Jennings said. "Those people were unarmed. As fast as we went after one, two others would appear out of nowhere and throw more rocks and horse shit at us."

"Next time?" the major asked. "The next time will be the last time. What the hell am I supposed to tell Colonel Sibley? The governor has already decided to put him in charge here and he doesn't take kindly to incompetent soldiers allowing Indians to continue stirring things up."

"Are your orders for us to shoot to kill? Sir?" the lieutenant asked, his voice incredulous, "Over pitched rocks and horse manure?"

"My order is don't let it happen again. I know you are new here, Lieutenant, but that's no excuse. You will not allow even one more of these animals to get away with anything like this. Next time, you tie and gag a few of those insurrection leaders and bring 'em back here for trial. It is incidents like this that make us appear to be weak."

"They were mostly young kids, boys and girls, Sir," the lieutenant insisted.

"Then, by God, bring me some trussed up kids and we will make an example out of them. Is that clear?"

"Yes, Sir."

With that, the major offered a quick salute. He was obviously still upset as he stormed from the briefing room with Lieutenant Harley close behind.

Lieutenant Jennings was an older man who had served in the regular army for nearly ten years. His field promotions had taken him as far as he could go up the military chain of command. His intention was to give it up after this enlistment and return to his family farm in Tennessee. For now, he remained content to follow orders.

"I'll meet you at the crossing, Harley," he called as Lieutenant Harley went out the door with the major. He gave them a few minutes to depart before following. His sergeant had the troop, twenty-five men strong, assembled and awaiting his orders.

"Where to, Sir?" the sergeant asked as he snapped to attention and saluted.

"Just a routine patrol, Sergeant," Jennings replied, "We will check out the settlement of French Crossing. We'll hook up with Harley's troop there. Rumor has it that the locals have been talking of an uprising."

"Yes, Sir." the sergeant said. He turned and walked quickly back to his mount.

It was his turn to answer questions from his men.

"Where to, Sarge?" a private asked him.

The private waited patiently as the sergeant sliced off a chew from his tobacco plug. As the lieutenant was mounting up to join them, he said, "We're off to French Crossing," he made eye contact with the private as he added, "real boring. Remember? From there, if like the last time, we go on to the trading post at St. Peter."

"Yes, Sir," the private murmured.

"The lieutenant says that the major thinks it's time we set an example or two. What better place than French Crossing and what better time than now?"

"That's why they pay us the big money," the private retorted with a grin.

"The way I've got it figured," the sergeant continued, "tomorrow, while we go on to St. Peter, Lieutenant Harley's men will go to the upper reservation. There have been a lot of complaints from the upper store and the major wants to make our presence known."

"I thought we had us a militia troop up that way," the private said.

"I guess we do," the sergeant replied. "Last time I saw Corporal Benning he said that they had settled in real good at the old schoolhouse. They're supposed to meet up with us at the Crossing tomorrow for a show of strength."

"Ain't seen Benning in a long time," the private said. "Not since he's been reassigned. Have you?"

"Not in a while," the sergeant answered, shaking his head in agreement, "not since he got re-assigned to Shepard's troop somewhere over around Redwood. Stockade duty, I think."

"The hell you say," the private said. "What do you mean, show of strength? Militia? How about a show of incompetence? What the hell is the major thinking? Doesn't he know their reputation?"

"Can't read the major's mind, Private," the sergeant replied. He leaned to one side to spit as he added, "It's a good thing, too."

"I heard that Colonel Sibley is on his way here," the private commented. "Do you believe that story 'bout the Injuns stealing a ton of money?"

"Hell, Soldier." the sergeant said as he paused to spit again, "don't make no matter to anyone what I believe, I just follow orders."

Their conversation was cut short as the lieutenant signaled the troop to move out.

The east side of the French Crossing settlement was nearly unrecognizable from only six months ago. The central part of town still had the same buildings and several newer ones had been built along the main road leading through to the river. Dozens of heavy canvas tents had been pitched in several long rows making for a number of neatly organized blocks known as Tent City. Merchants sold everything from dry goods and cloth to tins of kerosene and just about anything imaginable. Several tents also served as saloons. Some had signs that advertised fine whiskey and eastern whores.

The west side of the river was considered the Indian side and had remained nearly unchanged over the years. One large log structure, in particular, was still a meeting area for the old-time trappers and traders. It was a store and trading center located on high ground overlooking the crossing. An Indian man ran the place; it was one of the few places where Indians were allowed and could congregate without permission of the white man. It was within these walls that a most unusual meeting was going on.

Red Calf, still dressed in white man fashion, and the black Indian, Colton, were seated on one side of a long table made from rough sawn planks. Colton, now eighteen years old, was dressed the same as just about any settler traveling through. If not for his heavy armament, he could have easily passed for a Negro servant or perhaps a freed slave traveling west in search of better times. He wore a six-shot cap and-ball revolver and a huge bowie knife around his waist. The Spencer repeating rifle at his side completed his arsenal. Red calf was armed with a revolver and a similar rifle. These weapons were spoils taken from several defeated wagon trains.

 Sitting across from them were Tall Cloud and several other tribal chieftains. The man who ran the trading post was a friend who had fought beside Tall Cloud back during the great Indian wars. He was trusted and they knew they were safe in his establishment. A woman brought freshly made biscuits and a plate laden with pan-fried deer meat to the men. She listened with great interest as they discussed the current situation.

"You must lead us in battle, Tall Cloud," Colton said. "Our people still believe in you. You are the last of the great warriors remembered from the days of the great Indian wars with the whites. To you, our young braves will listen."

"What he says is true, my brother," Red Calf said. "Now is the time to strike while the white man is away fighting their own war in the east."

Tall Cloud remained reluctant to lead any kind of attack or hostile actions against the whites. Despite the white man's clearly weakened condition, he knew better than to underestimate their ability to seek vengeance.

"It was only a few days ago that my wife's cousin was hanged to death by the murderous bunch at the upper store!" Red Calf exclaimed, "For this reason, I have sent Marion and our child to live with relatives. They will be safe in the winter camp to the north. If anything does happen to me, I ask that you get word to them there."

Colton stood up. He commanded attention every time he spoke. His powerful manner and the way he talked, clear and to the point, was a trait that made him a well-respected spokesman,

"I was with Dakota when we returned to his farm. It seems like only yesterday." His voice grew louder as he continued; "his was a simple life. All he wanted was the life of a farmer. His wife, and his children, all were innocent of any thing the white man could possibly claim against them. We found them all dead. Never again are they to breathe, to speak, nor ever again to comfort our brother, Dakota. The unspeakable things done to them by the militia soldiers are pale compared to the revenge we seek. We must drive them off our land and write our own treaty."

Red Calf said, "Whether Tall Cloud leads us or not, we are at war. There will be no more peace. Even now, our brothers are assembling. Within days we will be ready. I have talked to Little Crow and others. They also know that the time for talk has passed."

"You must very carefully listen to me," Tall Cloud insisted. "I too hate the whites. They have brought only sorrow to our people. But I have seen their numbers. We cannot win. I beg you, my brothers, wait. Despite any strategy you may have, their numbers are too many."

Red Calf responded, "We could give you a week. Two weeks. We could give you three weeks and agree that if those responsible for hanging two of our own are not brought to justice, it will be up to us. But why?"

"Don't you see?" Colton asked. "This makes no difference to them. What are the chances that two of their own soldiers would ever be brought up on charges in a white man's court?"

"They will never give up Harley," Tall Cloud said in a resigned tone.

"Then we will do as we must," Red Calf replied.

Tall Cloud had nothing more to say. He and the other tribal chieftains left the table and started on their journeys back to their homes. Red Calf and Colton remained. As the older chieftains were leaving, they noticed a large group of young men, some armed with rifles, others with bows and homemade clubs, waiting silently outside. The word had spread. These young men were there to join up with Red Calf and Colton. The proprietor started ushering them into the meeting room in groups of ten to a dozen at a time.

As he climbed astride his horse, Tall Cloud said, almost as if to himself, "A week. A month. A year. He is right, it makes no difference. The whites will never change."

One of his companions nodded in agreement as he too observed the group of young men. "We must be ready. When it happens, you must lead."

"He is right, Tall Cloud," the other added.

There was no mistaking the sorrow in his voice as Tall Cloud replied, "This I know to be true. I will talk to Little Crow and devise a battle plan if it comes to that."

Red Calf and Colton spent the rest of the day talking to young men. Their reputation had spread and they were treated with utmost respect. The stories of the young black Indian had spread like wildfire among those present who wanted to fight the white man. Colton was viewed as being larger than life.

"When can we fight?" a young man asked. His face was anxious. He stood proudly with several others across the table from Red Calf. "Give us a chance. We have had enough talk. The white man's word is meaningless."

Another young man persisted, "When can we fight?"

Colton shook his head in agreement. It was late afternoon. He was standing looking out the window. He had a clear view of the river crossing below. He watched silently as a troop of horse soldiers pranced their horses across the shallow waters followed closely by two support wagons.

He called the other's attention to the scene at the crossing. "Look, down at the river, were we not just speaking of Lieutenant Harley?"

Red Calf and the others remained motionless as they watched the soldiers disappear from view on the road leading to the main settlement.

"When can we fight?" Colton asked softly, repeating the young man's question.

Red Calf looked at him with a questioning expression. He knew the serious look on Colton's face. He knew that his friend was forming a plan. He wasn't exactly sure what the plan would be or what Colton meant when he turned to the young men and said, "You ask when we can fight? I ask you. Is tonight soon enough?"

The army patrol, led by Lieutenant Jennings, along with their two support wagons arrived at French Crossing shortly before dark. Jennings was surprised to find that Lieutenant Harley and his entourage had already arrived and was set up for the night. They were camped several hundred yards from the last row of tents in an open area close to the river. He was pleased to find that the quartermaster and the cook from Lieutenant Harley's troop had been waiting for them. He was relieved to find that his troop wouldn't have to set up a separate mess tent.

After the soldiers were fed and the night duties assigned, they were allowed to roam about the area at will. There had been a lot of interest in the signs they had read on the way through Tent City that proclaimed eastern women and fine whiskey. For this reason, the soldiers had been very excited on the way to this campsite. In a very short time, their camp had been set up and they anxiously awaited orders. When permission was granted, most of them set out across the expanse of the clearing headed for the saloon tents.

Jennings sat with Lieutenant Harley at a small table after the men had been dismissed. The table was set up under a canvas canopy that the quartermaster had erected for the officers. He had a lot on his mind as he quizzed Harley.

"Are you sure it was a good idea to dismiss most of the men like this?" he asked. "What would the major say?"

"Hell," Harley retorted, "we're in town now and the major isn't here, is he?"

Jennings asked, "What do you make of all this?"

"Of what?" Harley responded. "There isn't a damned thing to worry about."

Jennings slowly twisted on his stool as his eyes took in the lights from the many lanterns shining along the wheel-rutted streets of Tent City. He said, "Here we are, trying to head off a possible insurrection and what are we doing? Giving the men an excuse to get drunk and whore around. That's what worries me."

"The men need a break," Harley said, "especially, now that they've been moved close within the new reservation boundaries. There hasn't been much of a chance for them to cut loose." He gave Jennings a calloused look and added, "This does give them that chance, right?"

"I guess so," Jennings replied. "You're the senior officer. Still, I think it's wrong to let most of them go. I'm nervous as hell over this whole deal."

"I figured as much," Harley said, "but listen, it's no secret that you are new here. I assure you that these dime store Indians won't do a damned thing. After you've been here awhile, you will get as bored as the rest of us."

"Tell me then, why is the major so worried?" Jennings asked, "Remember, I was there. It was my troops that got caught up in that ruckus where the Indians threw all that horse shit at us. It wasn't a pretty sight."

Harley leaned close and said softly, "Had it been me, we would have had a couple of very ignorant Indian funerals the very next day."

"How can you be so calm over this?" Jennings insisted. "Haven't you heard the gossip and stories about what happened a while back with the Indian, Brown Tooth?"

Harley was quiet. The short period of silence that followed caused Jennings to feel uncomfortable. He added, "Well? You've been here longer than me."

Harley's voice was shaking with an instant surge of rage as he nearly shouted, "That bastard is living on borrowed time! Of that you can be certain."

Realizing that he had struck a nerve and wanting to hear more, Jennings added, "How about the other two? The Indian, Red Calf, and the one they call John the Baptist? I'm sure you know about them as well."

"Yeah," Harley murmured, "I know all about those sons-a-bitches."

"What about the black Indian?" Jennings asked. "The talk is that you know him as well."

"I'll dance at that son of a bitch's funeral," Harley snarled. "They say Hell comes with him, we'll see about that." Harley's voice turned ice cold as he added, "You just go on feeling sorry for these heathens and it's sure to get you killed."

"It's not that I feel sorry for anyone," Jennings replied. "It's just that I've heard that you've had one devil of a time trying to catch any of them."

He was surprised when Harley abruptly got up and angrily stalked off.

Harley snapped over his shoulder, "What you need is to find yourself some whiskey and a woman."

"I think you're doing this all wrong, Harley." Jennings said. His voice loud enough to carry the distance as the lieutenant stalked off. "This is all going in my report."

The cook came to the table carrying a pot of coffee. "Sir?" he asked.

The lieutenant met the cook's concerned look with one of his own. "Thanks. What do you know about all this?" he asked as his cup was filled.

"About as much as you, Sir," the cook replied. He was obviously uninterested. "If it's all right with you, Sir, I'll be leaving for Tent City in a few minutes."

"Fine with me," Jennings said resignedly. "It's not like I'm in charge." He sat sipping his coffee, thinking that Harley should show a little more respect for the Indians.

The predawn light arrived with an annoying, light rain. It was just enough to make everything cold and wet. Lieutenant Jennings woke to a steady drip from a small hole in the canvas tent sensing that something was wrong. He got up, pulled on his boots and walked outside. About the same time, the quartermaster breathlessly approached,

"Sir!" he exclaimed, "Something ain't right."

A sergeant was rushing along the line of tents, his voice loud, rousing everyone.

"Bugler," the sergeant cried, "sound reveille!"

In a matter of only a few minutes, the soldiers were awake and assembled in front of the row of tents.

"Oh, damn," the quartermaster murmured.

Lieutenant Jennings felt a sinking sensation in the pit of his stomach as he noticed that their horses that had been staked out near the river were gone. Two soldiers were dragging a man's body back to the tent area from where the picket line had been set up the night before.

It was his turn to say, "Oh, damn." as he realized that all of the horses from both his and Harley's troops were missing. They had been stolen during the night while the men were in Tent City or passed out drunk.

He cursed softly as the sergeant reported. He nearly vomited as he got a look at the dead soldier. There wasn't much left of the man's head. In a matter of minutes the situation was clear. The two soldiers who had been assigned as the first night guards had been found near where the horses had been picketed. Obviously, no one had shown up to relieve them. Both men had died from having their skulls brutally crushed. When the roll was taken, Jennings was amazed to find that three soldiers were missing, including Lieutenant Harley.

He quickly organized the soldiers in a defensive position. "Lord have mercy," he murmured to himself as the reality of it all struck him.

"Sergeant!" he shouted.

"Yes, Sir."

"We need to find Lieutenant Harley right now."

"Where should I look?" the sergeant asked, still in shock from what had happened.

"Send a team, two men." Jennings said softly. "Try the tents that advertise women and whiskey."

"Maybe he's out rounding up the rest of the men," the sergeant said.

"Maybe," Jennings replied. He placed a hand on the sergeant's shoulder, "Am I wrong or am I the only one that can see what's really going on here?" he asked.

"See what? Sir?" the sergeant answered, obviously missing the context of the lieutenant's question.

"Never mind," Jennings said; his tone disgusted. "Have someone get the bodies loaded in one of the wagons and stay on full alert until we get back with fresh mounts."

Word of the incident had spread throughout Tent City. The immediate area was now alive with settlers wanting to know what was going on. Some were on foot and others on horseback as curiosity got the best of them.

"My God." a man shouted after seeing the two bodies, covered by a blanket, in the back of a wagon, "is this what the army calls protection?"

Jennings commandeered the man's horse right then and instructed a corporal from Harley's unit to ride hard and get word back to the fort at once. He did his best to regain his composure as he led a group of soldiers into the Tent City area to commandeer more horses. He wondered to himself if anyone else had noticed that the fuse had been lit and the Indian nation was about to blow sky high.

Lieutenant Harley had made a series of bad command decisions, and now, they were catching up to him. Lieutenant Jennings and a private from his own command were the ones to find him passed out in a whore's crib in the rear area of a tent saloon. The immediate area was deserted due to everyone's interest being focused on the events at the army's campsite. He awoke to the sounds of angry voices, and through blood shot eyes, determined that Jennings wasn't happy. The woman beside him remained sleeping soundly, exhausted from a long night of servicing several soldiers, and finally, the lieutenant.

"You will be court-martialed for this, you arrogant son-of-a-bitch!" Jennings told him angrily. "Make no mistake about that."

"What the hell are you talking about?" Harley growled, his temper surfacing, as Jennings physically rousted him out of bed. "What the hell do you think you are doing?"

"We've got at least two men dead, Harley," Jennings snarled. He tossed the lieutenant his clothes and said, "Get dressed." Then, he turned to the private, "You are a witness to this, soldier. Return to camp and inform the sergeant at arms that I am relieving Lieutenant Harley of his command."

"Just a minute there, Private!" Harley exclaimed, "Just a one damn minute!"

The private remained, as he was, unsure of what to do. Harley hastily got dressed and pulled on his boots saying, "I am your commanding officer, not Jennings."

"Not anymore, Harley," Jennings said, his tone still angry. "Thanks to you, all of our mounts have been stolen, men are dead, and panic is sweeping through the area."

Harley stood up took a step closer to the small table and his military service revolver as he reached for his hat. His smile was out of place as he adjusted the wide brim and said, "I guess we will just have to see about that."

Jennings once again turned to face the private who had remained frozen in place, unsure of what to do, "I gave you an order, soldier!"

The surprised expression on the private's face caused him to feel a chill as he realized that the private was staring over his shoulder at Lieutenant Harley. He heard the sound of a revolver being cocked back and turned around in time to see the smile on the lieutenant's face. He died instantly as a round struck him squarely in the forehead. The private stood; almost in awe, as Jennings fell to the floor.

"Sir!" he stammered.

The last words he heard were those of the lieutenant as he said, "It's a shame you two had to shoot it out just because he caught you with a murdered whore."

"Sir?" the private's voice was incredulous.

The sound of the first shot had awoken the woman. This second one caused her to screech and sit upright. She remained frozen in place, a blanket clutched over her breasts, a stunned look on her face. Her eyes widened in horror as the private dropped to his knees. She gasped softly as she saw blood soaking through his shirt. Another shot hit him in the throat causing his body to jerk once and hit the ground with a thud. She remained frozen in terror as the lieutenant whirled around and without warning drove his long knife deep into her chest. With a final gasp her body went limp. Harley withdrew the knife and slowly wiped it clean on the blanket. He watched intently, with a curious expression, as the essence of life faded from her eyes.

Lieutenant Harley hastily exited through the rear of the tent and hurried back to take command of his troop. He motioned to several soldiers who were mounted on confiscated horses. "Over here," he shouted. As they neared, he was glad to find that they were from his command. He stood in front of the first mount and took the reins from the soldier, "Dismount, I am afraid we've got even more problems now."

"Sir?" the soldier said, his tone questioning.

"Lieutenant Jennings," Harley said, his voice soft, "I just found him in a saloon tent. He's dead."

"What?"

"It seems he caught one of the men with a murdered whore and got himself shot." The lieutenant motioned towards the saloon tent where several men were now gathered. "It doesn't look good." He placed his foot in the stirrup as he added, "Let's keep the details to ourselves. There's no need in slandering any soldier over a murdered whore. I'll swear that those same damned stinking Indians that attacked us last night killed them both."

"Sounds right to me," the soldier said. "What now, Sir?"

"I need to get back to the troops, you two gather the bodies and bring them along. I'll have the report written soon and you both can sign it."

"Yes, Sir."

Harley urged his horse to a gallop. Several civilians had to jump out of his way as he made haste back to camp.

When the militia arrived a short time later, Lieutenant Harley greeted them with enthusiasm.

Fort Ridgley

This meeting was more than a routine officer's briefing. The major had a serious look on his face as he began,

"It looks like we will be declaring martial law," he said, eyeing the officers. "Colonel Sibley has Major Griffin on his way here to take over the militia and it looks like they're going to call up the tenth regiment."

Reports of attacks on settlers and soldiers were being logged in from all over the reservation lands and from as far away as the Dakota territories. There was no question in anyone's mind that the area could blow sky-high any day.

"Captain," he said to his second in command, his voice irate, "you will remain in charge here. Keep a close eye on things. The rest of us have a lot of ground to cover."

"Very well, Sir," the captain replied.

"This is serious, men," the major continued. "The war in the East is raging and now it looks as if we've got the makings of another one right here." He paused as his aide passed out several papers to the officers. His voice was angry as he continued, "These warrants are newly updated." He slammed his clenched fist hard on the table. Nearly shouting, he said, "I want these sons-a-bitches found."

Lieutenant Harley read down the list. A sadistic grin crossed his face as he noticed the names, Brown Tooth, Red Calf, John the Baptist and Colton Sage on the list. "My pleasure, Sir." he murmured.

"What did you say, Lieutenant?" the major said his voice still angry.

"Just reading the list of names, Sir," Harley said. "How about Tall Cloud? I know for a fact that he's been abetting these heathens since the beginning. I think he should be on this list too."

"Even Jackson has lost interest in Tall Cloud," the major replied.

"Any rules or restraints, Sir?" Harley asked. "We may have to rough up a bunch of these heathens and need to know that the government is behind us."

The major's answer caused him to smile again. "Just bring them in. I don't care how you do it." His tone softened a bit, "I appreciate the way you handled the incident with Lieutenant Jennings. I think it best if we keep the story as your report says."

"Thank you, Sir." Harley replied. The others nodded agreement as he added, "They died as heroes."

"From now on," the major said, "no more kid gloves with these animals. I'm told the governor himself has sanctioned any killing and is on record wanting these damn Sioux exterminated and driven out of Minnesota. We got it directly from him that President Lincoln will be ordering General Pope and Major Belmont back here as well. Let's hope we get a grip on things before they arrive."

Again, Harley's smile was sadistic as he added, "I want to be sure I've got it right, so let's be clear, some of these Indian squaws and kids are just lookouts for those heathen bastards. The men have to be sure that there will be no repercussions if they happen to say, trample a few of them with their horses before asking questions. Is that right, Sir?"

"That's right, Lieutenant." The major said, his voice intense, "Whatever it takes."

The meeting was dismissed even as a rider arrived with more bad news.

Chapter Nineteen

Merciful Heavens

Third week in August, 1862

All hell had broken loose. It was said that what set everything in motion was the killing of five white settlers by a group of Indians over a dare made by one young Indian to another to steal from a farm not far from New Ulm. It made no difference if the rumor was true or not. The hard facts were that settlers had been killed, the war was on, and no one could stop it.

Panic among the whites had set in overnight. Many tried to flee the area. In wagons and on foot, they made haste away from the reservation lands. Some of these settlers, armed or not, were set upon and ruthlessly butchered by warriors with years of pent up hatred to vent. There was no mercy shown and none expected by those on either side of this all-out conflict. Indian warriors were everywhere, their hearts as cold as stone, their frustrations and anger apparent for all to see. Word had spread like wildfire about the incident at French Crossing. Young men came by the dozens to join with the black Indian, Colton. By late afternoon the day after the incident, his was a force nearly a hundred strong.

In the heart of the main reservation, the government agent and trader, Myrick, and many others were dead after an argument had gotten out of hand over the distribution of food. Myrick, it is said, was found shot many times by both guns and arrows. Someone had stuffed his mouth full of grass and propped his body in a sitting position beside the same steps that Tall Cloud had been knocked down only a few short weeks before. This was said to be in retribution for his infamous statement; 'If they are hungry, let them eat grass and their own dung.' It is said that those had been his words when Tall Cloud, Little Crow and others had attempted to convince him to release food to their people.

There were those in the Indian police agency who were hated nearly as much as the soldiers themselves. Several were found hanged in the fashion of the white man. Two it is said, were found hanging from the same overhead timbers on the back porch area of main trading post store; the same as Cardinal the Carpenter and his friend had been.

The good, the bad, and the ugly of it all

It was shortly after daybreak when the heavily armed convoy made up of six wagons and a dozen armed men on horseback began their frantic journey towards safety. Many of their friends and loved ones had been killed in a late afternoon raid on their settlement the day before. Those who had survived the night had banded together and now sought the safety of Fort Ridgley. The bodies of their loved ones had been left where they had fallen as they fled for their lives. Many were seething with bitterness and grief.

About an hour after sunrise, these desperate settlers happened on a small group of helpless Indians using the same road. The Indians were non hostile and were also trying to escape the war that had broken out around them. It was like a nightmare. Their group was made up of over a dozen very old men and women and also several children, two of whom had to be carried. These people had been unable to keep up with the main throng of Indian refugees who had gone before them in the predawn darkness. They were simply trying to find a place of safety and to stay apart from the madness unfolding all around. They were in a wide open area when they saw and heard the whites coming. Too late to seek cover, they huddled together alongside of the road. Most were facing away, some kneeling in positions of supplication, as the wagons neared. The situation got ugly fast as two angry riders in the lead fired shots into their midst as they galloped past. Several women cried out from within the wagons, shrieking for them to stop.

It was then that the driver of the lead wagon urged his team to a fast pace and reigned directly into this defenseless group. This wagon was followed closely by a second. All save three or four of the Indians were sideswiped or run over by the wagons. The driver of the first wagon, a smooth shaven man, yelled in glee at this wanton act. As they distanced themselves from the carnage, he yelled to a rider alongside, "How's that for teaching them damned redskins a lesson?"

A woman from within the wagon yelled at them, "What are you doing? Those were old men and women." When there was no answer, she added, "We need to stop and help them."

"Help them," another woman said bitterly, shouting to be heard, "those animals deserved just what they got."

Despite the heinous acts against them by rogue Indians only yesterday, there were several people in each of the wagons who were aghast as they looked back at the sound of gunfire. Several of the men riding escort had stopped and were methodically executing those Indians who had survived.

They were travelling hard as mid-afternoon approached. Their convoy was still made up of six wagons and also a buckboard with three people they picked up along the way. The women and children riding in the wagons were hopeful that there were enough armed men to see them to the safety of the fort. In addition to a dozen mounted men, all armed with rifles, two or more well-armed men were in each wagon. They were confident that they would reach the safety of the fort soon. The road ahead disappeared from view around a bend leading to an area that was thickly forested. They were about ten miles from Fort Ridgley when they first saw the hostile Indians. The men leading the wagons stopped at the sight of the five

Indians on horseback waiting in the center of the road at the forest's edge. In the lead was a young black man astride a fine black horse. He was dressed as they were and looked out of place considering those painted warriors around him. He sat calmly holding a repeating rifle in the crook of his left arm with his right arm raised in a sign for the settlers to halt.

The wagons were within shouting distance when they came to a stop. The driver of the lead wagon was a local farmer with a clean-shaven face. His name was Tanner. He leveled his rifle and shouted, "Step aside, you damned heathens if you know what's best for you."

The black man ignored Tanner as he spoke in a raised voice, "Hear me well. Your choices are few. I urge you to surrender now. Lay down your arms. You will be treated humanely as prisoners of war."

The settlers were amazed to hear this.

"There will be no surrender you heathen son of a bitch!" Tanner snarled, "Step aside!"

"You have one other choice," the black Indian said, his voice loud, still calm. "Anyone who chooses may leave the wagons unarmed and go in peace." He motioned with his hand towards a path that forked off from the road. "This trail will lead them to the river. A short distance upstream they will find people who will escort them to safety and watch over them."

Those in the wagons exchanged worried looks. The man's calm, yet ominous voice had sent chills up and down their spines offsetting the heat of a late summer's day. For what seemed like the longest time, there was silence.

"Get the hell out of the way," Tanner shouted.

"They must leave now," the black man said, his voice loud and calm. "Those of you who choose to fight will be led, like sheep, to the place we have chosen. We will kill you there."

"Who the hell are you?" Tanner shouted, his rifle aimed and cocked, "I'll blow you clean out of the saddle."

"I know who you are Tanner. My name is Colton Sage. Today I will personally get four dollars' worth out of you."

Tanner gasped.

Colton continued, "I offer sanctuary to all." He lowered his right hand, took up his reins and added, "Only if they go now." Without another word, he reined his horse around and rode off. The four Indians with him turned their mounts as well and followed. The settlers sat motionless, stunned at what they had just heard.

One of the men in the lead shouted, "How is this for surrender?" He raised his rifle and fired. His shot struck the last Indian in line in the right shoulder, knocking him from his horse. Then, the other settlers at the front of the wagon train began firing. One of the Indians reined around and through the volley of gunfire, reached down and pulled the injured warrior onto his horse. It was nearly unbelievable that no other bullet found its mark as they quickly rode out of sight.

A strange calm came over the settlers as they sat in the wagons or astride their horses. Breathlessly they watched the road ahead where the Indians had disappeared. The settler named Tanner was sweating profusely as he wiped his forehead with a cloth bandanna. The silence was broken as someone said, "Let's not forget to reload."

A young mother holding a small child and seated between a young boy and girl quickly got up and carefully climbed out of the wagon. She waited anxiously for her children to climb down and join her. The boy nearly fell to the ground as he awkwardly got off the wagon carrying a large sack containing some of their possessions.

"What do you think you are doing?" a man with a rifle seated in the back of the wagon asked.

"Don't you know who that is?" the woman said breathlessly. "That's Lillian Taylor's boy. I urge the rest of you to heed his promise and come with us. The men can fight better if we are not around."

"Bad idea," another man snarled. "We need to stick together."

"My husband is back on the east coast because his mother died and he won't be home for a while," the woman said, her voice loud. "I intend for his wife and children to be here to greet him when he returns."

Without another word, she took the hand of the young girl and started walking. The boy stayed close, carrying the large sack slung over his shoulder. An older woman joined them. She said to no one in particular, "I also know Miss Lillie's foster son. I sure as hell don't want him or his heathen brethren shooting at me."

A young man and one middle aged man got off the wagons. Two other women and two children joined them. The started walking quickly following the others.

A man staying in the last wagon said in a contemptuous tone, "Cowards."

Several others exchanged worried looks. As the wagons were made to move out, a woman from the last one called, "Good luck and god speed."

Knowing that there were hostile Indians ahead, the settlers were on full alert as they once again urged the horses onward. They had no sooner reached the edge of the forest when gunshots and war whoops were heard from the rear of the column. Dozens of Indians, some mounted and some on foot appeared as if out of nowhere and began the attack. A woman riding in the center of the last wagon was killed instantly from a stray bullet to the head. One of the mounted men in the rear was dragged from his saddle by two Indians who seemed to rise from the ground itself and overpowered him. As the wagons gained a little distance, those who were watching could see clearly that the man was brutally killed by an Indian who wielded a double-bit axe.

The settler's horses were whipped onto a dead run as they desperately tried to outrun these screaming banshees from Hell. What they should have realized was that they were being herded to a location that had been pre-selected for their final stand. Soon, they would know that what the black Indian had said were words of truth.

The battle lasted for only a short time. The forces led by the black Indian proved overwhelming. When it was over, only four Indians were dead and several wounded. Of the many settlers, only two women, an older man and two children were left alive. They were herded a short distance from the scene and stood in terror as the young black man who had introduced himself as Colton Sage, sat his horse calmly and addressed them again, "There," he motioned towards the northwest, "you will find the same trail you were offered before. Go to the river, follow it upstream and you will be safely led across. My people will see that you are not harmed."

He gazed at their terrified faces and added, "None of this is what we wanted. You white people are the trespassers." He whirled his horse around and galloped back to the burning wagons. The survivors started walking quickly, hoping that his word was good. The settler named Tanner had been tied securely face down to a wheel on an overturned wagon. He called to them begging for help as they walked away.

The soldiers garrisoned at Gull Lake, commanded by an army major, were attacked the same day and were easily routed by warriors led by a fierce tribal chieftain and the wanted outlaw, Red Calf. They fled in panic and disgrace back to Fort Ridgley. The attack had come out of nowhere and in their hasty retreat they had left many weapons and supplies behind.

The major's forces re-grouped, re-armed and came to grips with reality. They were ordered back into the field early the next morning. This time, the major was confident that he would have an easy victory. He now had a prepared force of over fifty heavily armed men with two cannons in tow.

About the same time, Tall Cloud was preparing to attack Fort Ridgley. Watching from his place of concealment, he smiled broadly as the major and his soldiers rode out. He knew that those who were leaving, as well as those who remained, were about to receive long overdue justice. He and Red Calf, Colton, and Dove of Day had carefully planned a series of attacks designed to happen almost in unison.

A few miles away, a band of warriors that included Brown Tooth and John the Baptist were surrounding the settlement at a well-known lake. This would turn out to be another fierce battle. Others had gathered and were preparing an all-out attack on the town of New Ulm. The 'Black Bat from Hell,' one of Tall Cloud's most trusted advisors, was waiting with his band to greet the overconfident major. A lot of things were about to happen at once. These events would cause those who had referred to the Indians as 'a bunch of unorganized savages' to wonder just what the hell had happened.

The major's troop rode hard and fast in an effort to engage those who only the day before had caused them to retreat in panic. His plan was to set up the cannons on high ground overlooking the enemy camp. He obviously believed that his foes had merely gotten lucky the day before. He expected them to be lazing in their makeshift huts in the heat of the afternoon. He was confident that the Indians would become nothing more than easy targets for his men. His second-in-command, Lieutenant Harley assured him that this would be so.

They were thundering across a large open area that bordered the river when Harley, who was in the lead, signaled for them to slow, then, to stop. The road ahead was blocked by a series of burnt out wagons and the carcasses of several horses. The bodies of white settlers, men, women and children were scattered about. He sent his scout, a newly enlisted private named Orrin, who was a former member of the militia, to check the scene. He returned a few minutes later.

"Sir," Private Orrin said, breathless, "it was a massacre, just yesterday."

The troop continued to approach slowly. The major reined his horse alongside of Harley's. "What do you make of it?" he asked as his eyes took in the grisly sight.

"These people didn't have a snowball's chance in Hell," the lieutenant replied. "We can make a path through or we can take the river trail and go around."

"What do you think is best, Lieutenant?" the major asked, his voice nervous.

"The river trail would be the best choice, Sir." Harley replied. "The cannons will tow okay and despite a couple narrow canyons ahead, there's less chance of an ambush."

"You know this area better than I do," the major said uncertainly. "We'll follow the river."

Indicating the bodies, Harley asked, "What about them, Sir? We can't risk leaving men behind to bury them."

"We can send a single rider back to the fort for a burial detail," the major said. "You're right. Let's get going, we have bigger fish to fry." He felt nauseous as reined his horse around a wagon that had been turned over on its side. A man's charred body was still tied face down to the front wagon wheel even though most of the rope that held the body in place had been burned through. It was obvious that a small fire had burned slowly beneath the man causing a slow and agonizing death.

The column rode to the south, following the wide trail that led around a small forested hill. About a mile further on, the trail started to snake its way up a steep ravine. It was this narrow section with high natural walls on either side that the Indians had selected as an ambush site. Harley realized this when a young black man suddenly appeared, standing tall on a rock formation only fifty yards away.

"Harley," he shouted.

"Oh damn," the lieutenant gasped. He was instantly panicked as he recognized the black Indian, Colton Sage.

The expression on Private Orrin's face was one of complete bewilderment as he watched the lieutenant rein his horse around in a fit of panic and tear off at a full gallop back past the long line of mounted cavalrymen. Then, the Indians materialized like ghostly demons on either side of the ravine. To them it was like shooting fish in a barrel. Harley was shot twice, once in his lower right leg by a bullet, and an arrow was shot into his hip as he raced away without firing a single shot.

Most of the soldiers fought gallantly against these overwhelming odds. They were engaged by a deadly crossfire at close range. Only twenty men, some severely wounded were able to escape in a panic and make their way back towards Fort Ridgley. They split into two groups as they fled. A group of five cavalrymen, two of whom were badly wounded, overtook Lieutenant Harley whose horse was suffering from an injured foot. Harley assumed command and led the way in the direction of the fort. Back at the ravine, seven soldiers had been taken alive.

Playground

It was nearly dark when the group of Indian women and children passed by what had once been the school and mission ran by the white woman, Miss Lillie. The building, recently taken over and used as a military barracks by militia soldiers, was now a smoking pile of ash and rubble. A fierce battle had taken place here only a few hours ago. These hapless refugees stopped and stared in amazement at the sheer carnage.

The bodies of many whites and Indians were scattered everywhere. Faces, with unseeing eyes frozen in death, stared blankly. The playground area was now a macabre scene, an example of the evil that man is capable of inflicting on his fellow man. The militia soldiers stationed at this location had been taken completely by surprise in an early morning raid. All save a fortunate few who were killed in the initial attack faced the wrath of the Indians as they sought long overdue vengeance. The lieutenant and the sergeant called Collier were among those for whom death was an extremely long time in coming. The Indian named Friend, whose farm was in ashes across the lake, made sure of that.

The swing set, once a place of laughter and fun for children was now a tribute to the bitterness that had been simmering for years. The horribly mutilated bodies of three adult whites were swaying slowly back and forth, twisting and turning in the gentle breeze. The top rail was bowed downward in the middle from the weight. Two men and a woman had been hanged there. In the minds of the Indians, this was to serve as both a warning and a reminder of what had happened to their own only a short while ago. The victims had all been too tall to be hanged beneath the top rail of the children's swing set that was only about seven feet off the ground. To offset this, each victim's feet had been tied together and trussed behind in a bent position. They had then been lifted into the nooses. No dignity had been afforded the woman as her naked torso clearly showed evidence of horrible abuse. The men too, had been disfigured most gruesomely by the cuts of many knives. Mercifully, it appeared as if death had been but a short time coming.

The seven soldiers, who had been captured alive in the battle that had taken place only a few miles away, had been brought to this place. They were about to discover that everything they had ever heard, feared, or experienced about the savagery of the Indian people was soon to be realized.

This was another grisly scene that would be forever etched in the mind of the young Indian woman, Dora, who had survived the Sandi-yohi massacre with her sister, a wife to Spirit Keeper. She, and the others who were fleeing in an attempt to find safety for themselves and the children, were amazed to see these seven doomed soldiers who had been staked spread-eagle to the ground. The soldiers had been stripped to the waist, their boots had removed and they were tied securely to a long row of stakes. The row of stakes had been made straight by a length of rope that had been stretched tight to insure that they were in perfect alignment. It was a deliberate mockery of how the soldiers were known to have everything at their fort and even in the field, laid out in an orderly fashion. Several of the soldiers were only slightly wounded. Dora lowered her eyes in respect as the black warrior, Colton, galloped past followed by dozens of armed men. She turned her attention back to the captives and gasped aloud as she recognized Private Orrin.

The cries of those soldiers who were suffering from many wounds only served to excite and anger their captors. The chieftain, called Sharp One by many, was the leader. He spoke to the soldiers in broken English.

"Hear me, you soldiers who are damned." His voice, deep and heavily accented, carried far in the stillness of early evening. "As you have done to our people, we now do to you." He stood tall and proud as he left no question about what was to be expected. "When your white brothers find you, they will find justice." he paused and slowly brandished his long knife in the air making sure that each captive saw it.

"Shut the hell up, you goddamn heathen." A gutsy soldier shouted.

The soldier cried out in agony as a warrior kicked him hard in the ribs.

Sharp One smiled and continued. "Those of you who die tonight will be the lucky ones." He focused his attention on the soldier who had spoken, "For what you have done, your eyes will be open, but you will not see. Your hearts will beat, but you will not live. For what you have done, your minds will scream words, but you will be without the means to speak." He paced back and forth, eyeing each soldier. He paused long enough to straddle over and urinate on one of the doomed men. When he was finished, he said, "You will now pay for what you have done."

The woman, Dora, whose life had been spared by the condemned soldier, Orrin, only a few months ago quickly made her way closer. She dropped to her knees beside the helpless man and implored Sharp One to spare him.

"Have mercy, great one. In heaven's name, I ask mercy for this one." She soon realized that her pleas were falling on deaf ears. She said, imploringly, "At least leave him alone for now." She met Sharp One's pitiless gaze with one of feigned assurance as she added, "I will do what is right."

Sharp One kneeled to be at eye level. He eyed her knowingly. In a low tone that sounded regretful he replied, "He is yours to do with as you want until the dawn's light. Then, the will of our people will prevail."

Knowing what this meant, Dora remained motionless on both knees beside Private Orrin. The screams of the other men, staked helplessly to the ground on either side pierced the stillness and carried for a great distance as the Indians vented their frustrations. Each captive, in turn, was deliberately and slowly cut. Their screams of agony were silenced as their tongues were stretched nearly to the point of being torn out and pierced with long sharpened sticks to insure that they could not talk nor close their mouths. As full darkness descended, their stifled, pitiful moans, convulsions and unintelligible pleas for mercy filled the still night air.

In the dim light from the rising moon shining briefly through a break in the clouds, Dora's eyes locked with Private Orrin's. Although he hadn't been able to understand a single word that had been spoken on his behalf, he sensed that his would be a more merciful death. For now, his only discomfort was that of being tied spread eagle to the stakes. His eyes widened in appreciation as she poured cool, clear water from a small bottle onto his parched lips. When the water was gone, she placed the empty bottle on the ground and slowly reached for something concealed within her blouse with her right hand. With a damp cloth in her left hand, she gently covered his eyes. His murmured words, "Thank you," were destined to be his last as she mercifully plunged a knife into his heart.

As the stories were told and re-told, the black Indian, Colton, was said to have been in two or three places at the same time. The reports submitted by the major following his afternoon defeat, and the report written by the post commander concerning the simultaneous battle at the fort, both swore that the black Indian had been there.

The attack on the fort had ended in defeat for Little Crow, Tall Cloud and their band of nearly three hundred warriors. It was the mighty cannon fired with great accuracy that turned the tide of the pitched battle in favor of those within the fort. After losing nearly a hundred brave men, they retreated to fight another day.

September 2nd

The stagecoach was only a few miles out of Red River on its journey from St. Paul. Two men serving as armed escorts rode ahead. They had been hired due to rumors and reports of an Indian insurrection. So far, there had been no real evidence that they knew of, other than rumors, to reach St. Paul. The stage company always insisted that the coaches be on schedule and felt confident in hiring two additional armed guards. The two riders reined their horses to a stop when they came to a large tree that had fallen across the roadway around a sharp bend in the road. The driver stopped the stagecoach a few yards behind them. The shotgun rider climbed down to help as the two escorts dismounted. They heard a horse snort and looked up as a young black man approached riding a black horse. The man stopped fifty feet away and sat calmly in the saddle watching them. He was armed with a lever action repeating rifle that he held cradled in the crook of his right arm.

The driver saw him and shouted, "Hey. Boy. Get the hell over here and give these men a hand." He seemed upset that his command was ignored. "Lazy son-of-a-bitch!" he exclaimed. "You're one lucky nigger that this is a free state." He continued mumbling about dumb Negroes as the three men pulled together and easily moved the obstruction out of the way. His mumblings ended with a brief gasp as an arrow from out of nowhere drilled him dead center in his chest.

It really wasn't a fight at all. The whites both outside and inside the stage only had time to fire a few shots. In what seemed to be the blink of an eye dozens of angry Indians had emerged from the cover of the forest and killed the three white men. Next, they dragged the passengers, three young white women and two armed men from the stage. The men were dead in a matter of minutes. The horses were unhitched and the stage tipped over in the ditch. The three women, horrified, stood trembling silently awaiting their fate.

A short period of silence followed as the young black man approached. He eyed the women, uncertain as to what would happen. It was surprising that Friend hadn't killed them already. "Dakota," he said in the native tongue, addressing Friend, "I must ask mercy for the white women."

"Please," one of the women implored him, "you speak English. I know you do. I heard the driver talking to you. Please help us." She was a slender young woman with fierce blue eyes set narrowly in a pretty face. She wore her auburn hair in a bun like so many other women of the time. She had a ceramic cross pinned to the lapel of her blouse. Colton nearly gasped when he saw her; she so closely resembled his foster mother that she could have been a young Miss Lillie.

Colton's face was flushed as he said, "None of this is what we wanted." Sounding defensive he added, "I will do all I can."

"None of this is what we wanted either," the woman said, her voice intense, "and we can do nothing." The young woman continued to stand defiantly, her gaze fixed on him. The other two women stood trembling, embracing each other.

Colton looked at Friend, "Dakota, will you spare these helpless women for me?"

Friend's look of pure hatred towards the whites caused Colton to be taken aback as he answered in English, "You and your brother Red Calf, you are known for mercy. I am not." His voice rose, "if it is important to you, I will give you one, but only one."

"My friend," Colton insisted, his voice loud and firm, "these women have harmed no one. I ask that you listen to my words and spare them."

Friend's hateful gaze seemed to go right through Colton. "And who did my Lisa harm?" he asked. Expecting no answer he added bitterly, "Only for you will I do this."

Colton motioned towards several of the mounted braves including his friend Wild Fisher.

"Mount double behind these warriors," he said, addressing the women. Your lives will be spared. We will lead you to safety." Wild Fisher quickly reined his horse close to the woman who so closely resembled Miss Lillie. He stretched his arm towards her indicating that she take his hand and mount behind him. Others did similar with the remaining two women.

"Thank you," Colton murmured to Friend. In the native tongue he added, "I will wait for you near New Ulm." With that, he reined his horse around. He was followed by about half of the warriors and soon they were out of sight as they thundered around a bend in the road. After about a half mile of hard riding they neared an abandoned and still burning settlement. Colton indicated for Wild Fisher and the others to release the women. The women were let go roughly. Their confused and terrified expressions were such that Colton would never forget.

"I regret that we have no way to escort you to where other whites are safely held captive," he said. Then, indicating an area near the burning buildings he added, "Take shelter there. Remain quiet and out of sight." He felt a chill as his eyes locked with the young woman who so reminded him of his foster mother.

Still not certain of their fate, the women waited in terror as the Indians quickly rode past. Moments after the Indians were gone, they quickly made their way to the shelter of shed near a smoldering farm house. They hid inside and waited, hoping for help to come. Minutes later, a white man quietly approached their hiding place from the rear and indicated that they go with him. Soon, there were among a small group of survivors and well-hidden in a cabin deep in the forest.

Not all the settlers had left the area. Many had chosen to remain on their farms and in their homes as the events unfolded. One such family had chosen to stay with confidence. They had always been friendly to the Indians and believed that this would make all the difference should trouble brew. By the end of the third day of the uprising, they found out the hard way that their belief had been wrong. A family farm not far from their place had been attacked and all those within the farmhouse had been murdered by a group of rogue Indians. The men had been summoned to another farm a short distance away. The two women had insisted that they remain there, at home, with the children. They were armed with several rifles and still felt certain that they would be spared any hostilities. They were understandably scared half to death as a group of fived armed Indian men that they had never seen before cautiously approached their cabin.

One of the children had seen them out the window in plenty of time to warn the others. Knowing that the Indians had no way to know if there was anyone home or not, they decided to hide and wait it out. They all took shelter in a small root cellar, the trap door to which was located beneath the table and hidden from sight by a handmade carpet. They remained undiscovered, terrified, as the Indians ransacked the cabin.

Another story was told of a white woman who poisoned a large jug of corn whiskey with strychnine and left it for a group of three or four marauding Indians to find. After drinking the whiskey, it is said they died a most horrible and slow death.

There were also several accounts of Indians sheltering and protecting many of the settlers. There were many settlers that had shown care and compassion for the Indians over the years and had been instrumental in helping many of them through long and harsh winters. It was a fact that not all settlers were callous and evil towards the Indians. Those who had shown kindness in the past were now very glad that they had done so. Later on, similar stories of bravery and kindness and evil from both sides of the conflict were told.

Chapter Twenty

A Simple Minded Negro

The Indians had settled in for the night in a narrow and deep ravine that extended for nearly a half mile on the high ground about a mile to the north of the lake. This natural shelter was ideal to conceal their many horses and offered relative safety during the long night hours. Even though this was open country, the ravine could only be seen at a very close distance. From afar, the land just blended in with the far away foot hills. It was a safe bet that the soldiers would never see them. When the time was right, and when the soldier's slow moving columns were where they were predicted to be, they would be less than a mile from the ambush site and could be there in a matter of minutes.

Several miles away, on the first day of the fighting, the Indians had defeated and captured a white settlement located in a blind canyon. This is where they kept the majority of their prisoners. Over a dozen warriors, several of whom were wounded, had been given the task of guarding and protecting the growing group of captured whites being held there. Tall Eagle and Little Crow had insisted that whenever possible, if the whites wanted to surrender that they be allowed to do so. The black Indian was also in favor of this. It was said that his roving band was responsible for over half of all the prisoners being taken alive. This included five soldiers, two of whom were seriously wounded. It was out of respect for the 'Black Bat' that the captors refrained from killing them.

As darkness gave way to early morning light, those Indians who were sleeping were quietly awakened. They were all aware of their part in the battle to come. Several chieftains, including Tall Cloud and the black Indian, had carefully planned the attack.

This group, led by Colton, was over fifty mounted warriors strong and they were to be the second force to strike the horse soldiers. The timing was critical and they waited patiently for their scouts to return with the signal. Colton was confident that the attack would go well. He waited silently holding onto his horses' reins as full daylight swept over the land.

His close friend and second in command, Wild Fisher, slowly walked his horse over to stand next to Colton. He had a worried look on his face as he said, "Dove of Day has told me that this will be a proud day for our people."

"Let us hope he is right," Colton replied, "is he any better today?" He glanced over Wild Fisher's shoulder at a small shelter made of hastily erected branches covered by several blankets that Wild Fisher had just left. Only yesterday, Dove of Day had received a gunshot wound in his abdomen. He was holed up in the small shelter. It was certain that it was a mortal wound and he didn't have much time left.

"No," Wild Fisher answered, "no better. He wishes he could be with us. He is very weak and wants to see you."

"I fear he will die," Colton said softly, "today. He is very old and his wounds are severe." He passed his reins to Wild Fisher and turned and walked to the shelter. As he slowly went inside it seemed strange that Dove of Day did not greet him. He found out why, seconds later when he lifted a corner of the blanket from his dead friend's face. "Good bye, my friend," he said softly. His expression, as he returned to join Wild Fisher was all the telling that was needed. They continued to wait patiently for the battle to start.

Tall Cloud had positioned himself and his first strike force several miles away and even as dawn was breaking, they were stealthily moving into position to attack the horse soldier's column as soon as they were stretched thin on the road. They knew this would lessen the chances for the soldiers to use their cannon effectively.

Even though some of the terrain was open, the Indians seemed to disappear onto the ground as they sought cover on both sides of the road. They only had to remain out of sight and still and when the signal was given, they would rise up and the battle would be on. As full daylight came, and they took their final positions, they were now only about a mile from Colton's band.

John the Baptist and his group were positioned likewise only a half mile farther on and hidden in similar cover. Theirs was a more open position on the prairie. The Indians were hunkered down in small ravines and hollows. Most were afoot and those with horses had sought cover farther away from the road.

As predicted, the army convoy started out a short time after sunrise. Everything about them had been predictable. From the early morning bugles calling reveille, to the shouted commands of both the mounted and infantry forces, the day started the same as any other. A troop of mounted soldiers led the way. Almost immediately, the forces were strung out for nearly a mile as the soldiers, over fifteen hundred strong, mostly infantry, began the grueling journey in search of rogue Indians. The mounted horse soldiers gave a feeling of confidence to those foot soldiers as their trek began.

Tall Cloud's forces, nearly seven hundred strong waited patiently for the trap to be sprung. Then, something completely unexpected happened. Several Army wagons had split off from the main convoy only a half mile from where they had started and were being driven across the prairie to some other destination. No matter what the reason, this was something that could not have been planned for. They had gone only a quarter of a mile cross country when they accidentally stumbled onto the waiting forces of John the Baptist.

Once discovered, the Indians had no choice but to attack. Like screaming banshees, these fierce and unforgiving warriors were all over the few soldiers in those wagons. The soldiers were outnumbered and had no mounted escort for protection making this first skirmish of the day a decisive victory for the Indians. However, the victory was short lived as everything that followed went badly for them. The mounted soldiers arrived in full force only minutes later after hearing the rifle fire. John the Baptist was seriously wounded in the first few minutes of this next engagement and had to retreat.

Colton and his forces, upon hearing the firing thought it to be the signal for them to attack. They mounted quickly and within a very few minutes they were thundering across the prairie towards the sounds of battle. The soldiers had now had plenty of time to quickly move their cannon to high ground. They started firing on Colton's group even before the Indians knew they were that close. The mounted horse soldiers had already engaged John the Baptist's forces, most of who were on foot. The Indians were routed and scurried for the cover of thickets and the nearby forest close to the lake. The victory was easy for the mounted soldiers as they rode hard and fast after each group of three or four Indians as they split up attempting to escape a fate that was near certain.

During the thick of it, Colton led a charge straight at the cannon positions. Two artillery pieces were set up at the top of a small rise and two others were in a similar position about two hundred yards farther on. His followers, some of the bravest and most fierce warriors of all, rode hard beside him. His initial charge was started with at least two dozen Indians. Within minutes, the cannon fire had their numbers down to only a half dozen. The first cannon position was silenced and its crew dead after a short time of fierce fighting as Colton and his braves got off their horses and took on the gunnery crew in hand to hand combat. A round fired from the other cannon position exploded only a few feet from Colton and several others. Their horses were gone and now they were facing an overwhelming force of soldiers, both mounted and infantry.

The concussion from an exploding cannon shell had left Colton barely able to move. He fell to both knees and slowly looked around. Sound had stopped and everything appeared to be moving in slow motion. He watched and was nearly overcome by a feeling of sadness as the one remaining Indian with him was set upon and bayoneted several times by infantry soldiers. He watched as if in a dream as his friend was brutally killed. Other soldiers assuming that he was with their forces, rushed past him. These images were followed by a time of silence and then a blinding pain in the back of his head as his world went dark.

"What the hell is this?" a soldier leaning over Colton exclaimed, "This boy ain't no damned Indian." He looked past a second soldier and shouted, to no one in particular, "Hey, did you club this poor bastard or did the Indians do it?"

His question was ignored.

"Damn," said the second soldier, "you're right about him not being an Indian. Did you see him fight?"

"No, but look at him," the first soldier said, "He's covered in blood and wearing a cap and ball revolver."

Both soldiers had been brought back from the fighting in the East with their units to help quell the Indian uprising. Both were northern boys and proud to be a part of the effort to free the slaves. They only knew for sure that Colton was a Negro and that he was very young. They didn't want to jump to conclusions.

One of the soldiers bent down and removed the gun from the boy's holster. "All six have been fired," he said eyeing the revolver's cylinder. He paused and asked, "Hell, I just don't know. Did you notice him before now?"

"No," was the reply, "I didn't even see who it was that tried to cave in his skull. Let's tie him up and let the captain decide."

Colton had no idea at the time, but the only reason he wasn't killed on the spot was because of his appearance. The soldiers couldn't be sure what a young, well dressed and clean cut looking black man was doing on the battle field. Thinking it better to be safe than sorry, a soldier had clubbed him hard in the back of the head with his rifle stock. Soon, he was bound and thrown onto to back of a wagon for transport to Fort Snelling with several other captives.

The doctor at Fort Snelling checked him out upon his arrival. He thought that there had to have been some kind of mistake in the boy being labeled a war combatant. The young black man had a concussion and was obviously in a state of shock. The doctor's aide revived Colton with smelling salts.

"He's coming around, Doc," the aide said.

Colton opened his eyes and stared blankly around the room. His head hurt like crazy and at first he didn't know where he was. He could barely hear due to that cannon ball exploding so close to him but he could tell that the white men were trying to talk to him.

The doctor helped Colton to sit up. "Get the blood cleaned out of his ears," he instructed the aide as he checked each side of Colton's head. Then addressing Colton, he asked, "What is your name?"

Colton murmured something that sounded to the doctor like he was speaking French. He asked again, this time louder, "What is your name? Can you hear me?"

The aide said, "I think he said his name was Go Two."

Colton could barely hear him and offered no reply. In his weakened condition he had defiantly told them to 'Go to Hell.' His words were slurred and the doctor and his aide didn't understand what he really said. He closed his eyes and lay back down on the cot. The doctor recommended a hospital bed for him but to no avail. The soldiers were determined to place him with the other captives. The doctor noted in the medical report that accompanied Colton to the stockade, that he thought that there had been some kind of mistake in placing this young Negro with the enemy combatants.

Tall Cloud's forces had been defeated. Without the element of surprise, their entire plan had unraveled. In a matter of a few hours, the Indians were in full and fast retreat.

It was late afternoon when Tall Cloud and several others made their way across a large field towards several farm houses. They could hear screams of terror and pain from nearly a half mile away as they approached. A group of Indian warriors had captured nearly a dozen white settlers and were taking out their rage and frustrations on them.

When Tall Cloud saw that it was defenseless women and children who were being tortured and murdered he flew into a fit of rage. A warrior was getting ready to cut a woman with his knife when he looked up in time to see Tall Cloud approaching at a full gallop. Tall Cloud sprang from his horse and literally flew through the air and tackled the man driving him to the ground. His rage was intense. He nearly beat the Indian to death before being stopped by several of his own warriors.

He stood shaking in rage as he shouted for all to hear, "A self-respecting warrior would never do this. You must stop." He cut the bonds of a woman and another, a young boy. Their eyes were filled with terror not knowing what to expect as they were rejoined with several others who had been trembling close by.

"Escort them to the blind canyon." Tall Cloud said, his voice commanding. "Let it be known, I will kill anyone who does more of this to innocent women and children." The Indians did as they were told and herded the survivors towards the holding area. They picked up several more white stragglers along the way. They turned them over, unharmed, to those watching over the captives.

For several days after, it was more of the same. There were several small and intense skirmishes. Some were won by the Indians and some were lost. Tall Cloud soon realized that the war was over and that they had been defeated.

Word reached Red Calf that Colton was feared dead. An Indian gave them an eyewitness account of Colton being struck and killed by cannon fire in the same area that John the Baptist had been wounded. Although this saddened Red Calf, he insisted on seeing where it had happened. At the end of the third day after the fighting near the lake, the soldiers were mostly gone from the area. The bodies of those Indians killed still remained, left to decay. He was joined by Tall Cloud and they rode silently to the scene. They both recognized Colton's dead horse and the body of another Indian believed to have been with him. When there was no positive sign of a young black man's body, they both came away with hope in their hearts that the Black Bat from Hell had indeed survived.

Fort Snelling

Several of the prison cell blocks in the older part of the fort were below ground. These damp and dark places of dismay and lost hope were reminiscent of the old English torture chambers spoken of in stories. For what seemed like days at a time, the guards would never come near. When they did, it was to bring meager rations of food and water. The lamps in the corridor were lit only at those times. Since the current prisoners were Indians, no one said a thing about the conditions and no one cared. Colton was crowded into a small cell with three others. These small cubicles were designed to hold two prisoners, no more. The conditions were worsened when one of the men crammed in with them died. Since there was no natural daylight in that part of the prison, they could only assume that it was at least two or three days before the guards unlocked the door and dragged the dead man away. This same type of event happened in several other cells as well.

As the weeks and months went by, those confined were tried on charges of insurrection and murder. It was around the first week in November that the lower cells were emptied and those surviving Indians were moved to the upper detention cell row. It was much more sanitary and the cell windows allowed fresh air to circulate. During the times of what could only be referred to as 'mock' trials, they were fed on a regular basis. Once a week, they were even allowed to bathe in the corridor area. A single tub was hauled in and filled with water. A large bar of soap was provided and those who desired to bathe did so. Two buckets of fresh water was brought for each man. At first they had no idea why. Later, it turned out that a prison employee, a colored man named Cyrus, had taken it on himself to provide this ever so primitive comfort.

Colton was treated the same as the others. He acted mute and refused to talk to any of those who would question him about his role in the uprising. He was always quiet and never seemed to fully understand what was going on around him. It appeared as though he was quite harmless. For this reason, the guards and the prosecuting officers took him to be a 'simple minded Negro' and made written notes of that. On occasion he had uttered several words believed to be French leading them to believe that he must be from one of the northern settlements. He was logged in as being named 'Go Two' by the officials. Still, he was considered to be a captured enemy combatant and when his turn for trial came it lasted less than five minutes. He was declared guilty of insurrection and sentenced to life in prison. He was awaiting transport with a dozen or so others to the prison in Davenport Iowa.

Since its construction, the fort had employed several local civilians to do some of the more undesirable work. This included a limited amount of cleaning and caring for the detention area. One such employee was an older Negro man named Cyrus. He was a freed slave who had made his way west many years before. He owned a small house within sight of the fort and had worked here off and on for nearly twenty years. It was due to his efforts in bringing bath water once a week that caused him and Colton to build a friendship. Soon, he and several others on the outside of the fort's prison knew of Colton's true identify. It was one of the best kept secrets of the time. Had the officials known that he was the infamous 'Black Bat from Hell' he would have been singled out for sure.

From time to time, Colton would get word from the outside from Cyrus updating him on the whereabouts of Red Calf and Tall Cloud. Knowing that they could not break him out of this detention center, he determined to accept his fate and see how events would unfold. He took solace in knowing that they were pleased to know that he was indeed alive and well.

After they had been moved to the regular detention center, Colton could see the outside from his cell window. He shared the cell with several others. Looking out the window he had a clear view of the courtyard on the south side of the fort. Many Indian women and children had been herded there. Along with several old men, they were kept outside like livestock animals in a makeshift stockade. On quiet, clear nights, he could hear their moans and cries for help in the still night air. He knew that their cries and pleas for mercy fell on deaf ears with their white captors. This caused him to be more determined than ever to break out and somehow offer aid and comfort to his people. If he could get word to Red Calf, he was certain the he and Tall Cloud could help them.

It was a rare day indeed when the former slave, Cyrus, was doing work for the soldiers that caused him to actually be inside the cell block. He scraped and shoveled up the stained and dirty sawdust from the cell block floor areas and wheeled it outside in a wheelbarrow. The interior cell doors were all opened to allow him to do this. As he cleaned each cell, the Indians would simply wait in the corridor. The guards outside the one door into the cell block had no cause for worry. They paid Cyrus little or no attention and as a result he could talk openly to Colton. Cyrus didn't necessarily care for the Indians, but Colton being a Negro seemed to make him feel obligated.

"It's okay, you can talk freely," Colton told him. "I remember the last time we spoke, you were worried that the wrong people would overhear. These Indians don't understand a word of English."

"I know that, my friend," Cyrus responded, "is there anything I can do for you?"

"Yes," Colton said softly, "can I trust you to deliver a message."

Without hesitation, Cyrus said, "Yes, of course you can."

"I need you to get word to Red Calf," Colton said softly, "he has money and he needs to have someone buy supplies and medicines for our people who are penned like sheep outside these walls. Can I trust you to get a message to him?"

"Yes," Cyrus replied, "how do I find Red Calf? Some say he is already in Canada."

"He may be in Canada soon," Colton said, "but not for a while." He gave Cyrus instructions in how to get word to Red Calf. He cautioned, "There will be trouble for those involved if you talk to the wrong people. There is a money reward for the capture of Red Calf and I urge you to be very careful."

Cyrus placed his hand on Colton's shoulder and whispered, "Anything for you my young friend."

The way he said it caused Colton to ask, "Why are you my friend?

Are you a friend to all Negros the same as with me?"

Cyrus looked anxiously over his shoulder. The soldiers were unlocking the cell row's corridor door as he whispered intensely, "The soldiers are coming and just don't you forget to act simple minded. To answer your question, I consider you to be family. I know your father. I owe him my very freedom."

Colton gasped. Before he could say anything more, two soldiers were positioning themselves to watch as Cyrus was joined by another even older black man, to spread the fresh sawdust on the cell block floor.

Colton's mind was in a whirl as he tried to get a grip on his emotions. Cyrus had said that he knew his father. That meant that he must also know his given name. Despite his current situation and the horrible surroundings, his heart was strangely filled with hope as he resigned himself to face each new day with a well-defined purpose. Escape.

Chapter Twenty One

Black Indian – Red Heart (White Justice)

The Indians remained on the offensive for several weeks and were said to be victorious most of the time. There were those who viciously attacked and killed anyone non-Indian. Tall Cloud was furious at many of the tribal leaders as reports of the wanton slaughter of civilian women and children came in. He was powerless to do anything about it.

The end was near and the Sioux were put on the defensive after General Pope's forces arrived. It is said that most of these troops were led by a merciless major named Belmont who arrived with nearly a thousand soldiers. It was said that his orders were to eliminate the Sioux once and for all. Word was that even the Governor was in favor of total extermination. Combined with the existing forces, Belmont's soldiers delivered a crushing defeat to the remnants of the organized tribes. In a skirmish near a lake, remembered as the Battle of Wood Lake, the Indians suffered a major defeat.

The war was declared over by Tall Cloud, Little Crow and several other prominent leaders in late September. The Army honored their truce and dealt with them as they would have any other defeated force. After the terms of their surrender were accepted, the Indians released nearly three hundred white and half-breed prisoners. These were mostly settlers and travelers who had been captured and their lives spared. The soldiers then allowed the Indian leaders to remain free.

Another Sioux nation had been all but wiped out.

Red Calf and John the Baptist and several other rogue Indians reportedly headed north to Canada after the surrender. It was reported that Little Crow and others soon followed. The one called Friend was said to have died on the battlefield from wounds received during the thickest of the fighting. No one could say for sure at the time, but many rumors were abound about the fate of the black Indian, Colton Sage.

Still, remnants of the insurrection lasted for several months before the last shot was fired. The hundreds of Indian men who had been taken captive awaited a certain death as the white man regained control of the area.

The war had seen a complete rout of the town of New Ulm, the destruction of dozens of settlements and the displacement of thousands of settlers who fled to safety. When the final tally was taken, it was estimated that six to seven hundred white settlers were dead along with nearly four hundred soldiers and militiamen. Later on, when the many reports and incidents were calculated more closely, the numbers were lowered considerably.

It was said that the Indian casualties were estimated at over a thousand. As it turned out, this figure was said to be low as death stalked the subdued Indians from this time forth. The atrocities against the whites were still considered pale, by many, in comparison to the horrific acts of past violence and those acts of vengeance now being brought against the Sioux.

First week in December 1862

There were weeks of intense deliberations and what could only be referred to as mock trials by those in charge. It was finally decided that over three hundred captured warriors were to be put to death for their involvement in the uprising. Of these hundreds of men, only a few were of mixed blood. The record books in nearly every courthouse, local and federal, contained pages with lines and scribbles that changed names, places, dates and even charges against these condemned men. These alleged facts changed daily. No actual report had yet been accepted as official and final. A series of meetings between government officials, including Indian Agents, military officers and local authorities, were held to approve the final story. When this was done, President Lincoln was asked to approve the death warrants of over three hundred men.

Several prominent clergymen and many others wrote letters to the newspapers and to the president asking for clemency on behalf of the condemned Indians. After what was referred to as a 'review of tribal records,' President Lincoln's final order approved the executions of thirty-nine of the most heinous murderers. Some believe that he did this for political purposes thinking that European allies may have switched sides and supported the southern Confederacy had he allowed the executions of over three hundred captives. This figure, thirty-nine, was about to change. Later, when the 'dust settled and the smoke cleared,' conflicting reports surfaced that could no longer be whitewashed due to published newspaper stories and firsthand accounts. The order of events would forever be in dispute. The stories and rumors that were surfacing, both in the newspapers and in the official transcripts, would never add up with any degree of certainty. It was also believed that in spite of all the heinous acts and incidents of murder claimed to have been done by the whites against the Indians, not a single white man, soldier or civilian, was ever charged or convicted of any serious crime.

Most of the captured warriors and insurrection leaders were held in a stockade that had been hastily erected west of Mankato. The soldiers stationed to guard them were also faced with keeping these prisoners safe from the mobs of angry whites who repeatedly threatened to storm the place and 'put them god-damned heathens out of their misery.' Security was tight. Heavily armed military escorts traveled with the accused men as they were taken back and forth from the stockade to stand trial in Mankato.

At Fort Snelling, dozens of men were being held awaiting trial. Among them was a young black man. His captors believed him to be a 'simple minded Negro,' raised by Indians in the French crossing area who spoke no English. His name appeared in the first draft of their record books spelled, 'Go Two.' It is said that the only words he was known to speak to his captors when they asked his name were a few mispronounced French words and what sounded like "Go Two." Many of the other captives knew who he was but were determined to keep his identity a secret. Had the authorities known that he was infamous 'Black Bat from Hell,' Colton Sage, he would most certainly have been hung separately and sooner than the others.

The conditions at the stockade as well as at the fort were deplorable. At Fort Snelling it was said that hundreds of Indian women and children were herded into a large fenced area. They were forced to live in the open with only makeshift tents for shelter. Their food was almost always served cold, spoiled, or rancid and never on a regular basis. There was no one in authority for anyone to complain to. Their pleas for humane treatment, as usual, were ignored.

It was the last week in October when word came that three warriors who had refused to surrender had been caught trying to steal food from a farm near Redwood Ferry. Two of these men were killed and one was taken alive, only to be hanged by angry whites hours later. One of those killed was a young black man whose description closely matched that of the renegade Indian, Colton Sage. A white man had split his head open with an axe. The story had it that the soldier named Harley had been requested to view the remains and positively identify the man. It was four days before he showed up to do so. The body had been kept in a storeroom, wrapped in a soiled blanket. The natural course of decomposition made identification difficult. Still, Harley swore that it was indeed the 'Black Bat from Hell.' He did so after seeing that the body was dressed like a white man and wearing heavy leather work-boots.

Even before the trials were over, Lieutenant Harley had been promoted to the rank of Captain and awarded a medal. Several newspapers ran stories that claimed he had displayed unquestionable heroism during a battle in which he suffered two serious wounds. The newspaper story claimed that even after being struck by a bullet and an arrow, he somehow saved the lives of five fellow soldiers and led them through hostile territory to the safety of government forces.

When the story was told in the crowded cellblocks at Fort Snelling the one called Go Two listened intently. His sentence had already been passed down. Unable to find any direct witness against him, he was to be transported to the prison at Davenport, Iowa, to serve a life sentence along with nearly two dozen others.

Fort Snelling, December 24th, 1862

Major Belmont was present, along with Captain Harley, as the prisoners destined for the federal prison in Iowa were being led toward the three large wagons that would transport them to the rail station at St. Paul. The men were individually shackled with leg irons and handcuffs. They stood silently as the convicts filed past.

One of the prisoners stopped and turned to face them. Until this he had drawn no attention to himself. He stood tall and looked Captain Harley in the eye.

"You will die for all you have done, Harley," he said. Then, sounding like he had authority; he said over his shoulder to the guard, "Give us a minute, please."

The escorting guard stood still, surprised by the man's perfect English.

"It is I, Colton Sage," the prisoner continued. "Remember me? I am your Black Bat from Hell."

Harley's face lost all color. "You're dead!" he gasped.

"I have returned from the dead to tell all who will listen that you have no honor," Colton said as he continued to stand tall and proud before them. He made eye contact with the major and smiled adding, "we would have won and driven you and your horse soldiers back to the east had you not shown up with such overwhelming numbers."

Captain Harley was astounded. Major Belmont raised his right hand towards the guard who appeared to be about to strike Colton with his rifle stock. His voice boomed, "Wait, Soldier, let's find out what is really going on."

Colton continued to defy them. "I will see you dead. Harley. This is a promise I make to you."

"My God," Belmont murmured after seeing the shocked look on Captain Harley's face. "He is the one. He is the black bat."

"I'll be god-damned, Sir." Harley stammered. "I thought sure that dead nigger I looked at was him."

Major Belmont smiled. This caused Captain Harley to settle down a bit. He remained silent as the major barked an order to the guard,

"Bring this one inside." He turned to his executive officer, "We need to send a rider to Mankato and tell them to scratch someone off the list. Tomorrow we'll be sending them the thirty-ninth murderous Indian to hang." Major Belmont went back inside with his executive officer to write the orders for a rider to deliver to Mankato.

Colton was unshackled from the others and hastily chained to a support post near to the stairs that led up to the elevated porch area.

"Hey, Harley," Colton said, his voice filled with concern, "are you really this stupid? The major said to take me inside."

Captain Harley, always a coward at heart, walked over and kicked Colton hard in the midsection. "How's that for stupid," He snarled, "I've said it before and I'll say it now, I'll be dancing at your goddamn funeral." He drew his leg back to kick again. As he did, Colton shifted his position just enough to cause the captain to miss him and actually kick the support post. Still bent on antagonizing the captain, Colton said, "can't you even kick someone that's chained to a post?" He heard several soldiers laugh as he said it and knew that the captain was truly infuriated. Harley kicked him again, cursing, several times. Chained as he was Colton could only take it and pray inwardly that his turn for revenge would come.

December 25th

The army wagon was empty except for one man who was shackled and chained in the wagon's bed. His arms were slightly outstretched as each wrist was shackled to a short chain attached on each side of the wagon. His feet were likewise shackled. The driver sat alone as he urged the horses up a steep incline that wound between two heavily forested hills. Four soldiers, including Captain Harley, rode ahead and four soldiers rode close behind. This heavily armed escort was expecting no trouble. Soon, they would deliver the infamous outlaw and justice would be swift and final. It was certain that a death by hanging awaited this young black man known as the Black Bat from Hell. Several newspapers had picked up on the name and it seemed that everyone knew about this fierce warrior.

Word had been sent on ahead. It was said that even President Lincoln had been informed of this latest change to the list of those who were to be executed. The number of names still remained at thirty-nine with the intention of sparing some other poor soul in order for Colton Sage to take his place.

The soldiers in the lead disappeared around a bend in the road at the top of the incline. The wagon was close behind. As they rounded the bend, the driver reined the horses to a fast stop causing the rear guard to stop as well. A loud voice that could have easily been a commanding officer was heard, "Stay at ease, men. Do not draw your weapons."

All at once hordes of Indians were everywhere. Several dozen, mounted and armed with rifles, all pointed at the soldiers blocked the road ahead. More, also armed with rifles and some with bows stood among the trees on the high ground only fifty feet from the road. Before any orders could be given, any hope for retreat was dashed, as another dozen Indians, on foot, appeared as if out of nowhere surrounding the soldiers in the rear guard. They stood silently with rifles leveled and bows drawn back. The horse soldiers remained as they were, frozen in place, surprised at this unexpected turn of events. To their knowledge all of the Indian warriors had been disarmed or had already fled the area.

The wagon's driver sat with a slack-jawed expression and he wondered what would happen next. He was expecting orders or something from Captain Harley.

Harley was in a funk. There was no time to figure out a plan. The decision to fight or surrender was one that needed to be made now. He made it, without even speaking, when he recognized the outlaw Indian, Red Calf. As he threw up his hands, a wave of dizziness overcame him as he also recognized the most famous Indian of all, Tall Cloud.

It was Tall Cloud who spoke first. "We have come for our brother. In exchange for him we offer your lives. If you choose to fight, we will kill you all."

Red Calf positioned his horse next to Tall Cloud's. His voice was commanding and instantly obeyed as he said, "Soldiers. Place your weapons in the scabbards, dismount and stand there." He pointed to a small area of level ground.

Harley followed the command along with the other soldiers. As he dismounted, his face ashen, Colton spoke from the wagon, "Not you, Harley."

The Captain stood shaking uncontrollably. He silently handed his keys over to Red Calf who had dismounted and approached on foot. As he started to free Colton, the soldiers were made to lie face down. They were stripped of their ammunition pouches. The silence that followed was deafening. The sounds of the chains being removed and horses snorting and stomping was all that was heard.

Colton stood upright in the wagon bed.

"It is good to see you, my brothers," he said, addressing Red Calf and Tall Cloud.

They used the same shackles and chains to secure Captain Harley to the bed of the wagon in Colton's place. Colton mounted one of the captured horses. He threw the shackle keys away as he rode off. Several Indians got in the wagon and followed. Harley immediately started shouting and pleading for his men to come to his rescue. The soldiers could only remain motionless as they hoped that their lives would indeed be spared. The second ranking officer, a lieutenant was made to walk with the Indians for a short distance. He stood trembling in fear as the Indians filed silently by.

Colton led the way, riding hard for about a mile before he stopped. "What about our brothers in Mankato?" he asked, directing his question to Tall Cloud.

Bitterness filled the chief's answer as he replied, "There is nothing we can do. There are over a thousand soldiers. They are everywhere. These brave warriors," he paused and indicated the others who were waiting silently to see what was to come next, "are all that remain. To attack would be foolish."

"It is true, Colton." Red Calf said, nodding his head in agreement. "We were already traveling to the north country when we got word that you had been found and were to be taken to be hanged with the others."

Colton's voice was also laced with bitterness as he said, "There are still several things that I have to do. I know that you must be on your way." A look of pure hatred crossed his face as he gazed into the wagon and said, "It is time to take care of the coward, Harley."

"No, please, Colton," Harley pleaded from within the wagon, "this isn't what your mother taught you." He was in a funk, overcome with terror as he started sobbing. "She saved my life and yours, Red Calf." Harley sought help from Red Calf as he pleaded for his life. "Red Calf, please," Harley sobbed, "can you help me?"

His words fell on deaf ears and hardened hearts. Colton spoke softly to the Indians who had been riding on and in the wagon. "Quickly, gather as much dry firewood as you can."

The Indians did as instructed. They piled the firewood in the wagon around and under the hapless Captain Harley who was still sobbing in fear.

"Colton, Please," he begged, "don't do this, I beg you."

Colton dismounted and walked over to stand by the side of the wagon. He gazed for a moment at the captain, then asked, his voice serious, "You must have heard that all of us," he paused and looked first at Red Calf, then Tall Cloud, "we always do our best spare someone to show that we have the power of life and death and sometimes we even show mercy. Have you heard of us doing that?" He paused and then added, "Showing mercy?"

"Yes, yes. I have heard that," Harley blubbered. "Please, please show mercy."

"Today is no exception." Colton said softly, "except that we have already done that and you should be grateful, we spared your soldiers."

Harley had no reply. He could only sit and watch in horror as another Indian slowly broke some small sticks to serve as tinder to start a fire. Colton was mounting his horse. His voice was almost mirthful as he smiled and asked, "Oh, by the way, Harley, can we borrow a match?"

Expecting no answer, Colton reined his horse around and rode off slowly with Red Calf and Tall Cloud. One of the remaining Indians reached into the captain's shirt pocket and got out several matches. He reached out and struck one on Harley's belt buckle. Harley was unable to speak, overcome with terror as the match slowly lit, coming to life. The Indian's expression was serious as he placed the lit match into the tinder. As the flames started to catch on, several Indians paused to spit into the wagon as they walked by following their leaders.

After riding for about a quarter mile, Tall Cloud stopped and indicated for the others to do the same. Those Indians who were mounted reined to a stop in a semi-circle facing them.

"We must wait for the others," Tall Cloud said, "We need to go quickly. We now have enough horses for all to ride if we double up."

Colton said, "I have several things that I must do before I can go north." He turned to Red Calf and said, "Our people are being starved to death in a stockade alongside of Fort Snelling. We must get some money and buy supplies to smuggle in to them."

"Yes, we know what you mean, we got your request just last week," Red Calf said, "from your black friend Cyrus. But it is too late."

It was Tall Cloud who broke the news, "They are already being moved. Yesterday and today they are being led to the railroad where they will be loaded into box cars and taken to the place called Nebraska."

Colton shook his head sadly. "Then there is nothing we can do." Then, addressing Red Calf he said, "Still, I must find a way to contact Cyrus at the fort." In response to an inquisitive look from Red Calf, he added, "I'll explain when we have a chance to talk."

As if an afterthought, Red Calf reached into the large saddle bag tied to his horse. "If I am to travel with you," he said with a grin, "you need to stink less." He pulled out several articles of clothing and passed them to Colton. "Try these on," he said, "what you are wearing now is apt to attack and kill you at any time."

Colton was grateful for the change of clothes. He dressed in the new trousers and nice shirt. A dark brown waist coat completed his wardrobe. He strapped on a cap and ball revolver that Red Calf handed him and said, "Thank you my brother. Perhaps we should burn these old clothes in the wagon with our friend Harley." Colton smiled from ear to ear as another Indian walked close and passed him a wide brimmed, dark brown, felt hat. The hat was new and had a wide band with a small colored feather, also dark brown. He was pleased to find that it fit.

For some reason, at that moment there was a short period of silence. There was no wind and the calmness of the morning was broken by the sounds of Captain Harley's distant screaming.

Soon all the braves were assembled. Riding double, there were plenty of horses now that they had the newly acquired mounts from the horse soldiers. They rode in single file in an effort to throw off anyone who would try to follow their trail. Soon they came to a small stream. They followed it upstream, staying in the shallows and it soon branched off into another small creek that flowed into it. They rode like that nearly all day, knowing that they were leaving no tracks for the soldiers to follow.

The soldiers were feeling helpless and humiliated after giving the Indians such an easy victory. They had marched for about a mile towards Mankato when they smelled smoke.

The lieutenant was second in line. He spoke softly to the corporal who was in the lead and held up his hand indicating that the soldiers stop. He now believed that the Indian's words were good and wasn't worried about being attacked. Still, the smell and now the sight of smoke coming from around a bend in the road ahead cause him to show caution. Soon they came onto the abandoned army wagon. The horses had been taken and it had been filled with hastily gathered firewood and set ablaze. What was left of Captain Harley was still writhing and gasping in sheer agony in the red hot coals. He was still chained to the smoldering sides of the wagon. They could do nothing to help him since they had no keys for the shackles. Several soldiers did what they could to brush the hot coals and embers away from the captain.

Two soldiers were assigned to stay with him as the others hurried on to safety and to get more help. With no way to unchain the captain, the soldiers could only wait. They offered words of encouragement but could never be certain if their words were heard or understood. The awful moans and stifled screams of pain coming from the captain were almost more than they could stand. It was late in the afternoon when they decided to toss a coin. The loser of the coin toss used his knife to put the captain out of his misery.

Although their story was never in any real doubt, no one other than those soldiers present could claim that they had seen a single hostile Indian. It did appear strange that Captain Harley had been taken and an army troop had been disarmed and dismounted without a single shot being fired. It was a story that the officials thought necessary to keep to themselves. The last thing they wanted was for the remaining Indians to have a cause for hope, or for the local settlers to have any reason to doubt the army's ability to protect them and maintain control of the area. Still, rumors were flourishing.

If this latest story were true, and if a band of warriors were still at large, there was no real evidence to prove it. The Indians had disappeared like ghosts. Even though they tried, the soldiers were never able to pick up their trail.

December 26, 1862

It is said that each of the condemned men died with pride. As they were led to the place of their macabre execution, they began to sing. Even after the dark hoods had been placed over their heads and the nooses tightened around their necks, they continued to sing. It was a warrior's chant of death and a final display of their courage. This hanging was said to be the largest mass execution in United States history.

It is certain that many of these men did deserve their fate. Some heinous crimes had been committed and justice needed to be served. It is also believed that none of them got a fair trial by any standard.

Tying up loose ends

The Indians used all of their skill and tricks to remain undetected as they journeyed north towards Canada. The second day of Colton's freedom was the same day as the mass execution. Around noon time, Colton and Red Calf peeled off from the group near a settlement that had been destroyed during the worst of the fighting. It was late afternoon when they came upon an old friend. It was Red Calf who first smelled the smoke. It was coming from one of the farmhouses that still remained standing even though about half of it was burned to the ground. They approached cautiously and were nearly overwhelmed by the smell of roasting meat in the fireplace. A man was crouched down with his back to them in front of the fireplace. Even from this angle, they both recognized More Boy, a close friend.

"I heard you coming a mile away," More Boy said over his shoulder. "Come and sit. Food will be ready soon."

He stood up and gave them both an embrace.

"If the whites catch you, alone like this," Red Calf said, "they will kill you."

More Boy shrugged his shoulders, "Then I will die with honor."

"No need to die at all," Colton said, "You can join up with Tall Cloud and the others and be in Canada in just a few days."

"No," my friends, More Boy said softly. "I will stay. This is my land. I was born not far from here and I will keep killing the whites until they do get me."

Colton was ravenous, the prison food had been bad and he had nothing to eat other than a couple strips of beef jerky since the day before. He thanked More Boy several times as he ate his fill. They stayed the night there with their friend. At first light, they were on their way to Mankato. "I will wait here, my friends," More Boy told them. "In case you need me I will stay here another day."

They rode hard and made their way into Mankato by way of a back trail in broad daylight. They had never seen the place so busy. There were people and soldiers everywhere. Neither was worried about being recognized and dressed as they were neither was worried about standing out. They had both learned over the years that they could hide right out in the open with a higher degree of safety than skulking around trying to stay out of sight. Colton was hungry so they tied their horses to a side hitching rack at an eating establishment.

Inside, the eatery was dimly lit, suiting them just fine. A nice lady asked what they wanted and both ordered a steak and potatoes meal. There were several other patrons at other tables and no one paid them any mind. They visited quietly as their order was being prepared.

"To go to Fort Snelling," Red Calf said in a low tone, "would not be wise. Here in Mankato it is different. There are lots of civilians and farmers. Some are German, some English and some French. We can blend in here, but at the fort, I'm thinking that is a bad idea."

"I must see Cyrus," Colton said in a near whisper. "I need to ask him something." Responding to Red Calf's curious look, he added, "He said he knows my father. That means he must also know where he is and my given name."

Red Calf pursed his lips as if to whistle. With knitted brows he said, "I can't say as I blame you for wanting to know. My father was killed when I was a small child according to Tall Cloud. This is a good thing for you. We will go, but we must be very careful. You say Cyrus owns a house near the fort? That would be the best place to find him."

"Yes," Colton said, "the way he described it should make it easy to find."

As they waited quietly for their food, they could overhear other conversations going on around them. They were surprised to find out what was about to happen to the bodies of those Indians who had been hanged. They agreed to do something about it.

"We cannot let them take our fallen brothers and cut them up and make trophies of their remains. That isn't right."

"Agreed," Colton said.

"The shanties along the river still house some of our brothers," Red Calf said, "I'm sure someone there will know what is going on."

"Yes," Colton agreed, "they won't completely get rid of all of our people as long as there is dirty work still to be done."

"I am glad that More Boy will wait for us for a day." Red Calf said, "We may need him after all."

"Yes," Colton replied, "it would be a good thing if we could talk him into joining with Tall Cloud and moving to the safety of Canada."

The woman who had taken their order arrived with two large plates of delicious food. There was no more conversation as they both dug in.

As it turned out, they did need More Boy. When they learned that wagons were being loaded with the bodies of some of their fallen brothers, they had to act fast. The only real logistical problem they had was convincing More Boy not to murder the drivers and the doctor in charge when they stole the wagons. They happened upon about a half dozen other Indians who still hadn't headed north and with their help gave their brothers a proper Christian burial.

Family connections

The next task at hand was to get in and out of Fort Snelling undetected. They rode in slowly as darkness was descending. Looking at the fort from this angle gave Colton the shivers. It had been such a horrible place.

Finding Cyrus was easy. No one in the area was the wiser and they stayed the night as guests. Red Calf listened intently, as did Colton, as Cyrus told him about his father and where to go if he wanted to look for him.

"Your proper name really is Sage." Cyrus said. "Your mother took your father's last name as her own." He paused for a moment gazing at Colton's amazed expression. "The missionary named Earnest married them as Christians not far from here. Your father's given name is Rupert Sage. Your mother's name was Soft Water and her Christian name was Elizabeth. She was an orphan adopted into the Santee tribe. It all came apart when the slavers found them."

"How did this come to be?" Colton asked, "Why did not they flee to the safety of Canada or somewhere similar?"

"This I cannot answer," Cyrus replied, "only that your father, for a long time in his past, helped other escaped slaves to acquire their freedom. The Colton Township where you were born was known as part of the Underground Railroad. I was very sad when your father was caught and then to hear of your mother's death. Still, it was good news to find that the white missionary lady, Miss Lillie, had taken you in. Although I have never met her, she was known as a friend to all."

Colton listened somberly as Cyrus continued, "Your father helped me build this house shortly after we arrived here nearly twenty years ago. Since then, I have helped many of our people on their way to freedom. He and your mother have both sheltered here, with me, before you were born."

"Was my father born free?" Colton asked.

"No, he was born a slave, as was I. He was born into a plantation that was home for three generations to his family. He often spoke highly of the owners. Their last name was Anderson and they were said to be good Christians. No one ran away from their plantation. Money problems caused them to sell your father and several others."

Colton's face showed surprise at this news.

"We were both bought by the same plantation master's overseer at the same auction." Cyrus said, "Several years later, when it was discovered that your father had been helping other slaves to freedom, he had to make his escape. This is why the reward for him was so great.

He took four others with him, including me. He helped me in spite of the fact that I injured my knee the first day and could barely walk. I believe anyone else would have left me behind." Cyrus paused and continued, "The plantation master that we both escaped from called your father by another name. He named him Grant Washington. He was of great value because he could read and write and spoke several African dialects." Again he paused for the information to sink in. He added, "You must remember that your father was an owned slave. Owned and controlled by a harsh white master named Orville Thompson who had several sons. He was an old man then and is probably long since dead. If your father was returned to him, I fear his punishment would have been severe. His plantation is called Ashton Oaks and is located about thirty miles north and east of Atlanta."

Cyrus paused for a moment, then added, "The information I share with you now is what was known to me nearly twenty years ago. I have not heard anything about your father since."

"I must go to Atlanta and seek out this Ashton Oaks plantation," Colton said. "All my life I have wondered and asked questions. Until now, there have been no answers."

"Do as you must," Cyrus said, "but remember, where you are going is in the heart of slave country. And yes, as in most places, there are many good people there. Still, you must always keep in mind that nearly any white there can capture you, brand you, and claim you as their property. It is a danger you must be aware of."

Red Calf said, addressing Cyrus, "Our brother is determined to find out what happened to his father. He may even have other brothers and sisters. As a small boy, I knew his mother only briefly as did Miss Lillie. I can remember when he was around nine or ten years old asking Miss Lillie and myself questions about his mother and father that we could not answer. This is important to him. If anyone can go on a mission such as this and succeed, it is he."

The next morning they bade farewell to Cyrus. They still had a tidy sum of stolen gold from several of their past raids. They gave some to

Cyrus so he could continue to aid others and split up the rest. Red Calf insisted that Colton take the lion's share due to the journey before him. Then he headed for the northern border to be with his wife and child.

Colton's focus on life and survival had changed overnight as the information from Cyrus was told. It was with a fierce determination and hopeful heart that he headed straight for Atlanta Georgia.

Epilogue

The official record

It was reported that a last minute reprieve had been granted to one of the condemned men, changing the number of men to be executed from thirty-nine to thirty-eight. A conflicting account to this was the story that yet another reprieve was granted, to yet another condemned man, after he had been executed. True or not, this report insured that the numbers concerning how many men were actually hanged that fateful day would forever be in question by anyone not there at the time. There was also the story about the soldiers having to hang one of the men twice after a doctor determined that he was still alive. This story was made believable by newspaper and government reports. This event, a government official stated, accounted for the mix-up and gave assurances that there was never a thirty-ninth Indian. They would never admit that he was the one that got away.

The bodies of the thirty-eight men who were executed were said by some to have been buried near the river in a large, mass grave, at least most of them. It was said that some of the bodies were picked up the next day by a group of doctors from St. Paul for research purposes. The bodies destined for St. Paul were wrapped in white sheets and unceremoniously stacked in several wagons for the long journey. How many bodies were left buried in the mass grave and how many were taken by wagon, is still unclear.

The story goes that somewhere along the route to the railhead, three masked bandits held up the small convoy and the wagons and horses were stolen. The drivers and the lone doctor who accompanied them were beaten and robbed. They were trussed up and left beside the road. Those who heard this news chuckled thinking that it must have been a bunch of very stupid or incompetent highwaymen who were in for one 'hell of a surprise' when they uncovered their cargo and discovered what they had actually stolen.

Government officials denied the incident, stating that the report was false. Just before the government officials made this denial, a newspaper reporter from St. Paul had been about to run a story. It was his theory that the bodies had been stolen intentionally. He had personally interviewed the drivers and the doctor. They all claimed that a young, well-spoken Negro man led the trio of bandits and had done all the talking. Fearing that the public would mock him, the reporter never filed the report.

It was widely known that government officials had declared that the Sioux nation be removed forever from the Minnesota lands. The remaining Sioux were rounded up and forced to go to several different places. Many died on the way to these government sanctioned hellholes. Even more died from a variety of what should have been preventable causes.

Another Indian nation decimated.

The whites had won.

The Indian agents and those in charge of Indian affairs are the ones who many say should have been held responsible for the events that caused the uprising. It is believed that no white person or government official was ever held accountable for the harsh treatments and callous attitudes said to have triggered everything.

Another story is told about the Indian chief, Little Crow. It is said that he settled in Canada with many followers. There are those who say that he was killed a year and a half later after returning to the upper reservation area in an effort to steal horses. There were said to have been several witnesses. Those who had known him from his many years as an Indian leader thought it inconceivable that he would have returned in this way. A farmer, it is said, shot him dead and collected reward money from the government. It is a story that was sworn to be true by his close friend who had been along and had managed to avoid the gunfire. His friend, it is said, was later overheard mocking the white man for his sheer stupidity. "We all look alike to them," he reportedly said, "let them believe what they wish." His remarks caused many to seriously doubt the white man's version of the story.

Red Calf, still a wanted man, spent that first winter across the northern border in Canada with his wife Marion and their son, Taylor. A second son was born to them. His many skills as a builder and his education would soon insure that he could fit in with the whites and provide a good life for his family. He didn't know it yet, but fate would determine that his days of shared adventures with the black Indian were far from over.

Tall Cloud's wife took ill and died shortly after they arrived in Canada. Tall Cloud then headed west with several others to join up with the Sioux bands who still roamed the Black Hills. These tribes enjoyed many freedoms similar to the old days because the Black Hills area was protected by treaty. Tall Cloud's hope, despite the white man's certainty of broken promises, was that this land could truly be called home.

The End

NOTE: As you know, reviews are gold to authors. If you have found this book enjoyable, would you consider leaving an honest review on Amazon.com? Or you can email it to PressDept@oaktreebooks..com

About the Author

Frederick H Savage is a Wyoming author who has won many writing awards at the state and national levels. Categories include: adult fiction, children's fiction and poetry. He has won awards for works that deal with child abuse and neglect, children's issues, traditional poetry, Western themes and the Vietnam War.

He is a retired teacher and devotes as much time as he can to writing. Other interests include hunting and fishing and participating in VFW and American Legion activities.

Military service, US Army, Airborne Infantry. Served proudly in Vietnam.

CPSIA information can be obtained at www.ICGtesting.com
Printed in the USA
LVOW11s0012030516

486384LV00001B/96/P